W9-BMZ-333

THE
NINTH STEP

JACK LEIGHTNER CRIME NOVELS

Neptune Avenue

The Graving Dock

Red Hook

OTHER FICTION

Boombox

NONFICTION

*Storms Can't Hurt the Sky: A Buddhist Path
Through Divorce*

THE
NINTH STEP

A Jack Leightner Crime Novel

Gabriel Cohen

MINOTAUR BOOKS ✠ NEW YORK

A THOMAS DUNNE BOOK

A THOMAS DUNNE BOOK FOR MINOTAUR BOOKS.
An imprint of St. Martin's Publishing Group.

THE NINTH STEP. Copyright © 2010 by Gabriel Cohen. All rights reserved. Printed in the United States of America. For information, address St. Martin's Press, 175 Fifth Avenue, New York, N.Y. 10010.

www.thomasdunnebooks.com
www.minotaurbooks.com

Library of Congress Cataloging-in-Publication Data

Cohen, Gabriel, 1961–
    The ninth step / Gabriel Cohen.—1st ed.
        p. cm.
    ISBN 978-0-312-62501-6
    1. Leightner, Jack (Fictitious character)—Fiction   2. Detectives—New York (State)—New York—Fiction.   3. Murder—Investigation—Fiction.
4. Brooklyn (New York, N.Y.)—Fiction.   I. Title.
    PS3603.O35N56   2010
    813'.6—dc22

                                                    2010010451

First Edition: June 2010

10 9 8 7 6 5 4 3 2 1

For Reed

THE
NINTH STEP

CHAPTER ONE

Detective Jack Leightner was struggling to extricate half a bagel from his toaster when the doorbell rang. It was a day off from work and he just wanted to sit in his kitchen and eat breakfast in peace. He was tempted to ignore the bell, but it rang again. As he walked out of his kitchen, half his mind was preoccupied with remembering to unplug the toaster before sticking a fork in, and the other half was busy imagining what might happen if he didn't. Electrocution was a pretty rare cause of death, yet he had seen a few startling examples in his years with Brooklyn South Homicide.

The hallway of the house he shared with his elderly landlord was musty, and carpeted with a layer of Astroturf. (Mr. Gardner was a home fixer-upper, but he tended to improvise with found materials.) As Jack approached the door, he saw a vague figure standing outside beyond the frosted glass. The mailman? No, it was Sunday. He shook his head: maybe a Jehovah's Witness.

He opened the door. "Yes?"

A stranger stood there, a middle-aged, stoop-shouldered black man, several inches taller than Jack. He wore black pants, a white shirt, and a frayed gray windbreaker.

"Are you Jack Leightner?"

The man's cheeks were spotted with dark freckles, and the skin under his eyes was droopy. He looked like he had seen more than a few miles of bad road.

"That's right," Jack said. "How can I help you?" He lived in the quiet Brooklyn neighborhood of Midwood; one of its benefits was that unexpected visits were rare.

"Could I take a minute of your time? I don't mean to bother you."

Jack frowned. In his experience, people who said that they didn't mean to bother you actually meant to do just that. "Are you selling something? I'm sorry, but I'm not interested."

"No, sir," the man replied. "I'm not selling anything at all. Would you mind if I come in for just a minute?"

Jack crossed his arms. "Why don't you just tell me what this is about?"

The man bowed his head for a moment, and then he raised it. "With all respect, I don't think this is something you'll want to discuss out here on the stoop."

Jack didn't like the sound of that—it was something he often said before breaking the news to relatives of homicide victims. "I don't generally invite strangers into my home unless I know what they want."

The man stared at him for a moment, then sighed and shook his head. "Of course not. I wouldn't either." He looked away for a moment and watched a neighbor trundle her shopping cart down the street. The day was bright and sunny and a dogwood tree was blossoming above the sidewalk. (Later, when Jack recalled this day, he would envision this splash of pink, like a bomb going off.)

The stranger turned back. "I don't suppose you recognize me. I didn't think you would."

Jack's first thought was of the .45 service revolver sitting on top of his bedroom dresser. As one of only about a hundred NYPD members of service who had earned the designation Detective First Grade, and one of the most seasoned and determined of that elite bunch, he had helped send quite a number of men to prison. Very few had been accepting of their fate. "Excuse me for a second," he said. "I left something on the stove. I'll be right back."

"I'll wait," the stranger replied.

Jack ducked back into his apartment, grabbed his hand-cuffs and crammed them in his back pocket, and stuck the .45 in a pocket of his sweatshirt. It looked pretty obvious in there, which was fine with him. He returned to the front door.

The stranger was sitting on the stoop. He turned to stare up at the detective and immediately took in the new situation. "I don't think you're gonna need the piece. I'd just like to talk to you. Are you familiar with Alcoholics Anonymous?"

Jack nodded. "Why?"

The stranger took a wrinkled piece of paper from his pocket, lifted it close to his mournful eyes, and read aloud. "Step Eight: we made a list of all persons we had harmed, and became willing to make amends to them all. Step Nine: we made direct amends to such people whenever possible, except when to do so would injure them or others."

Jack felt his throat tightening. "Who are you? What do you want?"

The man folded the piece of paper and stuck it back in his pocket. He placed his hands carefully on his knees, looked away, and cleared his throat. When he looked back at Jack, his eyes were troubled and piercing. "You had a brother," he said. "I believe his name was Peter. I was the boy who killed him."

Jack felt a roaring in his ears and then the ground fell out from under him; he was hurled back to a warm November morning in 1965.

PETEY KEPT SINGING, "HELP Me, Rhonda." He loved to sing, Jack's two-years-younger brother, a lively thirteen-year-old with the biceps of a serious athlete. They were playing hooky, roaming aimlessly around Red Hook, their waterfront Brooklyn neighborhood. They had killed some time tossing pebbles at seagulls, out on one of the piers, and now they were strolling up Sullivan Street, past a vacant lot.

Petey was playing with a Spaldeen, and the little rubber ball took a bad bounce into the lot, beneath an old abandoned trailer. That's where he discovered the hidden case of Scotch, probably swag boosted out of a ship by some sly longshoreman.

They pulled it out, and were hurrying up the street to go hide the liquor in their friend Joe Kolchuk's basement when they were approached by two Negro kids, bigger and years older. Jack was holding the case. One of the strangers, wearing a green Army jacket, slammed Petey up against a wall; the other, a kid with a big Afro, demanded that Jack hand over the booze.

That was when Jack saw the patrol car moving slowly up the street, a couple of blocks away. And he said something he'd have a lifetime to regret. He stared defiantly at the kid with the Afro. "You gonna make us?"

Petey looked scared. "Just give it to them, Jack."

He held onto the case.

"I'm not gonna ask you again," the kid with the Afro said.

The patrol car was coming closer. Jack smiled. "Fuck you, nigger."

The others, including Petey, looked at him in disbelief.

"What did you say?" the Negro asked.

"I said, 'Fuck you and your nigger friend.' " It wasn't like he really had anything against black people—he ran with kids of all colors in the projects—but he saw the patrol car coming and he reached for the easiest jibe.

The kid who had Petey up against the wall pulled out a switchblade.

"Whoa," Jack said, going pale. "Look, I'm gonna hand it over." The cops were just a block away. He started to put the case down, and then he looked up the street and saw—to his horror—that the patrol car had pulled to the curb. The cops jumped out and went into a diner.

Petey began to struggle. And then Jack watched the kid holding his brother click the knife open and stab him. (He might well have stabbed Jack instead, if he hadn't been holding the case of liquor.) The guy only used the weapon once, but that proved more than enough. Petey put his hand under his shirt and it came out all covered in blood. He stared at Jack as if confused, and then he fell to his knees, and onto his side. He never got up.

The two assailants ran off down a side street, never to be found.

UNTIL NOW.

Jack's right hand closed on the grip of his .45. "Get up," he said, jaw clenched. "We're going inside."

His brother's murderer stood up slowly, hands half-raised. Jack looked around to see who might be out on the street, watching, but there was no one. He followed the man into the foyer, and took the gun out of his pocket. "Keep walking. Straight on through." He marched the man into his kitchen and ordered him to sit in a wooden chair, next to the red Formica table.

"Put your hands behind your back."

The stranger complied, and Jack cuffed him.

"You goin' to shoot me? Can't say as how I'd blame you."

Jack lifted the pistol and held it against the man's right temple. The stranger seemed oddly calm, but Jack's own breath had grown erratic, shaky. He closed his eyes for a second, saw red behind his lids, contemplated how good it might feel to apply a little pressure to the trigger. How it might put a salve on a lifetime of guilt.

After a moment, he opened his eyes. He had dedicated his life to catching killers, and he wasn't about to go over to the other side. "I'm not going to shoot you," he said.

The stranger's shoulders relaxed.

Jack scowled. "You dumb bastard. There's no statute of limitations on homicide."

"I know the law," the man replied. "And I'm not scared of prison. I'm just coming off a ten-year bid in Green Haven. That's where I found AA."

"Good for you," Jack said. "I'm sure they'll be thrilled to have you back."

The stranger shrugged. "You can do whatever you want with me. I ain't afraid of dying, and I ain't afraid of going back in. I've made my peace with the Lord." He bent his head down to scratch his chin against his shoulder. "There's just one catch. If you shoot me, or send me up, you'll never find out why I killed your brother."

Jack almost spat his reply. "I know damn well why you killed him, you piece of shit."

The stranger remained calm.

"As a matter of fact," he said, "you don't."

CHAPTER TWO

"Check it out," said Detective Richie Powker the next day. He held up a small plastic-wrapped package. "Little Debbie snack cakes! I used to love this crap when I was a kid."

The man stood in an aisle of a small deli on Coney Island Avenue, not far from Jack's Midwood apartment. The morning sunshine barely made it in through the grimy, advertisement-plastered windows.

Using his teeth, Powker ripped open the package's crinkly plastic wrap. "Don't worry," he said, grinning. "I'll pay for it." The detective from the Seven-oh house (the Seventieth Precinct), was a stout, shambling man with thatched red hair, a ruddy face, and the bulbous, veiny nose of a man who liked his whiskey. He was a good cop, though; Jack had worked with him on a mugging gone bad a year or so back. Now, again, as a member of the Brooklyn South Homicide Task Force, he was here to provide the local cop with expert help in dealing with the dead.

Jack noticed the picture on the snack package, a freckle-faced girl wearing a straw hat. A blast from the past. It reminded him of his own childhood, and then of course he was thinking of his unexpected visitor the day before.

"You okay?" Powker asked.

Jack rubbed his eyes. "I didn't get much sleep." He needed coffee—and needed to focus on his job.

Powker's eyebrows went up. "Some hot date action? You're divorced, right?"

Jack manufactured a polite smile but didn't respond. Over the other detective's shoulder, at the end of the aisle, he could see a couple of pathologists from the medical examiner's office crouched down, poking around the corpse of the day, a big Caucasian male. Jack caught a glimpse of the guy's pale face. (Then again, *everyone* looked pasty under these weak fluorescent lights.) Beneath the head, a pool of blood had spread out across the dingy blue linoleum. Jack gazed calmly at the scene. He'd get his chance to check it out soon, after the M.E.'s boys were through and Crime Scene had a whack at it.

He turned to his new temporary partner. "How long ago'd this happen?"

"About an hour."

"You talk to the clerk yet?"

"Briefly. He seems kinda shell-shocked."

The guy they were referring to, a plump young Indian or Pakistani, sat on a stool behind the counter, hunched over, hugging himself. He wore a Mets cap and a weak mustache and looked like he was fervently wishing that he had called in sick today.

"What happened?"

"He says he doesn't know. Some customer just went nuts on the vic here."

"Were they having an argument or something?"

"He doesn't think so. He heard some kinda quick commotion, and he looked up and the vic was already down." Powker took another bite of his cake, then brushed crumbs from the front of his too-small sports jacket. "At least we know who the dead guy was: we found a driver's license. Name's Robert Brasciak. He lived three blocks away, on East Eighth."

"Did the clerk know either of the guys?"

"He doesn't think so. He's new on the job."

"Any other wits?"

Richie shook his head. "Not inside the store."

Jack noticed that nobody seemed to be paying any attention to the clerk, even though the kid was clearly struggling with the trauma of having just witnessed a murder. He walked over to the counter. "You okay? You want some water or anything?"

The kid shook his head.

"Don't worry," Jack said, patting him on the shoulder. "We're gonna need to ask you a few more questions, but we'll get you out of here soon."

He returned to his partner's side. One of the pathologists, a gangly, bespectacled young guy chewing a big wad of gum, glanced up at the two detectives, then nodded at a bloody object on the floor, a few feet from the corpse. "That looks like your weapon. The rim of it matches the kosh in our friend here's head."

Powker grinned. "The *kosh*? Is that a technical term?"

The pathologist shrugged. "It is now."

In Jack's decade and a half with the task force, he had seen a great variety of instruments of sudden mortality: the usual guns and knives, of course, but also a World War I bayonet, a heavy gilded picture frame, a clock radio (thrown into a bathtub), a number of baseball bats (wood and aluminum), even a poisonous snake (an East African Gaboon viper, according to the zoo employee who had managed to bag it up). Today's weapon, though, was one of the most mundane he had ever recorded: a can of baked beans.

He glanced away, down the aisle of bright products arrayed in neat rows. A refrigerator case full of energy drinks and sodas; some bins full of unhappy-looking vegetables and overripe bananas. He frowned: here he was, assigned to the most humdrum case in the world, when there was another murder he desperately wanted to be investigating. The thing was, that one had taken place almost four decades ago.

Powker took out a notepad and started sketching the layout of the crime scene.

Jack returned his attention to his present surroundings. The place was like a thousand other New York delis, though the detective did notice a few items that indicated the specific ethnic makeup of the neighborhood: some fat green Mexican cactus leaves in the vegetable display, a product labeled Bakar Khani in the baked goods section. The front window was half-covered with beer posters and Lotto ads—bad sight lines for any potential witnesses who might have been outside.

"That reminds me," Powker said, following Jack's gaze. "My wife wants me to buy a bunch of tickets today. It's up to eighty-something mil."

Jack frowned. "The lottery's a sucker's game." Then, realizing that he had just offhandedly insulted his new partner's spouse, he held up a hand. "No offense."

Powker shrugged good-naturedly. "None taken. But I'm not gonna send you a postcard when we get to Acapulco."

Jack pulled out his own pad. "Let's see what else the register guy might have to say."

Just as they reached the end of the aisle, the front door opened and a young uniform, the First Officer on the Scene, poked his head in. "Excuse me, detectives. A guy out here says he's the owner. He's pretty jazzed up."

Jack nodded. "Let him in."

In marched a short, imperious-looking Indian or Pakistani wearing a long linen shirt over pajama-like pants. He glanced toward the back of the store, then stared at the detectives. "What on earth is going on?"

Jack stared back. "That's what we're trying to figure out."

The man peered down the aisle at the victim. His air of indignation deflated a bit. "This is terrible, terrible. Who is this man?"

Jack shrugged. "We don't know yet. Does the name Robert Brasciak mean anything to you?"

The owner shook his head.

"Would you mind taking a closer look at him?"

The owner looked away, uneasy.

"The sooner we can find out what happened here, the sooner your store can get back to normal."

The man followed the detectives down the aisle. From about six feet away, they stared down at the body. The victim lay faceup, with his eyes rolled back in his head. It was a hard-planed face, like that of a backstreet boxer, with an oddly small mouth, which hung open slackly, as if he was sleeping off a bad three-day drunk.

"You recognize him?" Jack asked.

The owner nodded gravely. "I think so. He comes in sometimes. A customer."

"Did you notice anything about him?"

The owner frowned. "Not a friendly man."

Jack sensed that he was holding something back. "What? Anything you can tell us might help."

"I think . . . he does not like us. Pakistanis, I mean. He will buy our products, and he will give us his money, but he does not respect us." He frowned down at the bloody floor. "This, ah, this mess here. Do the police clean this up? I don't want my people to have to touch this."

Jack nodded in sympathy. "We can recommend a professional service. They specialize in these matters."

The owner unstiffened a little more. "So what happened? Have you spoken to Aban?" He nodded toward the front counter.

"Your guy says he didn't really see what went on. And he says you don't have video surveillance."

The owner glanced at his employee, then lowered his voice. "Please, come with me."

Jack and his new partner exchanged puzzled looks, but they followed the man as he marched briskly down the left aisle, the one unpopulated by dead bodies, past a display of mops and cleaning supplies, through a back door, and into a dim hallway full of a sour foreign cooking smell. An open doorway on the right revealed a small storeroom packed with boxes and product-crammed shelves. The owner turned toward a closed door on the left. He pulled out a key, opened it, and gestured for the detectives to enter. They did, and found themselves in an even smaller room, not much bigger than a walk-in closet. An office. The owner marched over to a gray metal cabinet, pulled out another key, and yanked the door open triumphantly.

Jack and his partner stared at a small TV perched on the top shelf. On its little black-and-white screen, Jack could see a grainy bird's-eye view of one of the store's narrow aisles, facing toward the window, with the edge of the front counter just visible on the left. One of the M.E.'s boys stood up, emerging into view.

Next to the TV sat a VCR.

"Sweet baby Jesus!" said Powker.

The owner smiled, sheepish. "My employees don't know. This way, I can see if they are behaving."

"Is there a tape in there?"

"Yes indeed."

Jack grinned at his partner. "Maybe you just hit the lottery after all." The case might be wrapped up before lunchtime.

It took a few minutes of rewinding, watching customers pop in and out of the store like hyper little windup dolls, before they found the crucial scene.

First, the empty aisle. Then someone strolled in the front door. The picture was lousy, but you could see that it was a young guy, maybe mid-thirties, with a dark complexion and shiny black hair. Pakistani also, or Indian. (Jack had no idea how to tell the difference.) The guy picked up a shopping basket from a stack by the door, then walked toward the camera, casual and calm. He stopped to pick out a few items from the shelves, then drifted past the camera and disappeared from view.

Jack turned to the deli owner. "Do you recognize this man?"

The deli owner shook his head. "I don't believe so. Not a regular."

They returned their attention to the screen. Less than a minute later, the door opened and a big Caucasian walked in. The victim, alive. He ignored the clerk at the register, then ambled down the aisle toward the camera. He stopped to pick something off a shelf and stared down, reading the label.

The first customer returned into view, facing away from the camera. He walked a few feet down the aisle, looking at the shelf on his right, then looked ahead and stopped. The vic didn't look up. Maybe five seconds elapsed, Guy One just standing there, carrying his plastic shopping basket with his left hand, staring at the vic. Suddenly, he reached into the basket and lifted something out: it looked like the can of beans. He rushed forward. The vic just had time to look up, startled. Still holding the basket in his left hand, Guy One raised his right arm, then brought the can arcing viciously down against the victim's head. Once, twice. With the second blow, a small spray of blood flew out. The vic staggered back against a shelf. One more blow and he went down.

His killer stood there for a couple more seconds, staring, and then he stepped over the vic and rushed toward the door. As he came to the front counter, he dropped his shopping basket on the floor, and then he pushed through the door and disappeared out into a rectangle of bright sun. Once he was outside, he ran right: you could see him flicking past the posters in the window.

Jack rewound the tape; in reverse, the spray of blood looked like it was getting sucked back into the victim's head. He played the scene again. "You see that?" he said to his partner. "The vic didn't say a word before he got hit." He was thinking about what the owner had told them about the man disrespecting Pakistanis, but there was no evidence of that on the tape. "And I don't think the perp said anything either, or else the vic would've looked up."

Powker shook his head. "Weird. They didn't have time for any kind of argument, at least not inside the store. And if they'd been arguing outside, they wouldn't have just strolled in and gone shopping."

"So the perp walks around from the other aisle, and *bing*, he runs into this Robert Brasciak. The question is, did he know him? If not, maybe we're looking at an EDP." *Emotionally Disturbed Person*. Jack scratched his cheek again. "If he *did* know him, he must've had a hell of a beef."

* * *

THEY HAD TO WAIT for the Crime Scene Unit to show up, take fingerprints, and check for other evidence. Jack found himself thinking about yesterday's visitor again. "I'm gonna step outside for a little fresh air," he told Powker. He stopped by the front door to pour himself a cup of watery coffee, then paid for it at the cash register, along with some money for his partner's snack. He glanced down: the perp's shopping basket was still there on the floor. A liter bottle of Coke. Three oranges. A stick of butter. A couple of eggplants. Some ice cream. Hopefully the items would have picked up some good fingerprints.

Outside, the sidewalk had been blocked off with a reel of yellow crime scene tape. A couple of radio cars were parked at the curb, and their uniforms leaned against the hoods and shot the bull, awaiting instruction from the detectives. Their walkie-talkies squawked intermittently; the brakes on a city bus squealed as it pulled in toward the curb a few yards away.

Jack took a deep breath of the spring air and looked back at the store. Several tiers of cheap floral bouquets graced the front of the little bodega. A sign ran above: BEER, SODA, CANDY, COFFEE, LOTTO, CIGARETTES. Reflexively, the detective sought out the pattern. When you thought about it, he mused, the place was a regular pit stop for minor vices, for people seeking some reliable little hit of pleasure during their daily grind. And who could blame them?

He glanced down at his watch. The Crime Scene Unit could be delayed for a while, if their teams were busy with other cases. Sometimes the job seemed to be all about waiting.

A big truck came lumbering along Coney Island Avenue, which was a drab commercial stretch of car washes, auto parts emporia, international phone card stores, and humble Middle Eastern food joints that fed the many brown-skinned local taxi and car service drivers. Their wives strolled by, wearing bright saris or somber head scarves, surrounded by lively children. The area was home to Pakistanis, Bangladeshis, and other Muslim immigrants.

Jack stared off down the sunny thoroughfare, but in his mind's eye he was seeing a little street in Red Hook, watching a police car come along several blocks down, waiting for it to arrive. But it never would, no matter how many years he waited. No matter how many times he replayed the scene, his brother would always drop to the sidewalk, holding his mortally wounded side. One little moment in time, one split second when the whole world turned upside down. Jack had spent a lifetime obsessing about that random encounter, wishing he could go back and fix it, wishing he could pull the harsh words back into his mouth.

Only, the thing was, based on what the stranger had told him, it hadn't been random at all. Maybe he had been carrying this burden of guilt for nothing.

He sighed and turned; like it or not, he needed to go back inside and wrap up this silly bodega killing. Maybe the perp was nuts; maybe he had had some prior run-in with the vic. Perhaps the guy had been screwing his wife. Either way, it looked to be just another rinky-dink slaying, like a thousand others.

Routine—until the van came screeching up and the men in the protective bodysuits jumped out.

CHAPTER THREE

There were four of them, and they looked like deep-sea divers as they piled out of the vehicle, which was not at all like a typical NYPD undercover van (dented and unwashed). No, this was a shiny black ride that might as well have had signs painted on it: PROPERTY OF THE FEDERAL GOVERNMENT. The men—they all *looked* like men, though it was hard to tell, considering their bulky, hooded suits—wore oxygen masks. Jack's first thought was *biohazard*, but then he saw the yellow-and-black radiation symbols, which always reminded him of the fallout shelter sign in his elementary school cafeteria. The last man out carried a clicking device.

The NYPD uniforms guarding the perimeter tried to question this odd crew, but they ducked right under the tape.

Jack held up a hand. "Whoa! What the hell's going on?"

The man in front tugged at his mask; the rubber squeaked as he lifted it over his hooded head. An older guy with a bland, round face, wire-rimmed spectacles, rather stringy white hair combed over his balding pate. Grandfatherly. "You in charge here?"

Jack nodded. "NYPD, Brooklyn South Homicide. Now, who are *you?*"

The man pulled out an unfamiliar I.D. "Brent Charlson. Homeland Security."

Jack threw a skeptical glance back at the little deli. "You sure you got the right address?"

The man didn't bat an eye. "How long have you been inside there?"

Jack was definitely starting to get the creeps. "What's going on?"

"I'm going to have to ask you to clear out any personnel from inside. Immediately."

A street person, a big man wearing a wool watch cap, soiled sweatpants, and scrunched-up leather slippers, came shuffling around the corner. He stopped short when he saw the crime scene tape and the frogmen. "Yo! What's happ'nin'? Is this some of that *anthraps*?"

A uniform waved him away.

Jack watched the guy look back anxiously as he shuffled off. Any New Yorker who had lived through 9/11 and the subsequent anthrax mailings took the potential for terrorist activity very seriously. Even four years later, it didn't take much to get you worrying: any siren, a sudden halt on a subway train, an unattended knapsack.

He turned back to the Homeland Security agent. "So why are you guys here?"

The man gestured for his colleagues to move toward the door. "Call your supervisor," he said over his shoulder. And in they went.

Jack didn't like feds. Their Big Swinging Dick attitudes didn't impress him one bit. They were definitely not team players. He remembered a double homicide in Bensonhurst, a Mob case, where a bunch of FBI agents had actually started hauling away the bodies before the NYPD had even gotten on the scene. And 9/11 had made it starkly clear how uncooperative the different governmental agencies could be, with the Feebs and the CIA withholding vital intelligence from each other. Things had supposedly gotten better since then, each agency pledging to pull together, but everybody still liked a good pissing match. And the three-letter guys—FBI, CIA, NSA, DHS—were the cockiest of all.

Jack pulled out his cell and called Lieutenant Frank Cardulli, the head of his unit. "Hey boss, I've got a weird situation here at—"

Cardulli cut him off. "I know. I got a call just a minute ago from downtown. They say we have to let these guys do their thing."

"What's going on?"

"I don't know."

A second later the door of the deli swung open; out came the owner and his clerk, followed by Richie Powker and the M.E.'s crew. Looking anxious, they moved out past the crime scene tape and a good few yards down the block.

Ten minutes later, the boys in the bodysuits came back out. Their leader followed. "All clear."

"Was there a problem?" Jack asked. He couldn't imagine why there would be any radiation inside a deli, but he knew that he didn't want any on *him*.

"We didn't get a reading," Charlson said. "Not this time." He moved off toward the van.

"Whoa," Jack repeated. "You wanna tell us what this is all about?"

The man shrugged. "I can understand that you guys don't like anybody stepping on your toes, and I apologize for the inconvenience." He took out a card and handed it over. "If you find out anything about the perpetrator, I'm going to need for you to call me right away. And if you get a bead on him, I'm gonna really emphasize this: *don't try to bring him in yourselves.* There's a definite radiation risk. Call me and we'll take care of him."

Richie Powker made a face. "What's all this about radiation? The guy killed the vic with a can of beans."

The Homeland Security agent shrugged. "I know this must seem confusing, and I'm sorry, but I'm simply not at liberty to talk about this. Thanks for letting us do our job here; we appreciate your cooperation." He turned, strode away, and joined his colleagues in the van.

Off they went.

"*Simply not at liberty,*" Richie mimicked, sourly. "I hate feds."

Jack went back into the deli. The first thing he noticed was that the can of beans was missing. It took him another minute to discover that the videotape was also gone.

CHAPTER FOUR

As he handed over the admission fee to the New York Aquarium, out by Coney Island, Nadim Hasni noticed that his hands were still shaking. He willed them to stop, without success, but luckily the girl behind the ticket window seemed lost in her own private daydream.

Nadim moved into the cool interior of the entrance hall, grateful for the dim lighting and the near emptiness of the place. A weekday morning. On weekends the place was usually packed, full of tourists and New Yorkers out on family expeditions.

Nadim's nerves still jangled. It was a small miracle that he had managed to get here without being noticed or stopped, sitting on a public bus, in broad daylight, trembling. Well, it wasn't exactly as if he were covered in blood, though he couldn't help feeling as if he was. He thought of his windbreaker, how he had quickly stripped it off outside the deli, after he saw the red stains splashed across the front. He had folded it up, strode several blocks, then stuffed it deep into a trash can. Americans did not do things like this, he thought, throwing clothes away in public trash receptacles. He had straightened up and looked around wildly, but no one paid him any mind.

Now he walked farther into the aquarium's dark interior, past a tank full of gliding manta rays. They circled through the cool blue depths. Why had he come here now? He didn't know; he had simply seen the bus coming and gotten on, had sat there in a daze while it moved down Coney Island Avenue, all the way to the shore. He had gravitated like an automaton toward a familiar place, a place of comfort, where he could be inside, away from public view, in the dark.

He wanted a cigarette, desperately, but knew he wouldn't be allowed to smoke inside the aquarium. He also needed to relieve himself. He saw a sign for a men's bathroom and went inside. A man was holding his little son up over a urinal.

As Nadim zipped up his fly, he noticed—to his horror— that several flecks of dried blood still dotted the back of his right hand. He hurried over to the sink, turned to make sure the stranger was not watching, and scrubbed the blood away. It reconstituted under the water, bright red, like some terrible magic potion, then swirled away down the drain.

He hurried out of the bathroom and made his way out into the aquarium's center courtyard. After the dim interior, the morning sunlight blazed harsh overhead. With no particular destination in mind, he stumbled along a path between a series of outdoor pools: seals, walruses, penguins. . . . He groaned and punched himself in the thigh. What had he done? In one crazed, impulsive moment, he had ruined everything. He had spoiled the entire plan.

Across the way, a roar of applause went up from the arena for the sea lion show. The noise grated on him, and the thought of all the spectators; he ducked through another door, waited for his eyes to adjust to the darkness, and descended a flight of steps, thankful for the quiet. A floor-to-ceiling picture window afforded a side view into the penguin tank. Aboveground the creatures looked comical as they waddled along, but under-water they were transformed into startlingly graceful little torpedoes. Nadim watched for a few minutes, kneading his hands together. Enny had loved the penguins. But her favorites had been the jellyfish, those diaphanous, glowing pink and orange umbrellas, pulsing open and closed as they floated through the depths. His daughter had loved to watch the creatures, and Nadim had loved to watch her little face as she looked on, bathed in the blue light of their subterranean tanks.

He shook his head. The last thing he needed was to get lost in memories, but he couldn't seem to focus on what he needed to do now. Could he go back home? Would he *ever* be able to return home, after what he had done?

Light from the viewing windows rippled and shimmied against the dark walls. Nadim moved on to the next room, where he could see into the walrus pool. The big tank was filled with waving seaweed. A huge bull swooped down from the sun-lit surface. It zoomed up until its whiskered face was just an inch from the glass, flipped over, and zoomed away.

Suddenly Nadim saw before him the face of the big man in the deli, his rough, hard-hammered face, his odd little snapping-turtle mouth. He heard the man's gruff voice. Nadim looked down: his hands were shaking again. He sat on a bench in the middle of the dark room and tucked them underneath his thighs. His heart was thumping and he had to wait several minutes before it finally slowed.

A woman came in, holding the hand of a little boy. The child squirmed away from her, ran over to the window, and pressed his face to the glass. He gasped as the walrus swam right up and stared at him. Nadim wondered if it might give the child nightmares. Enny had had powerful bad dreams, per-haps because the other children teased her at school. Nadim remembered how he and his wife would rise in the middle of the night, stroke her forehead, tell her old folk tales to calm her down. *The Farmer, the Crocodile, and the Jackal. The Seven Wise Men of Buneyr.* And her favorite: *Heer and Ranjha.*

He pictured his daughter's face, plump and round, listening to that last one, that grand, doomed love story, her thick, round eyeglasses glinting in the low light of her bedside lamp. (Without them, she could barely even see her parents' faces.) She listened as they told her of the peasant musician Ranjha, and how he was prevented from marrying Heer, his upper-caste love. Heer's family married her off to someone else, but the young lovers still managed to elope one night. When her kinsmen recaptured her and took her back to their town of Rangpur, Heer cried out, "Oh, Lord, destroy this town and these cruel people so that justice may be done!" And then a fierce fire broke out and began to devastate the town.

At this point, Enny would always interrupt to ask, wide-eyed, why all this suffering was necessary.

It was her mother who answered, more often than not: "Because it was the will of Allah."

Nadim knew that others—Enny's fourth-grade classmates especially—had found her plain and bookish, had made fun of the hijab that covered her pigtails. Without mercy they had teased his daughter, who had proclaimed her wish to become a scientist—*a marine biologist,* no less—a girl whose ancestors came from a landlocked desert state! She had loved this place, this aquarium, had never grown tired of it. Had loved coming here with her father.

And now he had become a killer. What would she have thought of him? He would have explained to her, if he could. He had done it for her. For *justice.* Like the Christian Bible said. *An eye for an eye.*

He stood up and moved to the next dark room. He thought again of the plan. Was it too late? Perhaps not. He doubted that the deli clerk had gotten a good look at him. He had run wildly out of the store, but he'd had the good sense to slow down outside, and he couldn't recall anyone watching him go.

He stopped in front of another huge window, watching a seal rocket down toward the bottom of the tank, trailing bubbles, then spin around and corkscrew up toward the surface.

As if it were free.

CHAPTER FIVE

"Maybe we should just let them have it," said Detective Sergeant Stephen Tanney two hours later.

The man was Jack's direct boss. They were crammed into his little office, along with Frank Cardulli, the head of Brooklyn South Homicide. Richie Powker, new to the headquarters, was gazing at the walls, checking out the clusters of red pins, one for each murder of the year, covering a map of the borough, and the clipboards for each of the seventeen precincts in their region.

"I mean," Tanney continued, "if the feds want the case so bad, why not let it be their problem?" The young sergeant always reminded Jack of a Hollywood actor wearing a fake mustache and trying to play a tough guy; he was the kind of boss who couldn't appreciate the competence of his crew without considering it a challenge to his own tenuous control.

Lieutenant Cardulli listened patiently. He was a squat fireplug of a man, also mustached. Unlike Tanney, though, he had the squad's full loyalty and respect. The L.T. tugged at his earlobe. "Well, I guess Homeland Security *does* have the ultimate authority here, according to the bullshit Washington has handed down . . ."

"What about this radiation business?" Richie said. "I sure didn't like the sound of that."

Cardulli shrugged. "Let's not get all worked up until we know more. The feds are already on this, and we need to keep focused on our own mission." They were homicide cops, not specialists in counterterrorism. "Anyhow, this is probably just the latest false alarm."

The other detectives nodded. Ever since 9/11 and the anthrax thing, the whole country had been so nervous—color-coded threat levels going up and down, great paranoia about the mail and about unattended parcels, tiny towns in rural areas worrying about poison in their fishing holes—but it was hard to maintain that level of anxiety for long. Over the years since the big attack, after checking out hundreds of spurious reports, New York cops had learned to take new "threats" with a grain of salt.

Jack sat near the door. Over his shoulder came a bustle of phone conversations, file cabinet drawers slamming, scanners crackling. Business as usual out in the Homicide squad room.

Linda Vargas, another of the detectives on the Homicide squad, popped her head in. "You just got a call from Latent Prints. They didn't find any matches for your deli perp."

All of the detectives frowned. "This is ridiculous," Richie said. "All the feds need to do is give us a couple of frames from the security video. If we put out some posters of the perp, we can probably have this whole thing rolled up in a day or two."

Cardulli nodded. "I made that point. But Charlson said they don't want to broadcast word of the incident yet."

Jack leaned forward. "Does he already know who our killer is?"

Cardulli shrugged. "I just told you all I heard. I've asked

the chief of detectives if he can put a call in, see if we can get more cooperation."

"What are we supposed to do in the meantime?" Richie said. "Twiddle our thumbs?"

Cardulli crossed his arms. "They're obviously not making this easy for us, but they didn't say to drop the case. Far as I can tell, this is still an open one for the board." He was referring to the big erasable chart out in the squad room, which bore the names of the victims in current cases. He turned to Jack again. "What's your take on this?"

"I'm thinking about shopping."

Sergeant Tanney made a face. "What's that supposed to mean?"

Jack shrugged. "The perp was shopping for groceries in a deli at around eight A.M. Think about that. First of all, was he on his way to work?" Before the others could answer, he continued with his musings. "On your way to work, you buy a cup of coffee and maybe a bagel. You don't do your dinner shopping."

Tanney threw in his usual contradictory two cents. "What if he was shopping for someone else?"

Jack didn't blink. "There were a bunch of items in his basket. If he was shopping for someone else, he would probably have been looking at a list." He leaned forward and rested his elbows on his knees. "Another thing: you shop for food in your own neighborhood."

"But the owner didn't recognize him," Richie pointed out.

Jack nodded. "That's true. *Still*—he was buying ice cream and butter, and you don't grab those far from home."

Tanney scowled. "So what's your point?"

"First of all, maybe our guy's unemployed. Or he works nights—and what does that make him? A transit employee? A taxi driver? Anyway, I bet he lives within a few blocks of the place."

Cardulli stood up. "Why don't we start with what we know? We've got an I.D. for the victim. Let's see if anybody can tell us why some Pakistani would want to bash his head in."

THE SOUND INSIDE R. J. Stanley's brought back one of Jack's earliest childhood memories, when he had been spun in an undertow just off the beach at Coney Island. This new roiling cacophony came from the ranks of giant-screen TVs lining the back wall of the appliance emporium: the roar of the crowd from fifty displays of a boxing match, mixed with the sound of wrenching metal from a superhero action flick, mixed with dopey singing from Disney's *Jungle Book*.

"Christ," said Richie Powker. "I'm getting a headache and we've only been in here for thirty seconds."

Jack nodded. "Imagine *working* here." And that's exactly what he was doing, because this was where Robert Brasciak had spent a good number of his last living days on earth.

Red rubber mats led down the aisles of the big fluorescent-lit showroom, between stacks of microwave ovens and rows of stoves. The place smelled of plastic and metal. Salesmen in cheap khaki pants, pressed shirts, and dull-colored ties roamed their sections like tired lions out on a big synthetic plain; they perked up a little at the sight of the detectives, new meat on the sales floor, but not enough to rouse themselves. For the thousandth time, Jack was grateful for the constantly varied nature of his job: he got to roam the entire southern half of Brooklyn, checking out new scenery and new people every day. (Some of them were dead, of course, but still . . .)

At the sound of gunfire, he turned toward the back of the store, then relaxed: it was just a video game booming out over

a home theater system. A security guard in a blue blazer ambled over, a huge dreadlocked black man with the stolid, comfortable demeanor of a pro. "Can I help you guys?"

"We need to see a manager," Jack said.

The guard didn't ask why; Jack knew the guy had made
him and his partner as cops.

PHIL MANGIOLE, THE FLOOR manager, sat on a half-
size refrigerator in the back loading area, shaking his head. He
was a small, olive-skinned man with the anxious face of someone whose job depended on meeting monthly sales quotas.

"I can't freakin' believe it!" he said. "The guy was just
loading in the new Toshiba forty-seven inchers yesterday afternoon. And now? *Phfft—adios.* Man, what a fuckin' city! My
wife keeps pushing me to move down to the Jersey shore, and
I been resisting 'cause I'm from here, ya know, but shit like
this really makes you think. *Here today, gone tomorrow,* am I
right?" He looked up at the two detectives, as if expecting
praise for this deep insight.

Jack nodded, to be polite. He glanced around. The floor
in the back was plain concrete and the walls were grease-
stained cinder block. Piles of broken-down boxes and other
trash littered the room, and Jack—rather fastidious despite the
ghastly untidiness of his chosen career—looked on in disap-
proval. He noticed a hand-lettered sign on the nearest wall: DO
NOT RIDE ON CONVEYOR!!

"How long did Brasciak work here?" he asked, taking out
his notepad.

Mangiole shrugged. "I'm not sure. I got transferred to
this store about a year ago and he was already here. When I
first came, he was working security, but we both decided it
would be better if he switched to the back. He was okay with it

because the loading job paid better, which was good because frankly I wanted him off the floor. There were a couple of incidents."

Jack's eyebrows went up. "Incidents?"

Mangiole tugged at his chocolate-brown tie. "He, ah, he took the job *real* seriously. I mean, we want somebody intimidating out there, but he thought he was Chuck Norris or something. He was a bit lacking in the, whaddayacallit, *people* skills."

"How'd he do back here? Did he stay out of trouble?"

"Yeah," Richie said. "Or did he ride the conveyor?"

Mangiole smiled at the small joke but shook his head. "He wasn't exactly the fun-loving type."

"Did he get along with the other workers?"

The manager pinched his mouth with his fingers. "How do I put this? We, ah, we have a very mixed staff here. Very *urban*, if you know what I'm saying."

The detectives nodded. The employees were quite racially diverse.

Mangiole frowned. "Robert was not the, ah, most open-minded of individuals."

Powker crossed his arms. "You mean he was racist?"

Mangiole shifted. "Not to speak ill of the dead or anything . . ."

Jack scratched his jaw. "Sounds like he was kind of a problem. Why'd you keep him on?"

Mangiole pointed to a full-sized refrigerator sitting in the open mouth of a service elevator. "The guy could probably have bench-pressed one of those. He had some quirks, but he worked like a freaking ox."

"Did he have any enemies?"

"Well, I don't know about that, but I can tell you that he didn't seem to have a lot of *friends*. He kept to himself."

"Do you happen to have any Pakistani employees here? Or Indian?"

Mangiole looked puzzled. "No. Why do you ask?"

Jack shrugged. "Just curious."

CHAPTER SIX

This was the last place on earth Jack Leightner wanted to be.

After he and Richie interviewed some of the other salesmen at the appliance store, with little benefit to their investigation, he had given his colleague some advice about other avenues to pursue, and then he'd gone over to the Brooklyn D.A.'s office to give a deposition about another case. And then his shift was over, and he had started driving home, but he kept going, down toward the harbor, drawn back despite every instinct in his being.

He had left this place as soon as he could after Petey's murder; even though he was only seventeen, he'd managed to join the Army. He'd been shipped off to the Philippines, then Germany, eager to avoid his grieving parents, Petey's friends, the whole goddamn neighborhood offering him pity every goddamn moment. (He never told the full story of what happened that day—just that he and his brother had been mugged.) He had gone to the far reaches of the earth, but he had never outrun what had happened on this spot.

The trailer was gone, but the vacant lot was still there, where he and Petey had found the case of Scotch. It sat behind a Romanesque brick house of worship, now called the Red

Hook Pentecostal Holiness Church. Jack looked off down the street: the waterfront lay to the northwest, just a couple of blocks down. He turned and set off the other way, though his feet practically stuck to the sidewalk in rebellion, retracing the route he and his brother had taken on that fateful morning back in 1965.

The sky stretched over the waterfront—it always seemed more impressive here than elsewhere in New York City, a vast open plain sweeping high above the humble little two- and three-story brick houses. Jack walked up Sullivan Street to Van Brunt, which ran through the heart of Red Hook like the main street of some Wild West ghost town.

He plodded along past the Patrick F. Daly elementary school, named after a principal who had been killed in the cross-fire of a drug-related shootout back in '92. Ahead rose the red-brick towers of the Red Hook West public housing projects, where he had lived as a kid, back when they had been filled with longshoremen and pipefitters and welders, with Norwegians and Basques and Italians and even Russians like his own folks. Back when the mighty Todd Shipyards, just several blocks away, had built oceangoing steel behemoths, when this neighborhood had been packed with bars and restaurants and movie theaters. Now the shipyards were gone, the streets so quiet you could hear the sea breeze whisper past, the Red Hook Houses transformed into an inner-city ghetto.

The school looked like a minimum-security correctional facility. Jack's chest tightened as he forced himself to turn its far corner, onto Richards Street. He could almost feel the weight of the case of Scotch in his arms. He could hear Petey singing "Help Me, Rhonda," the way his brother would always get a song stuck in his head. Jack could picture him doing his impression of Norton from *The Honeymooners* or improvising some slapstick stunt to cheer up their often-depressed mother. He could even make their father laugh, when Max Leightner was not too deep into his cups. He had been a miracle, that kid, emerging from his screwed-up family like a bright plant rising from a dung heap. It wasn't until he was gone that the others realized how he had held them together—and then they all retreated in different directions: Jack's father into his drinking, his mother into her three-day periods of "lying down," and Jack himself into his torturous guilt. (And maybe into a career as a cop.)

He walked on, remembering how he and his brother had hurried that long-ago day, hoping to get their treasure to Joe Kolchuk's house before they were spotted by some family friend. They had laughed with the audacity of it, he and Petey, thinking they were almost home free, unobserved.

But they *had* been watched, as Jack had learned just thirty-two hours ago. Somewhere along the way a car had slowly cruised behind them with an Italian-American man at the wheel and two Negro teenagers sitting low in the back. His brother's killer and the friend he had brought along for backup—both members of Fort Greene's Black Chaplains street gang, a world away from their home turf. On Richards Street, the man had stopped the car and the back door swung open.

"That's them, boys. You know what to do."

Forty years later, Jack forced himself to continue on. Scraps of paper and empty potato-chip bags littered the sidewalk, challenged by big weeds pushing up through the cracks. A Puerto Rican woman and two little pigtailed girls emerged from the bodega across the corner, the kids laughing and skipping. He walked along a block of spavined little houses, their facades weather-beaten; old ornamental cornices ran along the rooflines. Take away the cars and the telephone wires, and the scene might have looked the same a hundred years before.

Jack trudged along, seeing how the upper windows of the houses filled with the bright gold of the late afternoon sun; white airplane contrails cut the blue sky above. And then, at the corner, he stopped and looked down. For the first time since his youth, he was standing over the spot where his younger brother had been slain. He stared at the sidewalk, half-expecting to see bloodstains on the cracked concrete. But the concrete itself had probably been replaced a number of times since that fateful day—a reminder that this was one very cold case indeed.

A flock of sparrows chittered loudly up in the branches of a scrappy little tree. Jack looked around. Across the way, a couple of the old houses had been sandblasted and renovated, maybe by some of the artsy types who had been moving in and trying to rejuvenate the neighborhood; they called themselves "urban pioneers." A block down was the corner where the diner had once stood, where the patrol cops had stopped in before they could witness two local boys getting jumped.

Jack stared down again. There should have been a memorial on this spot, a permanent one, a bronze plaque dedicated to a teenage kid who had been so cheerful, such a natural athlete, so full of life. The detective made a solemn vow: *I swear that I will find out who was responsible for what happened to you, Petey. And I will bring him to justice.*

Somewhere, maybe just a mile away—if he was still in this world—lived the man who had set this killing in motion. And there was no statute of limitations on murder.

Jack stood there a few minutes, musing. It was a strange thing: an Italian man and two Negro boys, together in Red Hook, back in the sixties. Like oil and water. *Mulignans,* the

Italians called their neighbors to the east, meaning "eggplants," referring to their dark skin. There was no love lost.

The boy with the knife, Jack's visitor yesterday, one Darnel Teague Jr., had never known the name of the man who had hired him. Dead tired, soaked with sweat, as he was getting off a shift as a dishwasher in a Fort Greene restaurant, Darnel had been approached by an Italian-American man, black-haired, medium height and build, maybe thirty years old. It had been very late, and the street was dark, and the man was sitting out front in a sharp-looking car, an Eldorado, maybe, or an LTD. He called out as Darnel walked out onto the sidewalk, but the teenager ignored him. The man called again, using Darnel's name this time. The boy approached the car cautiously, leery of talking to some strange white man at that hour of the night (or at any hour, for that matter), but the visitor quickly piqued his interest.

"Word on the street is that you're a smart kid. I bet you don't want to be a dishwasher in some shithole all your life."

And then Darnel was in the car, poised to jump out. The man drove them out of the neighborhood, up Atlantic Avenue, and then pulled over on a deserted side street. He made it clear that he knew quite a bit about Darnel, about his membership in the gang, about his juvie record: shoplifting, grand theft auto, possession of a homemade zip gun. (Ingredients: a piece of wood for the handle, a section of car aerial for the barrel, a strong rubber band. That sounded playful, except the thing could fire a .22 bullet. They came in very handy in rumbles with Red Hook's white street gangs.)

"I've got a project for you," the man had said. "We've got somebody over in Red Hook who needs to be taught a little lesson." He didn't explain who the *we* was, but—judging by the man's stylish car, his two-tone shirt, his heavy Italian accent—Darnel knew enough not to ask. But he *did* have one question. "Why don't you get one of your own people to deal with this?"

The man had not answered—he just reached into his back pocket and took out an envelope. "This is all the explanation you're gonna need."

Still wary, Darnel looked inside. Ten crisp fifty-dollar bills. And this was back in the sixties, when that had seemed like a fantastic amount of money for a young colored man. Hell, for *anyone* . . .

"What you want me to do?" he said.

"We just want you to shake a couple of kids up."

Jack, hearing the story decades later, had been frustrated by Darnel's vagueness. If he was going to reopen this case, he would need some definite ground for charges.

But then, according to the tale, the stranger had taken things a step further. He reached out, opened the glove compartment, and handed over a switchblade. "This might come in handy."

Now Jack stood on the corner where the schooling had been done, although he still had no idea what the lesson was supposed to have been. He thought about Darnel Teague, the teenager, and Teague, the man. All of his life and career he had nursed fantasies of what he might do if he ever ran into his brother's killer. One thing was sure: he had never imagined that he might just let the perp walk away, alive and scot-free.

It was nice to think that criminal justice was cut-and-dried: you caught the bad guys and put them away. But the system was riddled with compromise. Vicious criminals were allowed to plea bargain every day or were turned into confidential informants and sent back out on the streets. The principle was simple: you did what you could to land the biggest fish.

Jack's choice had been equally clear: he could exact revenge on one lone ex-teenager, or he could let the man go in exchange for the information he was mulling over now.

So he had let Darnel Teague walk out of his kitchen and back into the world. And now he ran his hand along his jaw, pondering. An Italian-American man, a black teenager. Brooklyn, 1965. Way back then, who would have dared to bridge the gap between the races? Who would have been bold—or crazy— enough?

He walked quickly back to his car.

"WHY DON'T YOU BRIGHTEN this place up a little?" Jack glanced around his old friend's office. "Open the windows, get some overhead lighting. . . . It looks like Don Corleone's den in here."

Larry Cosenza sat back in his massive leather armchair and shrugged. He was a handsome man, broad-shouldered, with a full head of bright white hair. "This is what people want. They think it means respect for the dead. You know how things are around here: it's not about change."

They were sitting in the Cosenza Funeral Home, in the heart of Carroll Gardens. The neighboring areas were gentrifying rapidly, with sushi restaurants and French bistros pouring in, with a flood of young hipsters who couldn't afford Manhattan rents, but the Gardens were a last remaining bastion of the old-school Italian ways. Out front, amidst dark perennial shrubs, cherubs sprayed water in a little aquamarine fountain, next to a statue of the Virgin Mary.

Larry placed his hands on his massive old desk. "*So*: to what do I owe the pleasure?" It had been years since their last reunion, when Jack had come to consult his childhood friend about another Red Hook case.

He stood up and wandered over to a credenza covered with sports trophies; his friend was sometimes referred to as the unofficial mayor of Carroll Gardens and his business evidently sponsored several local kids' teams.

Jack hefted a softball trophy. "You should have some of these for bocce," he said. The little local park still held a sandpit where old geezers in Members Only jackets and tweed caps could gather, tossing the heavy metal balls and reliving their glory days, when a sparrow couldn't fart in this neighborhood without the consent of the Mob and the International Longshoremen's Union.

"You didn't come here to talk about sports," Larry said.

Jack turned and came around to his chair in front of the man's desk. He sat down slowly, as if his joints ached. "I'm gonna tell you something, Larry, and I need you to keep it to yourself."

The funeral director shrugged again. "No problem."

"No, *really*. I need you to swear."

Cosenza's eyebrows went up. "You want me to prick my finger? What are we, kids again?"

Jack just frowned.

Cosenza's hands went up in surrender. "Okay, okay: I swear. Now what's on your mind?"

As Jack told the tale, he gripped the sides of his chair in order to keep his hands from shaking.

When it was over, Larry Cosenza sighed. "You're really bringin' up some ancient history here."

Jack shook his head. "It's not ancient to me." He leaned forward. "I need your help. You know this neighborhood as well as anybody."

Cosenza reached out to the leather blotter in the center of his desk and picked up a heavy glass paperweight. Then he sat back, staring into it as if it were a crystal ball. "Let me ask you something: what are you hoping to achieve here?"

"Achieve?"

"You looking for closure? That's what people yak about these days: 'Finding closure with the dead.'" Cosenza shook his head. "You and I both deal with this every day. And so you know the dirty little secret: we don't want 'closure.' We want them back. We want do-overs. We want to make things right because they weren't right the first time around. But the dead don't come back. They're gone for good."

Jack stood up again, restless, and paced the office, his shoes sinking into the thick beige carpet. "This isn't for me, Larry. This isn't *about* me. It's about Petey. It's about getting him the justice he deserves." He stopped and turned to his old friend. "I know he's gone, and I know nothing's going to bring him back. But that doesn't mean that I'm just gonna let the people who planned this get away scot-free."

Cosenza swiveled in his chair and looked out his office window for a moment. Then he sighed and swiveled back. "So what are you thinking?"

Jack nodded, glad to have his friend aboard. "I'm thinking, who would have gone to the blacks for help back then? I'm thinking Joey Gallo." While the rest of the big mafiosi of that era had kept to their own families and certainly their own race, Gallo had been a renegade. He'd been obsessed with expanding his criminal empire and saw a great opportunity in opening up dealings with the black community. He had taken a lot of flack for that from his own people.

Cosenza dropped the paperweight back on his desk. "You said the kid described the stranger as black-haired. Joe Gallo was blond."

Jack shrugged. "That doesn't mean he wasn't behind it."

Cosenza frowned. "Maybe, but he went upstate in 'sixty-one." The notorious Red Hook mobster had been convicted on extortion charges. "And he was inside for ten years."

"He still could've called the shots."

Cosenza made a face. "Yeah—but *why*? Why would a hotshot like that have it in for two harmless local kids? You wouldn't have been a blip on his radar."

Jack nodded thoughtfully. "I've gone over and over it in my head, and I can't even imagine a reason why he might have had any beef with Petey or with me. There's only one thing I can think of: he must've had something against my old man. Or *somebody* did."

Cosenza nodded. "I can't say that would surprise me. Your father could be a real tough guy."

Jack snorted. "He could be a total bastard, when he had a few drinks in him. Which was not exactly rare."

"So somehow he crossed the Mob?"

Jack shrugged. "If I knew, I wouldn't be bothering you."

Cosenza frowned. "Is this an officially sanctioned investigation? You got the NYPD behind you?"

"No. Why?"

Cosenza leaned forward. "I know you don't spend any time around here these days, but you can see how things are changing. Maybe you get the impression that there's only a few of these *made guys* left—that they're all ancient and toothless, and spend all their time playing the ponies over at the OTB. But I want to warn you, Jackie, as an old friend: you go sticking your nose in the wrong places around here, you might just find out there's plenty of bite in them left."

Jack waved a hand in dismissal. "They don't mess with cops."

"Unless cops mess with *them*. Anyways, I would think

you might wanna stay away from poking around these partic-ular parts."

It was hard for Jack to argue, considering that he bore the scar of a bullet hole on his chest—a souvenir of his last unofficial investigation in Red Hook.

"Can you just put out a few feelers, maybe find someone who knew my pop back in the day?"

Cosenza sighed. "It goes against my better judgment, but I'll see what I can do. Listen, you wanna come over for dinner tonight? Sandra would love to see you, and Lord knows there's always enough food on the table." He leaned forward. "Hey, are you single these days? Last time, I seem to remember that you were thinking about getting married . . ."

"I wasn't just thinking about it. I went out and bought the damn ring."

"So what happened?"

Jack squirmed in his chair. "It didn't work out." That was the understatement of the year. One fateful New Year's Eve, heart bursting with love, he had brought his girlfriend Mi-chelle to an expensive restaurant, gotten down on one knee, and popped the question. Michelle's response had been a bit un-orthodox: she announced that she was having an affair, jumped up, and ran out. She never came back.

He crossed his arms. "Why are you asking?"

"Sandy's cousin is coming over. You remember Trish, don't you?"

Jack grinned. "She's hard to forget." *Trish the Dish*. Back in the day, the neighborhood boys had followed her around wide-eyed, mesmerized by the wearer of the tightest sweater in Red Hook.

Larry waggled his eyebrows. "She's divorced now, you know."

Jack shook his head. "Sounds tempting. Some other time." He said good-bye, then went out and sat in his car. Home?

On impulse, he turned the ignition and drove off, not toward Midwood, but just east of it, to Flatbush. The Dhammapada Tibetan Buddhist Center was located in a rather rough section of the neighborhood, in an old brick building above a check-cashing joint. Jack had first visited the place a couple of years ago on official business, after a local teen accidentally killed one of the staffers by throwing an empty bottle.

The director was a little British nun. After the arrest of the young perpetrator, she had prevailed upon Jack to assist her in helping the kid. Normally he might have written her off as an armchair liberal, but she seemed to genuinely want to get involved, so he had—grudgingly—hooked her up with a sympathetic ear in the D.A.'s office. Every now and then, he liked to drop by and see how their little social experiment was going.

He pulled up in front of the center but was disappointed to find that the door was locked.

He got back in his car. And went back to work.

CHAPTER SEVEN

When Nadim's cell phone went off, the sound made him jump as if he had been poked with a hot needle. He dug frantically in his pocket, sure the other patrons of the little café would stare. He yanked the phone out and opened it to stop the ringing, even before he saw who was calling.

"Nadim? Is that you? Where the hell are you?"

Rafik-kahn, his boss. In a foul mood, as usual. Nadim pictured him ensconced in his Plexiglas-walled booth, sitting fat and lordly behind his desk like a rajah on the back of an elephant.

"Saabir dropped the car off half an hour ago," the man continued in angry Urdu. "Not you nor I, Nadim, neither one of us is making a rupee while it's just sitting at the curb."

Nadim pressed his free hand against his forehead. "I . . . I'm not feeling well. I think I ate something very bad for my stomach."

"Again with the sickness? I'm not running a convalescent home. How many times have you called in sick in just the last month?"

Nadim rubbed his eyes. How could he explain all these absences? If his boss knew what was really up with him, he'd be fired on the spot. "Tomorrow night," was all he said. "I'll drive a double tomorrow. I promise."

"Bah," his boss spat. "If I could put your promises in the bank, I could buy the Mohatta Palace. I'm warning you, Nadim: if you don't come in tomorrow night, don't bother coming back at all."

Nadim hung up. He really did feel sick to his stomach now. Life was turned upside down. He should have finished his shift in the car this morning, bought a few things in the deli, picked up a copy of the *Sada-e-Pakistan* paper at the local newsstand, come home to make himself some dinner, had a good smoke and a read, then pulled down the shades and gone to bed. But his usual deli had been closed for some mysterious reason, so he had gone to an unfamiliar one a couple of blocks away, and so had been set in motion this terrible deviation from his hard-earned quiet, anonymous path. He hadn't slept, had barely been able to keep down any food.

After passing a couple of hours in the aquarium this morning—*killing time* was the idiom, if he remembered correctly from his courses in English as a Second Language—he had wandered over onto Brighton Beach Avenue, in the neighborhood of the Russians. He had trudged aimlessly back and forth along their short main avenue, listening to their foreign tongue. They were aliens here in America too, though they were no longer looked at as public enemies. No, since the towers had fallen, that role had shifted toward men who looked like *him*.

He had walked until he could walk no longer, then drifted over to the beach and sat on a bench staring out at the ocean, wishing he had never come to this land of false promises, false dreams. The day passed slowly, so very slowly, but the sun did move overhead, and the afternoon shadows lengthened on the sand. Nadim contemplated returning to his apartment, but who knew what might be waiting for him? He wanted desperately to be back among his own people, to listen to Urdu rather than gruff Russian, but he couldn't risk arrest. He would never go back into captivity; that was one promise he had made to himself, one promise he would be sure to keep.

In the evening, he stayed in the café as long as he could, buying a cup of soup or a glass of tea now and then to keep the proprietor happy and avoid drawing attention to himself, but he knew he couldn't stay all night. He looked at the clock on the wall: just about now, he thought, he should have been driving someone to the airport or to some Manhattan rendezvous, should have been flowing along the dark streets of the city, safe in his driver's seat, in control of his destiny.

And now—glancing at the clock a half-hour later—he should have been stopping for a *karahi* and some *saag* at Tabeer's café on Coney Island Avenue, making idle conversation with Fayaz and Shafiq and some of the other drivers. Then back out on the streets, tracing the glowing pathways of the city, as they had been laid out beneath him that night twelve years ago when he had first arrived in this country, swooping low over Brooklyn in a huge airplane.

He emerged from the café bleary-eyed. A big poster on the side of a bus stop jumped out at him, a reminder of the city's severe vigilance after 9/11: IF YOU SEE SOMETHING, SAY SOMETHING. He hurried past, eyes down, avoiding the passersby. He thought of calling one of his fellow drivers, of asking for rescue or at least a couch on which to spend the night, but he would not risk implicating anyone else in his troubles. Agents of the government were everywhere.

He stopped in at a corner deli and bought a pack of cigarettes, even though the damned things were so expensive and it occurred to him that he ought to be saving his money now. He lit up, breathing the smoke deep into his lungs; it helped ease his anxiety.

He trudged back to the boardwalk. The night was fairly warm and people were still out, strolling along the weathered wooden walkway, chatting amiably, without any cares in the world. This place was too busy; Nadim walked west, toward Coney Island, until he found an unpopulated stretch of the walkway. Reeling with exhaustion, he found a bench facing the sea, lay down, and curled up. He couldn't risk staying out in the open like this for long, but maybe he could at least take a short nap.

He lay there as the night grew colder, chilled by ocean breezes, sleeping as if drugged, wracked by his recurring nightmares. His Enny came back to him, as she often did, that sweet little wraith, pressing her hand to her chest and coughing, coughing, imploring him, *Help me, Abbu. Please help me.* Then the dreams turned violent. One ended with Nadim covered in blood, and he jolted awake, shocked to find the sky brightening slowly with the dawn, then jolted again by the sight of a stocky policeman standing at the foot of his bench. The officer tapped Nadim's foot with a nightstick.

Never, he thought. I will kill this man—or myself—before I allow them to cage me away again. He tensed, prepared to launch himself up off the bench.

But the policeman just yawned. "Can't sleep here, buddy. Gotta move on." And then the man actually, miraculously, sauntered off toward the rising sun.

CHAPTER EIGHT

"Let's go," Richie Powker said. "There's no one home."

"One more try." Jack pressed the doorbell again, then waited a few seconds. Finally, he turned away; he was walking down off the stoop into the bright morning sunshine when he heard a sound behind the door.

The house was ramshackle, leaning to the left, with a threadbare little front yard and crumbling shingles on the roof. The old woman who opened the door was not in much better shape. Her hair poked out of her head like dry straw and her face was scrunched into what looked like a permanent scowl. "Whaddaya want?" she said.

Jack called up to her. "Is this Robert Brasciak's residence?"

"Who wants to know?"

He pulled his badge out of the pocket of his sport coat. "We're with the New York Police Department. About Brasciak."

"There's no one here by that name."

"That's funny," Jack said. He pointed toward a little pile of mail resting on the front porch. "There's a couple of letters and bills for him. Are you a relative, or his landlady?"

The woman scowled. "I was his landlady, but he doesn't live here anymore. He moved away last year."

Jack didn't believe her. "We'd just like to take a quick look at his apartment."

The woman crossed her arms. "I ain't stupid. I watch the TV. You need a warrant."

"You're right. We *would* need a warrant. If he was alive."

The woman took a step back. "What are you talkin' about?"

"I'm sorry to break the news: he was found dead yesterday morning."

The woman's right hand flew up to her cheek. "But he owes me two months' rent!"

Jack didn't bother to comment. In his time with Brooklyn South Homicide, he had witnessed just about every possible reaction to the news of a murder.

"What happened?" the woman asked.

"We're investigating what looks like a homicide."

She pressed a hand to her chest. "Who did it?"

"That's what we're trying to find out." Jack and his partner trooped in past her, into a front hall that was decorated with flowered wallpaper more faded than the owner's housedress. "Which way, ma'am?"

Grudgingly, she pointed to a doorway. They followed her down a dimly lit, narrow stairway to another closed door. She reached into the pocket of her housedress and took out a key ring. As she turned the key, she looked back at them with a puzzled expression.

"What is it?" Jack asked.

"The door was unlocked. He never leaves it that way."

Jack flashed on the image of the feds piling out of their van. "Has anyone else come by asking about Robert?"

The landlady shook her head. Jack frowned. Maybe the feds had dropped by without bothering to ring the bell. This landlady seemed like a tough watchdog, but these locks were old and not very effective; it would have been a simple matter to slip in while she was out. He started thinking about radiation: What if there was something nasty beaming little rays behind this door? In that case, he hoped the feds *had* paid a visit.

She turned the knob and pushed the door open. The reason for her wariness soon became obvious: the basement apartment was devoid of windows.

"Nice illegal rental," Richie noted dryly.

"You're not gonna turn me in, are ya?"

Jack saw a big chunk of her income disappearing in her panicked eyes, and he adopted a reassuring tone. "We're not here to make any problems for you—as long as you tell us the truth." He and his partner wandered through the apartment while they asked her more questions. They didn't stumble across any atomic bombs in the making, which was certainly a relief.

"Any idea why someone would have it in for your tenant?"

"He kept to himself. I don't know nothin' about his personal life."

"You ever hear any fights or arguments going on down here?"

"He never had company, not that I know of." She stared at Jack. "Was it a nigger that killed him? Robert could never tolerate the niggers."

Jack frowned at the casual slur; the last thing he needed right now was a reminder of his own teenage stupidity. "It seems like it might have been a Pakistani or an Indian." He watched carefully for her reaction.

Her eyebrows went up. "Well, *that's* a surprise. Those people seem pretty quiet. Family types."

Jack turned back to his survey of the apartment. He wished he could tell if Brasciak might have had a little company post-mortem, but even if the feds had tossed the place, they could hardly have left it in more of a mess. It was a real bachelor dump, with empty beer cans scattered around, overflowing ashtrays, clothes strewn about. It looked as if it hadn't been renovated since the seventies or eighties: the wallpaper was silvery, and there was a wall-sized photo mural of Manhattan at night in the little living room, which offered just enough space for a beat-up leather couch, a big-screen TV (employee discount?), an elaborate video game controller, and a weight bench and some dumbbells. The gray wall-to-wall carpeting smelled funky, like spilled beer and mildew. A poster on the wall bore a picture of a Hispanic-looking hoodlum holding a white woman in an arm lock. Crosshairs were superimposed over the man's face, and Jack realized that it was a shooting gallery target.

"Did Brasciak have family?" Richie asked.

"Not that I know of."

"How about girlfriends?"

"I don't think so." The landlady's nose wrinkled as she gestured at a pile of lurid porn magazines on the coffee table, along with a spread of well-thumbed copies of *Soldiers of Fortune* and *Small Arms Review* and a bunch of candy wrappers.

"Did he have problems with any neighbors?"

She shook her head. "He didn't go outside much."

Jack wandered into the kitchen. The refrigerator was nearly empty, except for some beer and big cans of bodybuilder's muscle powder. He passed through a back doorway: the bedroom was more like a walk-in closet, just big enough for a mattress on the floor, which smelled of sweat and foot odor.

As Jack returned to the living room, a phone rang up-stairs and the landlady trundled off to answer it.

"What do you think?" Jack asked his partner.

Richie shook his head. "You know what this reminds me of? When I was a kid, I used to dream about being grown up. I thought it would mean that I could eat candy bars and watch TV all day, and no one could stop me."

The detective picked up one of the porn magazines, flipped through it, then tossed it back onto the coffee table. "This must be a pretty weird part of working in Homicide: you look through everything in people's houses. Like, they go off to work, never expecting that they're not gonna come home, and all their stuff is just layin' there. My mom always used to tell me that thing about making sure I went out with clean under-wear, in case I got hit by a car and had to go to the hospital." He frowned. "Man, I wonder what the crap in *my* house would say about *me*." He shrugged. "I guess I don't have any big secrets lying around, though." Richie sighed and sat on the edge of the couch. "I keep thinkin' about those feds. They certainly didn't leave us a lot to work with."

Jack shrugged. "It could be worse. A *lot* worse. We some-times get dump jobs, a decapitated body in a Dumpster, or out in a marsh off the Belt Parkway. Sometimes we can't even get fingerprints. Look at the bright side here: we know the vic, and we've got a big jump on identifying the perp."

Richie wrinkled his bulbous nose. "There are tens of thousands of Pakistani or Indian men in this city."

"Yeah, but we know our killer is not black or white or His-panic or Chinese. We can cross about eight million potential perps off the list." He headed for the front door. "We may be looking for a needle in a haystack, but at least we know what the needle looks like."

Richie chuckled. "You must be a glass-half-full kind of guy."

Jack smiled. "A glass half-full of needles."

IN HOPES OF RECOGNIZING their suspect, the two detectives spent the rest of the morning staring at computer databases: any files that cross-referenced zip code and country of origin, and provided photos. They found no matches for their mysterious Pakistani or Indian in 11218 or 11230. Searching citywide—not to mention the rest of the state and nearby New Jersey and Connecticut—might take days, so they decided to leave the computers alone and follow an old but trustworthy motto: *Get Off Your Ass and Knock On Doors.*

"I told you this wasn't going to be easy," said Richie, later in the day.

The two detectives had just walked out of a little Pakistani café on Coney Island Avenue, half a block from the deli crime scene. Outside, the weather was pleasant, but the agreeable aromas of spring were damped down by the avenue's usual odors of motor oil and car exhaust.

The café owner, a mournful little man with a bushy mustache, had not offered a single remotely useful piece of information. "Please, sirs, I saw nothing," he'd said, eyes wide. "I will do everything possible to cooperate, but I saw nothing."

The man wiped down the counter with what seemed like a suspicious amount of nervous energy. In front of him lay steam table vats of mysterious entrées, orangey-red, pale yellow, muddy brown. The food looked oily, Jack thought; his digestion was already not the greatest. The place was tiny and narrow, with just a few humble tables and fluorescent lighting that reminded him of the Kings County morgue. The only decoration was some garish film posters of brown-skinned he-men with impressive pompadours and veiled women with sultry eyes.

Jack pulled out a Polaroid of the victim in the deli. "Do you recognize this man?"

The owner took a nervous peek. "No, sir."

"Have you ever seen him?"

"Never," the man replied, too firmly, in Jack's opinion. If the victim lived just a few blocks away, he had probably walked past here any number of times.

The owner wrung his hands. "I am sorry I cannot assist you."

Jack noted a layer of sweat on the man's upper lip, despite the moderate temperature inside the café.

Richie handed over a business card. "Thanks a lot. Please call if you hear anything about what happened yesterday."

The owner nodded vigorously. "Yes, sir. Of course. Anything I can do to help."

Now the two detectives were out on the avenue again, empty-handed. Jack took out a pack of gum and offered it to his partner. Then he unwrapped a stick, popped it into his mouth, and squinted off down the avenue. "I think that guy seemed kinda hinky."

Richie scuffed something off the bottom of his shoe. "He was just scared."

"That's what I mean. Why would he be scared if he doesn't know anything?"

Across the street, a yellow cab emerged from the open front of a car wash and a little crew of Mexicans rushed forward to dry and buff it. Richie walked to the curb and leaned against his car, an unmarked Crown Vic. Jack followed.

"You ever work a case around here before?" the local detective said.

"A couple. You don't get many murders around here, what with all the devoutness." The neighborhood, thick with East Asian Muslims, butted right up against Midwood, thick with Hasidic Jews.

Richie scratched at a little food stain on his tie. "I been workin' this beat for eleven years, most of that on patrol. You know they call this Little Pakistan, right?"

Jack nodded. Brooklyn was dotted with all sorts of intensely ethnic enclaves: former Russians in Brighton Beach, Chinese in Sunset Park, Poles in Greenpoint . . .

"When was the last big case you worked here?"

Jack thought about it. "I don't know, maybe five years? We had a nasty triple homicide over on Avenue C."

Richie nodded. "I remember. A guy killed his wife and his stepkids." He glanced around. "The thing is, the neighborhood has changed a hell of a lot since then. From the Pakistani point of view, it really hit the skids. Lots of stores and restaurants have closed down. The biggest mosque, not far from here"—he gestured south down Coney Island Avenue—"used to be so full that they'd have people praying on rugs right out on the sidewalks. Now they can't even come close to a full house."

"Why?"

"Two words: Nine-eleven. Before that, you couldn't find a parking space because there were so many Pakistani people here shopping, eating, praying . . ."

"And now?"

"Almost half of them are gone."

"Why?"

"After the World Trade Center went down, the feds ordered the community here to do 'special registration.' There were lots of Immigration raids. Tons of people got deported, and others skipped to Canada or other places because they were afraid of getting deported. Or arrested."

"For what?"

"For any kind of suspicion. It was a lousy time to have brown skin. It still is. That's why our friend in there"—he nodded back at the café—"wasn't eager to take a look at the photo of our vic. The people around here are petrified of getting caught up in something that has nothing to do with them. They just wanna keep their heads down and go on with their lives. Nine-eleven totally screwed them over."

Jack frowned. "I know most of the hijackers were Saudis, but weren't some of these people involved in the bombing of the Trade Center in 'ninety-three?"

"Some were, yeah, some newly arrived radical types, but most of these people were not at all happy with them, even before the bombing. The newcomers took over some of the mosques and forced the more moderate imams out."

"You seem to know a lot about this stuff."

Richie shrugged. "Like I told you, I've been working this turf for a long time."

Jack sighed and stretched. "Let's keep going."

And so they did, walking in and out of Laundromats, gas stations, auto parts stores, seeking anyone who might have any information related to their case. No matter how many times they assured people that they were not feds, that they had absolutely nothing to do with Immigration, every time they interviewed a Pakistani-American, the result was the same: a look of barely suppressed panic, a clamping down.

Two hours later, they stopped to take a break and sit in a coffee shop for a few minutes.

"Well, whaddaya wanna do?" Powker said as they settled

onto a couple of counter stools. "I guess we can go back and keep working on the Brasciak end of things."

Jack frowned. They had already discovered that their victim was unmarried, didn't seem to have any wives or kids in his past, had a decent credit rating and no criminal record.

"This is ridiculous," he said. "What a waste of time!"

"I told you," Richie said. "You can't hold it against them. They're just afraid of getting deported."

Jack shook his head. "I'm not talking about the Pakistanis; I'm talking about that fed. I think maybe he already knows who our perp is, while we're wandering around here like a couple of mopes. It burns me up—it's disrespectful of the NYPD, and it's totally pointless. Aren't we all on the same team?"

"Nothing new from your boss?"

Jack snorted. In typical fashion, Sergeant Tanney had been told what to do, and then had meekly gone ahead and done it. "He says he called again today, but the feds didn't call back."

Richie sighed, then picked up a menu. "You gonna get something to eat or just coffee?"

Jack rested his elbows on the counter, thinking of a little boost of sweetness to counter the futility of the day. Statistically speaking, after the first forty-eight hours the chance of solving any homicide case dropped like a stone.

CHAPTER NINE

After the day's tour of duty was over, Jack drove back to Cosenza's funeral home. A wake was about to begin and the deceased's family and friends were filing in, squat old women packed into tight black dresses, gangly teenagers squirming under the pressure of unfamiliar suit collars, and big beefy men with mullet haircuts demonstrating their manly handshakes and slapping each other on the shoulder. A couple of professionally grave men, employees of the home, stood at attention at the sides of the front door, hands folded over their crotches, doing their best not to look bored.

Across the street, Jack saw Larry Cosenza step outside for a moment, and he pushed himself away from the hood of his car and called out.

Cosenza looked up, startled. A little too startled, perhaps . . . He glanced up and down the street, then gestured at Jack. *Inside.*

"How about putting up some nice track lighting?" Jack teased as they walked back into his old friend's somber office. "Or some pictures of the beach?"

The funeral director pretended to be irked. "Hey—I don't

come over where *you* work, tell you how to use your goddamn sheriff's badge."

Jack chuckled. "The place looks great. Really." He settled into an armchair.

Cosenza picked up a tray of Italian pastries from his desk. "Want a *sfogliatella*? They're left over from a wake, but still nice and fresh."

Jack picked out one of the shell-shaped pastries and bit into it, savoring the ricotta filling, with its hint of orange peel; he held his hand under it, but a few flaky crumbs still ended up on the rug. The taste was like an instant time machine back to his childhood. Which, of course, reminded him of the reason for his visit. "I don't mean to bug you, but have you had a chance to think over what we talked about? You got any leads for me?"

Cosenza sat deep in his chair, dug a finger in his ear, then turned and looked out the window. "*Leads*. Christ." He turned back to Jack with an embarrassed look. "I'm sorry, but nobody around here wants to rehash ancient history."

Jack felt all his own amiability ice over. "I told you: there's nothing ancient about this for me. I've been living with it every day since I was a fucking kid."

Cosenza grimaced. "I'm sorry for that, Jack. Really I am. But you asked for my help, and I'm helping you. I'm telling you the best course of action here: you need to let sleeping—"

Jack nearly launched himself out of his chair. "Don't say it, Larry. Don't ever say that. We're talking about my brother."

Cosenza raised his hands in apology. "I'm sorry. But I'm looking out for you."

Jack stood up. "Did somebody tell you something, Larry? Did somebody ask you to warn me off?"

Cosenza sat back and raised his hands. "Just let it go.

There's no good going to come of this, not for you, not for anybody."

Jack stood silent for a minute. "All right. I get it. You still live here. You've got a wife and kids, a business." He shrugged. "Don't worry about it."

Cosenza stood too, a pained expression on his face. "Hell. Don't go away mad."

Jack just gave him a disappointed look, then turned and walked out.

HE DIDN'T GO FAR.

He got back in his car and drove a short distance west through Carroll Gardens. On Court Street, he passed the old hiring hall, once presided over by the Longshoremen's Union in close conjunction with a string of Mafia capos; the big boxy building had even featured a stained-glass portrait of Albert Anastasia, chief executioner of Murder, Inc.

The place was now a medical center for elderly dockworkers. The rest of the area had not changed much, though: old Italian bakeries remained, a butcher's, a coffee shop, the St. Mary's Star of the Sea Church. Jack continued on toward Red Hook, toward the waterfront, toward his childhood.

As soon as he crossed the elevated Gowanus Expressway, the rows of small but dignified brownstones, homes to generations of Italian families, gave way to the rough and tumble world of the Red Hook Houses, big redbrick hives, booming with gangsta rap. Deeper in, nearer the harbor, he passed vacant lots full of weeds; parking lots full of yellow school buses; small factories and machine shops. To the south, the old Todd Shipyards lay fallow, a wasteland of crumbling brick.

Jack dug down in his memory, trying to dredge up

names of neighbors from long ago, or people his father had worked with. There was Pat MacEgan, pipefitter, one of his old man's drinking buddies—Jack remembered coming across him one night on Van Brunt Street, rooting around in the backseat of his car. Jack asked what he was doing; the man answered, "I can't find the goddamn ignition." And there was Al Garbarino, shipyard purchasing agent. (Al's big story, repeated way too many times over shots of Seagram's: how he had bet the same number for six years in a row, then given up in disgust—only to have that number hit big the very next day.)

Other names eluded Jack, like minnows in murky water, partly due to his middle-aged memory but mostly because he had gone to such lengths to dissociate himself from Red Hook after Petey's death.

He soon discovered just how well he had succeeded in losing touch. At what had been Pat MacEgan's house, a tousled hipster girl with black-rimmed eyes and a nose ring answered the bell. Another stranger—an old woman—answered the door at Al Garbarino's house: she informed Jack that the unlucky gambler had died back in '87.

He drove north. The neighborhood changed, became more residential, though still quiet. Back in the day, this had been such a bustling area! He passed Union Street, which had been jammed with pushcarts selling fruit and vegetables, except in winter, when they'd sell hot chestnuts. The area had hopped with bars, and movie houses, and social establishments, like the Impala Club, which had been a block east, above Nino's Pizzeria.

Old landmarks caused memories to bloom. There was the

corner where Bobby Salesi lost three fingers when a zip gun blew up in his hand. There was the home base of the Kane Street Stoppers (a teen gang who sometimes rumbled with the Black Chaplains) and their younger cohorts the Kane Street Midgets. It had been a tough neighborhood all right; Jack recalled hearing some punk refer to his switchblade as a "Red Hook boxing glove." Jack passed various churches—Brooklyn had once been known as the City of Churches—and remembered how the local mobsters had run gambling games there, "collecting for the saint."

Wiseguys. The neighborhood had been full of them. He would see them on the corners or in front of their social clubs, resplendent in their two-tone shirts and camel hair coats and fedoras with wide brims. These days, it was hard to imagine how intense their control over the neighborhood had been. Sure there'd been patrol cops walking around, wielding their nightsticks if a kid got out of line, but many of them had been in the pockets of the Mob. And if two neighbors had a beef with each other, they wouldn't take it to the police or to the courts; they'd go to a "table," a sit-down with the local capos, who would tell them what to do, like neighborhood kings. You needed their permission to get work on the docks, but also to open any kind of business, and then you had to offer up tribute, including a regular cut of the profits, as well as a few bottles of booze or a turkey at Christmastime.

Jack circled back into a part of the neighborhood now known as Cobble Hill. Its genteel brownstones brought unbelievable prices these days, and he saw yuppie mothers pushing expensive baby carriages along the quiet streets. The Gallo brothers had once lived in a tenement here; the entrance, he recalled, had been presided over by a midget named Armando, whose claim to fame was that he had been an extra in the film *Samson and Delilah;* Jack could still picture the little thug clearly, with his high hairline and heavy brow. But Armando was not the most unusual feature of the operation. Joey and his brother Larry had bought an aging lion, perhaps off the same movie set, and kept it in their basement. If someone owed them too much money, the brothers would tell him to go down in the basement and "talk to Leo." (The threat had proved remarkably effective, but the lion had not lasted long; it stank up the place, and soon the Health Department came to call.)

The Gallos were flamboyant, public men; they threw silver dollars to the neighborhood kids, let them swim in their backyard pool, and played the big shots during local religious feasts, as John Gotti would do a couple of decades later in Queens. But their charm had major limits. They made most of their considerable profits by demanding protection money from the local businesses, the tailors, the shoe stores, the butcher shops. The misery these men spread was beyond estimation; if you crossed them in any way, your days might become a living nightmare. Your neighbors would avoid you, you couldn't work, couldn't feed your family—and worse, you had to live in fear of a sadistic beating or even death.

Jack's father had escaped Communist Russia, and he already knew plenty about brutality before he ever hit these shores. The old man had often been drunk and angry, but he was also a hard worker. He had grudgingly surrendered the tributes and bribes, but he warned Jack and Petey that if he ever saw them going near the gangsters, he would light into them with his heavy leather belt.

Jack remembered that threat, but now he was troubled by some other, deeper memories rising from the murk. Perhaps his father had not always been so set against the thugs. When Jack had been very little, some late nights he had peered out his bedroom window and watched his father get into a long dark car filled with men. Who were they? Where were they going? And why didn't his father come home until the next morning?

Somewhere along the line, those midnight trips had ceased, and his pop had begun to avoid the mobsters like the plague. And somehow, evidently, he had managed to seriously piss them off.

If Joey Gallo had been behind the lesson administered by Darnel Teague, the mobster had long ago received his just deserts: he had been gunned down in Umberto's Clam House on Mulberry Street in '72. But if it wasn't Gallo, who could it have been? Jack remembered what his father had once told him: loud men like the Gallos received all the attention because they craved it. But it was the quiet men, the ones you never heard about, who really held the power.

He sat there in his car, in the newly gentrified neighborhood, with its exorbitant real estate and its rich young Wall Streeters, who seemed to be the only ones who could afford it anymore. Who was left from the old dark days?

He knew that he could just go over to the NYPD's Organized Crime Unit and ask. But he thought of his brother and the justice Petey was owed. He thought about how he might never find enough evidence to make any official charge stick. Finally, he thought of the unregistered snub-nosed Charter Arms .38 Special that he had found during his career as a patrol cop and kept in the back of his closet. If he finally found the man responsible for his brother's death, maybe it would be best if word had not gone out that he had been looking for him.

CHAPTER TEN

"It's pepperoni, no cheese," Jack said, later that evening. "Just the way you like it."

He set the pizza box down on the coffee table in front of his landlord, along with a cold six-pack of Schaefer beer. The old man's rather dingy front room was illuminated only by the flickering blue light of his huge old battleship of a TV.

"I like cheese," Mr. Gardner replied. He held his stomach. "It just don't like me." He sighed. "I'm too old to give up all'a life's pleasures. Speakin' of which—" He started to push himself up from his battered, duct-taped old La-Z-Boy recliner, but Jack put a friendly hand on his shoulder.

"I'll get it."

Mr. G had difficulty walking these days, not just due to his age but because of a stroke he had suffered back in 2001. The man had once been quite robust, but his illness had stripped away the excess pounds and age had shortened him by several inches; now he looked like a bewildered garden gnome, staring up at the world through Coke-bottle-thick eyeglasses. And though he had once been an avid home fixer-upper, he now spent most of his time parked in front of his living room window, staring down at life on the block, a life he could no longer participate in. Or he sat in front of the television, which was currently blaring the local evening news.

Jack went into the kitchen, with its worn linoleum and time-browned, parchmenty window blinds. He reached up into the cabinets for a bottle of Seagram's 7 and a couple of delicate little shot glasses made of pale green glass. Mr. Gardner had brought them back from Naples, which he had visited while in the Army, back in World War II.

Jack returned to the front room. He cracked open a couple of beers, poured two shots of whiskey, and then he and his friend carried out their usual ritual.

"*Cin cin,*" he said.

"*Salut,*" Mr. Gardner replied from his throne by the window. The old man raised his glass toward a sepia photo on top of the TV, a portrait of his late wife—a rather horsey-looking woman, but very kind—then he and Jack clinked glasses and drank.

Jack served up the pizza and they ate in silence for a few minutes. This was one reason he liked coming upstairs to visit; they could sit in a friendly quiet, without feeling a big need to gab. It was good to have some company in the evenings and restful to be sitting here, with the TV just distracting enough to take his mind off his current cases.

A loud car commercial ended and the news anchors came on—a man and a woman who both looked like slightly over-the-hill models for a department store catalog. Their usual forced joviality was not in evidence tonight: a big orange banner headline in the background read NEW TERROR THREAT. The woman stared gravely into the camera and announced that the Department of Homeland Security had raised the color-coded warning level "based on NSA intercepts of a higher-than-usual level of foreign chatter picked up among suspected terrorist-

sponsored organizations." She didn't say if any specific information had actually been overheard, and Jack had to wonder
what the point of the alert might be. It certainly raised some
tension in him and the rest of the viewing audience but didn't
give them anything concrete to look out for or to do.

"Why ain't they caught that bin Laden guy?" Mr. G said,
disgusted. "These guys got their heads up their asses. They
should send you over there, Jackie—I bet you'd bring him back
on a platter in a coupl'a days."

Jack smiled, grateful for the vote of confidence, but he
couldn't help thinking about the recent talk of radiation right
here on his home turf, not more than a mile or two from where
he and his landlord were sitting. What the hell had that been
about? Could it have something to do with the news report he
had just heard? Well, whatever was going on, the three-letter
guys already seemed to know about it, and he figured that the
NYPD's own new counterterrorism squad must be on the case.
(As long as they were all talking to each other, which was not
exactly a sure bet . . .)

After a while, Mr. G began to snore. Jack roused him
gently and helped him back to his narrow old widower's bed.
(Otherwise, the man was liable to spend the night in his armchair.)

Downstairs, Jack glanced at his watch: it was too early
for his own bedtime, and he felt restless, agitated, as if he'd
drunk too much coffee. He wandered through the few rooms of
his apartment, turning his own TV on but then turning it off.
He went into his front room, picked up a newspaper, tried to
read a little, then let it drop. He turned off the lamp and sat
there on his couch, in the dark, watching through his windows
as the frothy, newly budding spring trees trembled in an evening wind.

He thought—as he rarely did after almost twenty years—
of his defunct marriage. He certainly didn't miss the sniping
and arguing at the end, but he remembered how sweet it had
been to come home from a late tour and find his wife in bed,
to kiss her and wake her, to make sweet love with her in the
middle of the night. Or just to slide into bed next to her sleeping body and put his arms around her.

He squinted down at the faintly glowing hands of his
watch. Not too late. He took out his cell phone and made a call.

"Ben? Did I wake you?"

"*Dad.* It's only ten-thirty. Is something wrong?"

"Nothing's wrong. I just called to say hi. How're tricks?"

"I'm fine. Listen, if it's nothing important, I'm kinda in
the middle of working on something right now."

Jack's son was an aspiring filmmaker. He said that he
made "experimental documentaries," though Jack could never
really figure out what that meant.

He frowned in the dark. His kid didn't have much time
for him. He couldn't complain, though. It was karma, right? He
had always been out working so hard when Ben was little, and
then the kid had resented him for the divorce. He tried not to
sound irritated. "No problem. Listen, how about we have lunch
soon? Maybe Friday?"

"Yeah, sure," Ben said, clearly eager to get off the phone.

"At the coffee shop?"

"Sure. Okay. Gotta go."

"Take care," Jack started to say, but the kid had already
hung up.

Conversations with his son were like eating meals that
consisted solely of appetizers.

He set his cell phone down and lay back on the couch,
staring up into the dark. After a few minutes he felt his eyelids

growing heavy, but he didn't get up. He often conked out here on the couch. Why not?

Soon he was fast asleep.

THE POOL IS VAST but crowded. Kids splash, adults lounge on the sides, sunbathing under the Red Hook sky. Dreamy music plays in the background: Connie Francis, "Where the Boys Are."

Petey is next to Jack, and they hold their breath and plunge under the water, swimming in the sunlit blue like dolphins, trying to make it across without coming up for air. Jack feels as if his lungs might burst, but he makes it to the other side, where he fountains up, gasping. Strangely, the sun has disappeared behind lowering clouds, and he sees kids pulling themselves up out of the pool and families hurrying toward the exits; he suddenly realizes that Petey is nowhere in sight. Jack plunges back under the water, searching for his brother. When he comes back up, the whole huge pool is empty.

And then somehow he is up in the F train, riding the elevated tracks out of the Smith–Ninth Street station, and he is an adult again, clad in his work clothes, and the train comes around the bend high above Red Hook, and he sees dark storm clouds marching across the harbor, above the Statue of Liberty. The train starts to head down into the tunnel before Carroll Street, and Jack begins to panic: something bad is heading toward the city, something very bad—it involves radiation—and he is desperate: he must find Ben and make sure the boy is safe. Then he notices that his son is in the same subway car, sitting farther down, and Jack feels better, but then his heart jolts again. Michelle! *His girlfriend is in the city, at work, and he has to reach her, to rescue her . . .*

HIS EYES JOLTED OPEN. Morning sun. He was lying on his couch; in his bedroom, the alarm clock was going off. He couldn't get up though, not right away. The dreams were still with him, and he felt bruised, as if he had taken several punches to the face.

Michelle again. He didn't even know where she was living these days, since that fateful night when she had bolted from the restaurant. He both dreaded and hoped that he would run into her someday. New York was a city of eight million people, but it still happened all the time—you turned a corner and bumped into somebody who had been your best friend in third grade, or some distant relative you hadn't seen for years. Someday when he least expected it, he was going to look up and see her striding through a crowd.

When that happened, how would he behave? Would he just act out of hurt and anger and say something cruel? Or was it possible that somewhere, deep down inside, he might be able to find a small kernel of forgiveness?

He had no idea.

He ran a hand over his face, and then he swung his feet over the side of the couch and stood up to face the new day.

CHAPTER ELEVEN

On the outside, the Seven-oh house looked a bit grander than most, with its beige stone façade, its arched front windows. On the inside, it was like every precinct headquarters in the city: anxious, beaten-down citizens sitting in the waiting area; a beefy, supremely unfazeable sergeant planted like a bullfrog behind the front counter; everything pervaded by a smoggy atmosphere of hope fading into despair.

Jack found Richie Powker sitting at his desk up in the detective's squad room, which was crammed full of gray desks and filing cabinets and the journeymen and women of the investigative trade. The detective had a little burrow over in the corner, dug out of stacks of manila folders, old newspapers, and mug shot books. He barely looked up when Jack walked in; he was hunched over, staring intently at his computer screen.

"What's up?" Jack said.

Richie didn't answer at first; he typed something in and waited a moment. Then he leaned in closer to the screen.

"What'cha doin'?"

The detective looked up. "I've been casting the net out there. Remember what you were talking about, how our guy went shopping in the A.M.? How he might have some night job, like a cabbie? We've sure got a lot of Pakistani drivers living around here. I've been looking through a database from the Taxi and Limousine Commission. Take a look at this."

Jack came around the desk and saw a driver's license up on the screen: a male, thirty-four years old, with black hair and a rather severe brown face. He peered closer; he hated to admit it, but even for a veteran detective it was often harder to identify suspects of other races. Blacks and Asians condemned it all the time, this "they all look alike" mentality, but he had seen scientific studies about the phenomenon, known as the *cross-race effect*: people of *all* races were usually better at identifying differences in facial features among members of their own group.

It certainly didn't help when you were trying to work from two-day-old memories of a grainy little security video.

"The age and height seem right," Richie said. "I think it could be our guy. Whaddaya think?"

Jack exhaled. "I don't know. It *could* be . . ."

"This is interesting." Richie tapped at his keyboard, then pointed at a new screen. "It says here that several passengers registered complaints about this hack. I looked into it: he's been brought up on charges a couple of times."

Jack frowned. "The perp's fingerprints didn't turn up on any criminal database."

"I know—but these are just TLC hearings, not court cases."

"What was he brought up on?"

Richie gave Jack a significant look. "It seems he has a bit of a nasty temper—and a tendency to pick fights. Oh—and he lives five blocks from our deli."

THEY TOOK BACKUP WITH them, two other detectives from the Seven-oh, tagging along in an unmarked Dodge

Charger. First they stopped off at the hack's home address and warily approached the front stoop. It was a small brick row house with garish chrome railings. No one answered the bell.

Next stop: the place of employment. The taxi office was on a small side street just off Coney Island Avenue, next to a shoe repair shop and a little Mexican bakery. Jack and his partner parked twenty yards down the street and got out of their car, while the other detectives remained in their vehicle at the far end of the block, keeping an eye on the incoming traffic.

The bakery had a picture window full of birthday cakes topped with plastic princesses and Power Rangers; as he walked by, Jack inhaled an inviting sweet scent tinged with cinnamon. Then came a high chain-link fence topped with one meager strand of barbed wire, enclosing an asphalt lot which held three yellow cabs, with spaces for maybe five or six more. Next to it stood a small open-doored garage and a freestanding little office. Jack knew that its modest appearance didn't mean that the business was not worth much: every cab had to bear a licensing medallion, and each of those cost around four hundred grand.

A mechanic in oily overalls, a compact brown man whose biceps bulged beneath his cutoff shirtsleeves, stared out at the detectives from the shade inside the garage. They ignored him and proceeded into the office, a small, grubby room made smaller because it contained a Plexiglas-protected booth, inside of which sat the dispatcher, a plump man with a pockmarked face and heavy black eyebrows.

He looked up at them, took in their sports jackets and their confident demeanor. Jack, a relatively small man of Russian Jewish heritage, could often pass for a civilian, but Richie carried the meaty look of a law enforcement officer in his very genes.

"TLC?" the dispatcher said. He didn't exactly look surprised, and Jack thought of his driver's previous run-ins with the Taxi and Limo Commission.

Jack pulled out his badge. "NYPD. You own this business?"

The dispatcher nodded.

"We need to talk to you about one of your drivers." Jack held up a computer printout of their suspect's driver's license.

"What is this about?"

"It's a routine matter. We just need to ask him a couple of questions."

The dispatcher frowned. "He'll be done around eight."

Jack held his ground. "We need him now. Would you please call him in?"

The dispatcher considered the request for a moment, then shrugged. His thought process was so obvious that it was almost visible: he could put up a fuss and risk getting hassled himself, or he could cooperate. And why not? The drivers worked freelance; if they got into trouble with the law, that was their problem.

The man reached out, pressed something, and spoke into his headset, rapidly, in Urdu. Jack hoped he wasn't warning their suspect away.

The dispatcher looked up. "He just dropped a fare at the airport. He'll be here in ten minutes."

Jack smiled. It was at least a twenty-five or thirty-minute trip to the nearest airport, but the dispatcher bullshitted by sheer force of habit.

The two detectives sat down on bare metal folding chairs.

"I love what they've done with the place," Richie muttered. The office was depressing: cigarette-burned wall-to-wall carpet, not a single picture or other decoration, just a little pile of well-thumbed foreign movie magazines. "You think our guy might be armed?" the detective wondered. "I know he doesn't own a registered piece."

Jack shrugged. "Maybe he's got another can of beans."

Richie snorted. "We should'a went out and bought some hot dogs. We could have ourselves a barbecue." The detective sat back and clasped his hands across his ample stomach. His eyelids drooped. A true veteran: they were awaiting a possible murder suspect, but the man stayed calm.

Jack glanced at his watch. Restless, he resisted an urge to flip through one of the foreign magazines. He knew the backup would call if they spotted anyone approaching the office, but he kept his eyes fixed on the little front window.

Finally, his cell phone vibrated. He glanced at its little screen, nudged Richie, pulled out his gun, stood up, and moved to the side of the door.

A shadow moved past the window.

The door swung open, revealing the face of the driver in the photo. The Pakistani peered in at the two detectives. He started to turn but saw the others closing in behind. And then he bolted, not back toward the street but straight ahead, into the office, knocking Richie aside, darting around Jack like a football running back, yanking open a side door, and hurling himself through. The detectives exchanged startled looks, then rushed after him.

Out in the lot, their quarry careened about like an animal in a trap. The fence designed to keep thieves out proved quite suitable for keeping murder suspects in.

The mechanic stepped outside the garage, but when he saw four cops with guns drawn, he raised his hands and stopped still.

The suspect dashed around behind the parked taxis. He

scrambled up on the hood of one, then hurled himself high onto the fence at the back of the lot. He scrabbled to the top but got caught in the barbed wire, where he was suspended, gasping and struggling.

Gotcha, Jack said to himself. He turned back to the mechanic. "We're gonna need to borrow some bolt cutters." Once he got the tool, he turned to one of the other detectives from the Seven-oh house, a wiry young guy who looked like he spent a lot of time at the gym. Without a word, grinning, the DT took the cutters from Jack and started climbing.

A minute later the detectives had their suspect pressed, panting, against the hood of a taxi. One of the Seven-oh detectives cuffed him.

"Fahad Marashi," Richie said to him, "you have the right to remain silent. Anything you say may be used against you in a court of law."

CHAPTER TWELVE

"I have *applied*," the suspect said, bearing an expression of great anguish. "I have applied, and applied, and applied."

"What are you talking about?" Jack said patiently.

He and Richie were standing in a drab little interview room over at the Seven-oh house.

"I don't *want* to be illegal," the driver said. "I wish to vote, pay taxes, all of this."

"You want to pay taxes," Richie said, grinning. "Well, that's a great start for an honest interview!"

Jack had zero interest in their suspect's citizenship status, but it seemed like it might make a useful bargaining chip. He sat down and clasped his hands together. "Monday. In the morning. What were you doing over at the S & R deli on Coney Island Avenue?" *Don't ask the suspect* if *he was there; ask* why *he was there. Let the guy at least place himself at the scene.*

But Fahad Marashi's eyes widened. "Monday? *Monday* you are asking me about? I was in Charlottesville, Virginia! For my cousin's wedding! He works at the university, in the mathematics program."

Richie scratched his ear. "You have any proof of that? Witnesses? A bus ticket?"

Marashi brightened. "Witnesses, tickets, yes! And I can show you photos, on the Internet!"

"Why'd you run then, when you came into the taxi office just now?"

The man's eyes widened. "Why did I run? Because you were chasing me!"

IT DIDN'T TAKE LONG to confirm Marashi's alibi. And then Jack and his partner stood outside the precinct house and watched the cabbie stride quickly, joyously away. They were on a homicide case and could not be bothered with immigration matters. What the hell, a hardworking guy—why bust his chops? The detectives took their setback philosophically. A lead didn't pan out? Just part of the job. *Adios, amigo. Vaya con dios.*

Jack shrugged. "Let's do Plates at the Scene."

On a busy thoroughfare like Coney Island Avenue, at rush hour, *someone* must have seen their perpetrator walk out of the deli, likely with bloodstained clothes. As part of their routine that first day, the detectives had jotted down the license plate numbers of any cars parked outside. Now they would begin the tedious job of tracking down the drivers, asking if anyone had been near the scene at the time of the murder. Criminal investigations, even of homicides, were rarely glamorous; they tended to involve a lot of slogging along, poring through files, canvassing for witnesses, praying that some small, significant detail might pop out of the mundane mass. After almost two decades as a detective—with Homicide, with Robbery, with other units—Jack knew that full well, but still, by the end of the tour, he was nearly cross-eyed with the tedium of the task.

"You wanna grab a beer?" Richie asked, standing up and throwing his sports jacket over one shoulder.

Jack thought about going home to his empty apartment, about watching TV while eating cheap takeout food.

"Sure," he said. "Why not?"

THEY WENT OVER TO Monsalvo's, a little bunker of a place Jack sometimes visited on the edge of Midwood. It was far from any precinct house, so he didn't have to listen to shop talk after work; he could just park himself on a stool like the resident old-timers and watch a ball game in peace.

Pat stood behind the stick, a ruddy-faced young man, son of Pat Senior, the night barkeep. The dim interior was lit by a couple of neon beer signs, a string of Christmas tree lights, and old TVs above each end of the bar; their light flickered in the big glassy eyeballs of a deer head mounted on the back wall. On a shelf above the register, some little statuettes—Jimmy Durante, W. C. Fields—stood patiently underneath a Spanish moss–like coating of dust.

"A couple of cold ones," Jack called out, but Richie overruled him.

"Just a seltzer for me. With a squeeze a' lime."

Jack didn't say anything—a man's drinking habits were his business and his alone—but he couldn't help cocking an eyebrow.

"I don't drink," Richie said. "It's not an AA thing or anything. I just don't go for the stuff." He smiled ruefully and pointed at his face. "I know: the nose fools ya."

Jack did his best to avoid comparing it to the veiny, bulbous schnoz on W. C. Fields.

"It's not drinking," Richie said. "It's a skin condition. It's called rosacea. Millions of people have it. And everybody assumes we love the sauce."

"Well, *that* sounds like a drag," Jack said.

Richie shrugged. "Hey—it ain't fatal. But it is a bit of a curse. If it wasn't for this, I would'a made commissioner by now." He laughed at his own joke, causing a couple of old-timers at the far end of the bar to tear their gazes away from the TV. Pat delivered a pint of seltzer; Richie raised it and began to declaim:

> *Here's to the camel, whose sexual desire*
> *Is greater than anyone thinks.*
> *One night in a moment of madness*
> *It tried to make love to the Sphinx.*
> *But the Sphinx's posterior opening*
> *Was clogged with the sands of the Nile,*
> *Which accounts for the hump on the camel*
> *And the Sphinx's inscrutable smile.*

The old-timers set down their beers and clapped.

Richie bowed. "Just 'cause I don't drink doesn't mean I can't enjoy a good toast."

Predictably, this set off old regular Tommy McKettrie, a wrinkled, long-retired bus driver sitting a few stools down. He stood gravely, adjusted an imaginary necktie, and raised his glass of whiskey. "Here's to the bee that stung the bull, that started the bull to bucking. Here's to Adam who ate the first apple, and started the whole world to—"

"Eating apples," Pat stepped in, dryly fulfilling his role in the miniature ongoing drama that was Monsalvo's.

Richie grinned. "I *like* this joint."

Pat shrugged and wiped the bar with a wet rag. "We can't *all* have good judgment." One of the old-timers signaled and he went off down the bar.

"*So*," Richie said to Jack. "If I remember correctly, I'll only be graced with your presence for a little bit longer."

Jack nodded. "I have a couple more days to work exclusively on this." That was the way it worked: the Homicide Task Force detectives got assigned a certain number of days to work a fresh case with the local precinct detectives, and then they had to go back into the squad's rotation, subject to catching fresh murders. "But I'll still help out whenever I have time." Jack took a sip of his beer and snorted. "Like I've already provided such invaluable assistance."

Richie shrugged. "Some cases are easy; some ain't. We don't get to pick and choose."

Jack nodded. "You got *that* right. You know what this case reminds me of? I had a job, a little while back, we had a gun that went overboard from a boat and we had to call in the Harbor Unit. The scubas went in; they've got this thing called a rope line. It's murky as hell down there at the bottom, and apparently you can't even see your hand in front of your face. So they stretch out this rope, maybe a hundred feet, and then they move along it, holding onto it with one hand. With the other, they just grope around."

Richie nodded. "Sure sounds like our situation right now."

Jack made a face. "The thing is, it seems to me that this Charlson fella is up there on the surface, with a really nice sonar unit." He shook his head. "I can't believe that this department rivalry crap still goes on."

"Nothing new from your boss about getting more cooperation from the feds?"

Jack snorted. "Here's the thing about Tanney: He cares the world about all the externals of the job—performance reviews, getting promoted, playing it smart with department politics.

Most of the time, though, he barely gives a rat's ass about the only thing that's really important, as far as I'm concerned—and that's the actual *work*."

Richie nodded. "I hear that. How about Lieutenant Cardulli? He seems more sympatico."

Jack shrugged. "He is. But Tanney is so insecure that if I say anything to the Loo, he'll make a big stink about me violating the chain of command."

He waved to the bartender for another beer. "I'm gonna shut up now. I hate cops who sit around and gripe all the time. We're freakin' lucky, no matter what happens: we get to work in the greatest city in the world, on the greatest police force. And—despite all the pencil pushers—we've still got the best damn job."

Richie's cell phone trilled. "Excuse me," he said. He took the call, then hung up and turned back to Jack. "The wife. I gotta go. See you tomorrow, okay?"

Jack nodded and raised his glass in salute. "It's good working with ya." He pictured his partner going home and spending the rest of his evening at home with his wife: a red-haired woman, Irish maybe, rather stout and busty.

He decided that he would stay on just long enough to finish his second beer. (He wasn't much of a drinker either.) So he sat there, while the old-timers chatted amongst themselves, and the sports channels played with no sound up on the TVs, and Pat restocked the beer coolers for the night shift.

He thought about cases. They might be baffling for a while, but when it came down to it, the solutions were simple. He didn't have to plumb the deep mysteries of the human heart or ponder why things played out the way they did in the grand scheme of life. He didn't have to explain why good people died young or bad people died old, or why it was so damn hard for parents and their kids to get along. He just needed to come up with concrete evidence to prove one simple fact: person x killed person y. That was the job.

Sometimes, when the bigger mysteries—love, family, what the hell he was doing on the planet in the first place—started to weigh him down, the only way to find some relief and release seemed to be to connect the dots and solve one of the solvable puzzles. To make a little sense of *something*; maybe even provide a bit of cosmic justice. Take one killer off the street; give the friends and relatives of one victim some sense of balance and fairness and possibly even peace.

Right now, though, he wasn't making progress on any front, and even being in Monsalvo's, this friendly, dumpy little bar that often provided a small oasis from life's big concerns, wasn't doing him a whit of good.

It was time for a little direct action.

BY THE TIME HE reached his destination, the late afternoon sun was glowing golden orange against the top stories of the little brick buildings, Brooklyn's magic hour.

Joey Gallo's old block might have turned into overpriced yuppie real estate, and humble little Smith Street here was now a paradise for young hipsters, a row of trendy bars and boutiques. But there were still a few places where the old-timers held sway. Aside from tossing bocce balls or betting on the ponies at the OTB, little old men who had been big shots in the Mob's heyday stood around chatting in groups with their hands clasped behind their backs over on Court Street, or took their wives to fancy dinners at the Fontana di Trevi restaurant, with its parking valets and starched white tablecloths. And they still whiled away the time in a few remaining social clubs like this one.

The three-story building had an unassuming brick façade. There was no sign out front—just a blacked-out picture window and an old metal door with a diamond-shaped little window cut in the center, blocked by a faded red curtain. It would have been very easy to miss, distracted as you might be by the flashy boutique next door and the French-Asian restaurant on the other side.

Inside, it looked as if nothing had changed for the past fifty years, and certainly not since the only other time Jack had been here, two years earlier. The same old geezer in a beige leather sports jacket finally admitted him after making him wait outside; the same beefy guys in track suits were playing dominoes at a card table in the middle of the room; the place still reeked of cigar smoke and looked like a grubby 1950s basement rec room. And John Carpsio Jr., the man Jack had come to see, looked exactly the same: a small, trim, middle-aged man, with wire-rimmed spectacles and a rather nondescript, putty-colored face. The Mob boss was behind his club's wet bar, puttering around with a fancy espresso machine. At first, he barely acknowledged Jack's presence; he looked down at his machine with disgust. "I can't believe I paid two grand for this piece 'a shit—I can get better coffee out of a ten-dollar stovetop son of a bitch." He looked up. "Well, well, well. Lookit who's slummin' in the old nabe."

He and Jack had a bit of a history. They had both grown up in Red Hook and even attended the same elementary school, though they were several grades apart. A couple of years ago, the detective had inadvertently done the criminal a favor, and then Carpsio had tipped him off on the whereabouts of a killer. But it pained Jack to even look at the man. "Can we talk?" he said.

Carpsio shrugged. "So? *Talk.*"

Jack's shirt collar felt tight and he tugged it away from his neck. "This, ah . . . this isn't an official visit."

"You been jonesing for a game of dominoes?"

"Not exactly." Jack looked around: the others in the club were yards away, and the TV overhead—showing some kind of afternoon spouse-versus-spouse freakshow—was loud enough to mask their conversation. Still, he hated even mentioning Petey in public, in this shithole. "The last time I was here, you said that you remembered my brother. And what happened to him."

Carpsio shrugged. "Of course. He got shivved by some mooley." *Mooley*, for *mulignan*. "That kinda crap didn't happen in Red Hook every day."

"No," Jack said, nodding. "It didn't."

"I told you: your family should'a let us handle it," Carpsio said, and there was no doubt who he meant by *us*. "We would'a taken care of them punks by nightfall."

Jack crossed his arms. "But see, here's the thing. I happen to know for a fact that it wasn't just some random mugging. There was someone from the neighborhood behind it."

Carpsio's eyes narrowed and his whole manner changed. "*Someone from the neighborhood.* What the fuck are you saying?"

"I think this had something to do with my father. That he pissed someone off."

"So what are you comin' to *me* for?"

Jack raised his hands in a placating gesture. "I'm not saying that you or your, ah, *friends* had anything to do with it. I was just hoping you might have heard something about my father that would help me make sense of this thing."

Carpsio drew himself up. "That last time you did me a solid and I was glad to repay the favor. But I don't know what the hell you want from me here. You want I should tell you about your own old man? You think I know more about him than you do?"

Jack shrugged. "You were older than me. Maybe you heard things."

Carpsio shook his head. "I'm only two, t'ree years older than you, guy."

"Look: this is ancient history. I've been thinking about who might've been in cahoots with any black guys back then, and the only person I can think of is Joey Gallo. He's been dead for over thirty years, so I can't imagine that there's any harm in talking about him, right? I just want to know what happened. Did you ever hear anything besides the official story?"

John Carpsio Jr.'s eyes were like ice and they didn't give away anything. But his next words did.

"Listen up, Leightner, and listen good. You did me a favor once, and I'm gonna do you another one right now. And this one is on the house. Get the fuck out of this neighborhood and stay the fuck away, unless you've got some kinda official business that's got nothing to do with this cockamamie bullshit." He stood up, indicating that their little talk was over, but he had one final word. "You go poking a stick around in a goddamn hornet's nest, don't come cryin' to me if you get stung."

Jack walked toward the door, bearing one small grain of satisfaction. He hadn't had much of a plan, coming in here, but he had figured he would do exactly what Carpsio had just said: poke around in the hive with a stick and see what flew out.

Now he knew for sure what Larry Cosenza had only hinted at: this story wasn't ancient history at all, and some thug much more alive than Joey Gallo was directly involved.

CHAPTER THIRTEEN

The morning sun was bright on Coney Island Avenue and Jack shaded his eyes, thinking that it was time to dig out his sunglasses for the season. The light made him squint as if he had a bad hangover, which he didn't; he simply had not enjoyed a good night's sleep ever since he received his surprise visit from Darnel Teague.

"Excuse me, ma'am," Richie said, addressing a plump Pakistani woman in a bright blue sari, pushing a shopping cart stuffed with laundry bags. "I'm with the New York Police Department. We're looking for people who might have passed by here at about this time on Monday morning."

The two detectives were out in front of the deli again: it was always a good idea to return and canvass an area at the same time of day that a crime had been committed. That was the best way to find someone with a regular routine—commuting to work, making deliveries—that might have brought them by this spot at the same hour on the earlier date.

The woman looked up at Richie suspiciously. She raised her hands—"no English"—and then pushed her cart off down the block.

Jack stepped out in front of an elderly Caucasian man stooped over with scoliosis; he wore a heavy tweed coat more suitable for the middle of winter. "Excuse me. Do you live around here?"

The man squinted up. "Yah. Why?"

"Is there any chance that you might have passed by here at around this time on Monday morning?"

"You cops?"

Jack nodded. "We're checking out an incident that took place here that day."

"The murder, huh? *Terrible*. This whole neighborhood's gettin' shot to hell."

Jack brightened. "Were you around?"

The old man shook his head. "Nope. But I'll tell you somethin'." He turned and pointed at the far end of the block. "Ya see those windows on the second floor? With the red curtains? Ya know why they're red? I'll tell ya: they got hookers in there! And nobody's doin' a goddamn thing about it!"

Jack refrained from frowning. "Thanks very much for the tip. I'll pass it on to the vice squad."

"My pleasure," the man said. "You know, my grandson wants to be a cop."

"That's great," Jack said, pulling out his cell phone. "Sorry—I gotta take a call." He moved away; he didn't really have a call, but he didn't relish the half-hour monologue he was in for otherwise. The old man tottered off.

Richie wandered over. "It's after nine. Whaddaya wanna do? Should we go back to the Brasciak angle?"

Jack shook his head. They could keep going, digging deeper to see if they could come up with anything else, but he kept thinking about the fed in his radiation suit.

He squared his shoulders. "I think I'll take a little trip

into Manhattan. Pay a visit to Federal Plaza. Our Homeland Security friend."

Richie's eyes widened. "You think that's wise?"

Jack shrugged. "I don't know if it's wise. But I'll be damned if I'm gonna keep plugging away in vain here, when this Charlson jerk could just save us the trouble."

Richie nodded—"Let's go"—but Jack put a hand on his shoulder. "It's okay. I suspect some fur might fly here, and there's no need for you to get caught up in it."

The veteran from the Seven-oh grinned. "Hey, I've got my twenty in. They wanna bust my balls, let 'em try."

AS JACK DISCOVERED WHEN he took another look at Charlson's business card, the man's office was not actually downtown in Federal Plaza (next to the FBI and City Hall)—it was in midtown, near Grand Central. As the two detectives got out of their car a couple of blocks away, they could see the building, a forbidding black monolith rising high above Third Avenue. Jack was staring at its tinted windows when a voice called him up short.

"Hey, mister!"

He paused in the flow of pedestrians. An old homeless man wearing a stained green Army jacket was sitting on the sidewalk, leaning back against the front of a Starbucks coffee shop and staring directly at him.

"Hey, mister," the man repeated. "I'll bet you three bucks I can tell you where you got your shoes."

The crazy offer snapped Jack out of his musings about federal agents and their arrogance. He stepped out of the pedestrian flow and confronted the stranger. "Whaddaya mean? You're gonna tell me I bought them in New York or something?"

The homeless man shook his head earnestly. "No, sir. I can tell you *exactly* where ya got 'em."

Jack thought for a second: he had bought his footwear in a little store in Bay Ridge one afternoon when he'd been out there on a case. He looked at his partner and they both chuckled. Jack turned back to the stranger. "Okay, sure. If you can pull this off, it'll be worth three bucks."

The man grinned. *"You got 'em on your own two feet."* He held out his hand.

Jack laughed, pulled out his wallet, and handed over the money, with absolutely no hard feelings. He had to give credit where credit was due.

Inside the skyscraper, the detectives took an elevator up to the State Office of Homeland Security, which looked like an impressive, well-funded government headquarters, with its official seals and photo of the president in the lobby.

An elderly blonde sitting behind a reception desk offered up a starchy smile. "May I help you?"

Jack flashed his tin. "I'm Detective Leightner and this is Detective Powker. We're here to see Brent Charlson."

"Do you have an appointment?"

Jack crossed his arms. "Nope. But it's urgent."

The receptionist picked up her phone. "I'll try his office." She dialed. "Hi, Deb. I've got a couple of NYPD detectives here asking for Mr. Charlson." She listened. "Leightner. And Powker. From—"

She looked inquisitively at Jack.

"Brooklyn South Homicide."

She repeated that, listened for a few seconds more, then hung up.

"I'm sorry—Mr. Charlson is not in the building right now."

"I don't think so," Jack replied.

Her smile curdled. "Excuse me?"

Jack leaned over the desk. "I just called his office about thirty seconds ago. And he answered the phone." He had hung up as soon as he heard the man's voice.

The woman rose from her seat. "Could you wait here a moment?" She disappeared through a side door.

Jack turned and grinned at his partner. "As my son used to say, we seem to be about as welcome as a screen door in a submarine."

After a minute, the door opened and the receptionist returned. "You'll need to go up to seventeen."

Up they went. This floor looked anonymous, no seals anywhere, not even signs on the doors, except for the suite numbers. Jack raised his eyebrows and gave his partner a grin. "Either we're on the super-duper top-secret floor, or this guy is just some flunky."

BRENT CHARLSON DIDN'T LOOK at all put out by the sudden visit.

"Sorry about that," he said briskly, offering them a seat in his office, with its rich wood paneling and plush blue carpet "Our gorgon downstairs might be a little *too* efficient."

Jack didn't believe the receptionist had anything to do with it, but he held his tongue. Instead of sitting, he walked across the surprisingly large corner office to take in the views of midtown skyscrapers and the shining East River. By the looks of things, Charlson was hardly a flunky.

"What can I do for you?" the man said pleasantly. Jack would have expected him to ask if they'd had any success in tracking down the deli perp, but Charlson just waited. Jack didn't take a seat; he preferred the psychological advantage of standing, as he would in a more routine station house interview. He stared down at the fed, who sat back in a swanky executive chair with his hands steepled together and a mildly curious expression on his face. *Grandfatherly,* Jack thought again.

"My partner and I have a bit of a problem here," he said. "The thing is, we've got a murderer walking around our city right now. And it really troubles me that we're out there pounding the sidewalks, looking for this guy, with what seems to be incomplete information."

Charlson considered this statement thoughtfully. "I want to assure you gentlemen that I'm not out to disrespect you in any way or to maintain any secrecy that's not absolutely necessary." He didn't continue.

"Okay. I'm glad to hear that. Maybe you could explain why secrecy is necessary at all."

"Were you on the job in 'ninety-three, detective?"

Jack nodded.

"I don't know how much you remember about what happened back then, with the first attack on the World Trade Center, but it was a major cock-up. The men who plotted that bombing had been under surveillance by the FBI for some time, but the surveillance was dropped just months before the attack. And there were confidential informants who were handled quite poorly."

Jack leaned forward. "What are you saying? There's some kind of terrorist plot going on here?"

Charlson took off his glasses and rubbed his eyes. "I can tell you that we're in the middle of an investigation. But this kind of case is incredibly sensitive. You bring too many people into the loop and lives get jeopardized. Or plotters hear about surveillance and they go deep into hiding."

Richie entered the conversation. "We understand. But

we're not some rookies, running around shooting our mouths off. We know how to run an undercover operation. Do you know who our perp is? Did you already have him under surveillance?"

Charlson spoke carefully. "We know who the man is."

Richie gave Jack a look, then turned back to the fed. "No offense, but you're making it sound like he's some kind of high-level terrorist or something. The fact is, he killed a guy right out in the open. With a can of *beans*. He doesn't sound very smart or stealthy to me."

Charlson fixed the detective with an eagle eye. "You know how we caught the first bomber in 'ninety-three? Shortly after the attack, he returned to the car rental place where he had ordered the van they filled with explosives. He asked for the deposit back! Now, that doesn't sound very smart or stealthy either, but that man and his comrades succeeded in blowing a gigantic crater in the basement of the North Tower."

"All right," Richie conceded. "But you've got our guy's picture on videotape. Why don't we just put it out there? We can probably scoop him up within a few hours."

Charlson shook his head, as if he were talking to a child. "You're not listening. If we spread the word that we know who this man is, his compatriots will go underground. And then we may *never* be able to stop them."

Richie remained unimpressed. "How do you know this guy is even involved with anything? I work in Little Pakistan. I've seen how these people get implicated, called terrorists, just because somebody doesn't like 'em and calls in a bum tip."

Charlson stared at him, incredulous. "You live in New York City and you want to argue with me about whether this sort of threat is real? Where were you on Nine-eleven? Do you know how many funerals I attended that month, detective?"

Reluctantly, Richie backed off.

"There are radical Islamic fundamentalists plotting in this city right this moment," Charlson continued. "Make no mistake: these people will do everything they can to harm us and destroy our way of life. I check my intelligence reports very carefully. And I'm not about to let good information go to waste, as it did in 'ninety-three." He gripped the edge of his desk. "I can promise you one thing: if something terrible goes down here, it's not going to be because I just sat back and let it happen."

Richie leaned forward, ready to go another round, but Jack intervened; he didn't want the fed to get defensive and shut them out. "So why did this guy kill our deli victim? What was that about?"

Charlson shrugged. "I have no idea. These people are very highly strung. They're angry—that's why they become terrorists. Maybe your victim just looked at him the wrong way."

Jack scratched his cheek, disappointed. He had hoped to at least have the reason for the killing cleared up. "Listen," he said. "I understand what you're saying about a need for discretion here. We won't broadcast the guy's picture. We won't even send his name around. But we need to get him off the street. Why don't you help us out, and we'll be very tight-lipped about what's going on, and we'll bring him in real nice and quiet?"

Charlson frowned. "I don't think you appreciate the dangers here. Are you equipped to deal with high levels of radioactivity? Do you know what radiation sickness does to a person?"

What Jack knew was that Charlson was eager to get credit for the arrest—typical fed—and he decided to play his bluff. "No problem—we'll just call our Emergency Services Unit and let them deal with it."

Charlson didn't buy it. "You don't have the proper equipment."

Richie frowned. "What's all this stuff about radiation, anyhow?"

Charlson remained impassive; he wasn't going to give an inch.

Jack was done. "You know what? I'm sick and tired of all this agency rivalry and hush-hush bullshit. We'll just find this guy on our own. And then maybe we'll let you know about it, a few days later." He stood up.

Charlson sat staring at him for a good long time. Finally, he moved closer to his desk and lowered his voice. "All right. You can sit down, detective. I'm going to swear both of you to complete and utter secrecy. If you're indiscreet and the slightest word of this investigation leaks out, *anywhere*, I'm going to personally make sure the NYPD takes away your badges. *And* your pensions. Is that understood?"

Jack and his partner nodded.

Charlson turned to Richie. "Would you please get up and lock the door?"

CHAPTER FOURTEEN

"I'm going to let you in on a very interesting little tale," Brent Charlson said. He reached into his pocket, took out a key, and unlocked a drawer of his desk. He pulled out a red manila folder and laid it on the leather blotter. "This story begins in the Gulf of Aden. Do you know where that is?"

Richie shrugged. "I'm gonna guess it's not near the Long Island Sound."

Charlson smiled benignly. "That's right, detective. In fact, it's about eight thousand miles away. The gulf connects the Indian Ocean and the Red Sea, and it's a crucial shipping lane for that part of the world. It runs past Somalia, unfortunately, which is a notoriously unstable country, overrun with radical Islamist rebels. The coast is very popular with pirates, who like to dash out into the gulf in speedboats and hijack commercial ships. Then they sit tight and demand large cash ransoms."

He adjusted his eyeglasses, opened the folder, and stared down. "On December eighteenth of last year, one of these pirate crews took control of an Iranian merchant ship in the gulf. Supposedly, the vessel was laden with iron ore and 'industrial products.' Our investigation shows that the ship was owned and operated by the IRITC. That stands for Islamic Republic of Iran Transport Corporation, a state-owned company run by the Iranian military. After the pirates seized control of the ship, they sat back and demanded a ransom of two and a half million dollars."

Richie interrupted. "Why wouldn't the ship's owners just go in and take it back by force? You said they were connected to the military, right?"

"Very simple: if the pirates were attacked, they could sink the ship. The potential loss might be much greater than the ransom demand. It's a difficult problem." Charlson sat back and steepled his hands together again. "Now, incidents like this are practically routine in the gulf—they get hundreds of pirate attacks every year. But what happened next was not routine. Not at all. While the Iranians were trying to decide what to do, the Somalis went poking around the cargo containers, just out of curiosity. After several days, some of them started to get very ill. They lost their hair and got mysterious skin burns. And then they began to die off, one by one."

Jack whistled. "That wouldn't be radiation sickness, by any chance?"

Charlson nodded. "That's exactly what it was."

Richie squinted. "The Iranians were transporting stuff for a nuclear power reactor? They're hoping to build a bomb, right?"

"Good guess, but no." Charlson stuck the folder back in the drawer and locked it away. "Now we're getting into some very sensitive intelligence matters, so I'm afraid I'm going to have to skip over how we found out about all this. But the gist is that the ship was actually hired by a company in Pakistan. A front for a group of Islamic fundamentalists. And it wasn't bound for Iran at all." He paused for dramatic effect. "Guess where it was headed."

Jack grimaced. "The port of New York?"

Charlson nodded. "Unfortunately, that's correct."

Richie frowned. "They already have a nuclear weapon? And they were trying to transport it over here?"

Charlson shook his head. "A standard nuclear weapon or its components wouldn't give off that level of radiation. That's the good news."

Jack winced. "And the bad?"

Charlson leaned closer. "Are you gentlemen familiar with the term 'dirty bomb'?"

"I CAN'T BELIEVE THIS!" said Richie as he and Jack descended in the elevator. "Here I was thinking we had caught the most ordinary case in the world, some stupid neighborhood beef, and now it turns out that—"

"*Later*," Jack said, gesturing with his eyes at the other occupants. "Let's discuss it on the way home."

They rode the rest of the way down in silence, mulling over what they had just heard.

Outside, Jack glanced back up at Brent Charlson's office tower. Even under normal circumstances, he was not big on spending time in Manhattan. As a kid, he had grown up with a view of this borough right across the East River, but like many Brooklynites, he didn't feel much need to visit. The center of New York City was just *too much:* too crowded, too tall, too loud, too fast-paced. Brooklyn felt more comfortable, a low flat plain of family homes, of neighborhoods where people knew and looked out for each other.

Today he was especially glad to be leaving. He wanted to get back on familiar turf, where he knew how to do his job and didn't have to worry about world politics or any of this spy business. He couldn't avoid it now, though—he had insisted on becoming more involved, and now he was, and it was a damned heavy weight. He looked up; the midtown skyscrapers felt as if they were pressing down on him, as if—at any second—bombs might go off and the buildings would come thundering down.

"Christ," Richie said as he settled into the passenger seat. "What I wouldn't give for a nice simple domestic violence case! Or somebody popped by a drug dealer."

Jack pulled out into the busy stream of traffic moving up Third Avenue. "This is gonna be tricky," he acknowledged. "We're supposed to find the guy, but without making any damn noise." He pondered what Charlson had told them. The fed had never really gotten around to explaining how their suspect—named *Nadim Hasni*—was tied in with the terrorist plot. The detectives had been about to press him on it, but the man had left for a briefing.

Jack had been stunned by 9/11 of course, but he had never really believed that Islamist terrorists might explode a nuclear weapon in New York. There were simply too many innocent Muslims living here who would be killed too. But a dirty bomb—a bomb made with conventional explosives, with radioactive isotopes added so they would be dispersed in the blast—was another thing. It would have a limited explosive impact, so it could be targeted much more specifically, and the initial release of radiation might only kill a few hundred or thousand people. Still, the psychological impact on the entire country would be hard to even imagine.

"So why do you think this Hasni guy killed Brasciak?" Richie said.

Jack sighed. "I don't know. It doesn't exactly sound like a smart thing for a terrorist to do, killing one person out in broad daylight. With such a stupid weapon, no less."

"This is really eating me up," Richie said. "Charlson says

our guy's a car-service driver, so he would be in that database I was looking at. I don't know what happened. I guess I just missed him."

"Don't worry about it. There must have been, what, forty or fifty thousand licenses in there? Anybody could've missed one face. Think about when we show people mug shots: their eyes glaze over after the tenth one."

Soon they were zooming down Broadway toward Chambers Street. As they came up the ramp onto the Brooklyn Bridge, both men fell silent. An NYPD squad car with flashing lights was permanently parked at the base of the bridge, a rather weak effort to discourage terrorist activity there. Maybe it made the general public feel better. As Jack drove across the span, the water of New York Harbor sparkled in the sun. He kept his eyes fixed straight ahead. He knew that if he glanced right, he would see the skyline of lower Manhattan also shining in the sun—with a big gaping hole where the towers had once stood.

"Hey," Richie piped up. "I know what we should do. Let's just send this Hasni guy a letter." He told a story about an NYPD sting operation in which they'd scooped up a number of mooks with outstanding warrants by sending them notices to come in and pick up unclaimed tax refunds. Ah, the criminal mind . . . Under other circumstances, Jack might have gotten more enjoyment out of the tale.

"Where ya goin'?" Richie asked a while later, in Brooklyn. "The car service is on Coney Island Ave."

Jack turned off Church Avenue onto a small side street. "I know. I just wanna see where our guy lives."

Richie frowned. "Charlson said we should stay away. They've got the place covered."

"Don't worry—I'm just gonna breeze right past."

And so he did. Nadim Hasni's block was nothing special: just a line of modest little aluminum-sided row houses. Jack spotted some neighbors as he drove along: a trio of tiny Mexican kids vying to heave a basketball toward a homemade hoop, a couple of women in Arab headdresses. There was a big plate-glass window in the middle of the block—a Laundromat, Jack saw as he cruised by. He peered for house numbers above the concrete stoops. *There.* The one with the sign for the doctor's office on the lawn. He grimaced. *Adolescent Gynecology?* What the hell was that?

"That must be the surveillance vehicle," Richie said, nodding at a shiny black van with tinted windows parked a few yards down.

Jack kept on driving and turned left at the next corner. With satisfaction, he noted a traffic light two blocks away: Coney Island Avenue. His theory about their suspect living close to the deli had been right on the money.

CHAPTER FIFTEEN

At that moment, though, Nadim Hasni was nine miles away, in Jackson Heights, Queens, walking out of a subway station into a burst of sound.

Overhead, above the rusty green metal trestles of the elevated 7 line, a train made a rackety thunder as it left the station. On Roosevelt Avenue, in front of Nadim, cars honked as they navigated a complicated and very busy intersection. The sidewalks were packed, the passersby speaking an amazing babble of different languages. He heard Urdu, Hindi, Pashto, Punjabi, and several unfamiliar tongues. The faces were mostly brown: Indians and Pakistanis and Bangladeshis, but also Mexicans and Tibetans and Ecuadorans, with an occasional pale Russian mixed in.

As he hurried across the busy avenue and reached the far side, a happy memory came to Nadim. He and his wife had come here on weekend expeditions from Brooklyn, bringing their excited young daughter, and they had walked on both sides of her, holding Enny's hands and swinging her up and over the sidewalk, on their way onto Seventy-fourth Street, into the heart of what tourists called Little India, though it was actually a shopping destination for people from all over the subcontinent.

While his neighborhood back in Brooklyn had been decimated after 9/11, here things still bustled with the energy of a
bazaar in Karachi or New Delhi. Nadim remembered his shock
when he had first seen this place: Pakistanis shopping next to
Indians, Muslims eating in restaurants right next to Hindus.
Back home, they fought bitterly, clashing over religion and
borders, but when they came to New York, they discovered that
what they had in common was more important than how they
differed: here they were all minorities, brown people in a white
country, all *Desis*, children of the South Asian diaspora.

Every weekend they thronged these few blocks, which
were like a carnival bursting with tastes and smells and sounds
from home. Nadim remembered how Enny used to practically
shake with the excitement of it all. They would take in a Bollywood movie at the Eagle theater, then gorge themselves on
the grand Indian buffet at the Jackson Diner, then stroll along
the strip to window-shop. The drabness of the low brick buildings was concealed under an intense mosaic of bright signs
and colors: the brilliant magenta, purple, and yellow fabrics
of the sari shops; the gleaming gold necklaces in the jewelry
stores; the rows of fruit and vegetables outside the Patel
Brothers supermarket, where you could buy a twenty-pound
bag of basmati rice or chapati flour. The street was also a riot
of sounds: a boisterous Bollywood soundtrack blaring from
the front of a DVD shop; some Indian hip hop thumping from
the window of a passing car; the fantastic, lopsided rhythms of
Bhangra romping out of the doorway of a CD store. Nadim's little
family would inhale the street as well: the warm sugary smell of
roasting nuts, the aroma of frying samosas, the familiar blends
of masala spices. At the end of the day, they would cap off their
adventure with one last stop: a visit to Kabir's Bakery, where
Enny would get to pick a sample from the prodigious array of

dense, milky sweets, and Nadim would always get a helping of *rasmalai*, the dessert that always transported him back to his childhood, to the safety of his grandmother's kitchen.

Enny had loved this place, loved it all. Nadim had too, and today he had hoped for a brief distraction from all his troubles here, but he could not find it. His nerves were stretched too tight. To make matters worse, he had to keep a constant eye out so he wouldn't run into his ex-wife, who lived just a few blocks away. He lit a cigarette and took several deep drags, but today the smoke just seemed to make him more jittery.

He saw loving couples and happy families, with their hopes of bright futures. Once he had been part of this world, an adventurer in this rich fresh land, a member of this great shared family. Now the passersby seemed alien to him, misguided, lured by golden baubles and sugary sweets. By a false, cruel dream. What future could he make for himself here?

The street had turned into a tense gauntlet, and he needed to escape. He was almost at the end of the block when two big speakers outside a CD shop blared on: pounding drums, shouted chants, skirling pipes. Nadim froze in the middle of the busy sidewalk, caught in an internal whirlwind, his mind torn open by jarring white light, by screaming, by jagged blasts of sound.

He stood there, unaware of his surroundings, until he felt cool drops on his face. He looked up: an April shower.

The passing streams of shoppers ran under awnings for shelter.

Nadim, unstuck, moved on.

AARIF'S APARTMENT WAS SO sparse that it was a wonder he even owned four chairs for the gang to sit on.

Nadim was grateful for the quiet and the calm, up here

THE NINTH STEP | *107*

near the top of this ugly brick building, two blocks from Seventy-fourth Street. While his host made tea in his kitchen nook and they waited for the others to arrive, Nadim had a smoke while he padded about the little studio checking out photographs of Aarif's extended family, in Rawalpindi. This was one reason for his comrade's spartan life here in New York: he sent a lot of his earnings back home. Most of the rest went toward the realization of their plan.

Nadim looked back to make sure that Aarif was out of sight, then edged over to the front window. Down below, Thirty-seventh Avenue held a fair amount of pedestrian traffic, but he saw few white faces, and none looking up at the building, none who seemed like undercover police. He still felt shaken, but the hard knot of tension that had pressed against the bottom of his breastbone for the past four days eased a bit. It was starting to seem possible that he might actually walk away from the incident in the deli unscathed, that he might even be able to return to his apartment and his normal life. *And*, of course, to continue working toward the plan.

He spotted Husain and Malik hurrying down the sidewalk in the light spring rain, the former young and bookish, the latter handsome and stylish with his sporty sweatshirt and gelled pompadour.

Aarif—gaunt, stern-faced, always a bit sour—came out of the kitchen with a tea tray. He wore drab brown and beige clothes; though he was not yet thirty, he managed to convey the tired authority of a village elder, and had become the de facto leader of their little group. He set the tea down on a side table, then began to unroll the *sajadas* and spread them on the floor, pointing east toward Mecca.

As soon as the others arrived upstairs, they had a quick cup of tea, then made *wud'u*, the ritual ablutions, then knelt down for the *Asr*, the late afternoon prayer, as the sound of the *adhan* wafted in through the window from a *masjid* down the block. As always these days, Nadim felt like a bit of a fraud as he went through the motions, but they were so deeply ingrained in him that he could have performed them in his sleep. Halfway through the second *raka'ah*, he snuck a peek at Malik, whose eyes looked glazed; Nadim sensed that he wasn't the only one who was putting less than his whole heart into the ritual. He felt a twinge of guilt again: he had spent the past couple of nights on Malik's couch. The last thing he wanted was to get anyone else in trouble, but he and Malik didn't work at the same place and they lived in different boroughs. He hoped that there would be no way to tie the two of them together in case the incident in the deli caught up with him. One thing he had learned recently: everybody on the planet had to have somewhere to sleep every night, and you didn't want that to be a park bench or a cardboard box out on the street, not if you could help it.

When they were done, they rolled up the *sajadas*, stowed them away, and got down to business.

"I have great news," said Husain, in Urdu. "Since last we met, I went home for a week. And I talked to my uncle, the one with the factory in Peshawar. He says he will come in for half a *crore*."

Nadim and the others whistled. That was over sixty thousand dollars!

"I hope you have not discussed this on the phone or by e-mail," Aarif said. The others turned to him.

"Why not?"

"Didn't you hear about Tajmmul?"

"What happened?"

"He was taken away. The CIA was tapping his calls back

home. This is how it works: they hear you talking about any kind of big money transfer, and *kudha hafiz!" Good-bye.*

Husain's face fell. "I e-mailed my uncle to say thank you last night."

Aarif scowled. "Let's hope you're still around for our next meeting, *yaar.* Let's hope we all are. Just use better sense in the future, all right?" He turned to Malik. "How about you?"

Malik reached inside his jacket and handed over a thick envelope. Nadim knew that it would be full of cash.

And then it was his turn.

"And you?"

His heart rate jumped. "I . . . I am continuing to save. I should have my portion ready . . . soon. Very soon." He didn't mention the fact that he had not gone to work for the past three nights, that Rafik-kahn would surely not take him back. But that was okay. There were hundreds of car service and taxi companies out there, and drivers came and went. He would find new work just as soon as it was safe.

Aarif scowled, but then he turned to the others. "No matter. Husain's uncle's share puts us very close to what we need. I think we're ready to move forward."

CHAPTER SIXTEEN

It wasn't every day that a veteran New York detective like Jack Leightner saw something he'd never seen before.

Nadim Hasni's former father-in-law sat at one end of the dining room table. The old man had a face like burnished, cracked teak, with piercing blue eyes. He paid Jack and Richie Powker absolutely no mind. He picked a cigarette out of a pack in front of him, made a fist, tucked the filter between his middle and ring fingers so that the cig projected up like a little chimney, fired it up, and then inhaled through one end of his chambered fist. Was this some Middle Eastern custom, or just a personal invention? Jack had no idea.

After their drive-by of Hasni's residence, on the way back to the Seven-oh house, the two detectives had stopped off to interview the man's employer at a Pakistani car service on Coney Island Avenue. The owner, a heavy, ill-tempered man, offered little useful information. He told them that Hasni had not come to work for the past few nights. They tried questioning him about Nadim's habits, friends, etc., but the man waved a hand in dismissal. "I have many drivers. Their life when they are not at work? Not my problem. I don't need this bullshit. If you see Nadim, tell him: don't come back."

Back at the Seven-oh house, the detectives hunkered down for a little computer search. Having a name for their suspect made all the difference. Without it, they might as well have been searching for a ghost; with it, every new bit of data gave him more corporeal form. Nadim Hasni, they soon learned, was thirty-two years old. He had arrived in the States back in 1993, on a tourist visa. He had applied for a green card years later, after marrying a U.S. citizen, one Ghizala Mamund, but it had not come through by the time they divorced in 2003.

The detectives searched through every database they could think of and called every contact who might be able to provide more information, at the Department of Motor Vehicles, the Taxi and Limousine Commission, utility companies, the city's Department of Finance . . .

When they finally ran out of sources, Jack turned to his partner. "Let's go for a drive."

Ghizala Mamund's residence, in Jackson Heights, Queens, was one of a row of modest homes with muddled architecture: drab brick façades topped with fussy mansard roofs, and red-tiled front awnings peaked like Swiss chalets. A skinny, serious-looking young girl, maybe nine or ten, answered the doorbell for Mamund's apartment. She wore a plain, high-waisted brown dress over a pair of blue jeans. Her hair was tied back in two braids, and she wore a little metal stud in one nostril, and a bead necklace.

"Is your mother home?" Jack asked.

The girl stared, wide-eyed.

"Do you speak English?"

She frowned. "I'm not supposed to talk to strangers." She sounded like any American kid.

"It's okay," Jack said. He held up his badge. "We're not

strangers; we're policemen. And we don't need to talk to you, just to Ghizala Mamund."

"She's not my mother," the girl said solemnly. "She's my auntie."

"Okay," Jack said patiently. "Is she home?"

The girl chewed her bottom lip for a moment. "Wait here," she finally said, and then she quietly closed the door. A minute later, she came back and led them into this dining room, where the old man sat, smoking his odd improvised hand-pipe and gazing off into the ether. Jack wondered if he might be blind. "How you doing?" he said, but the man didn't respond.

The dining room did double duty as a parlor; it was decorated with the kind of cheap but pretentiously ornate furniture you could buy on the installment plan in a discount showroom, and smelled powerfully of foreign spices. Jack noticed a stack of schoolbooks on the dining table, next to an open notebook. Moving away from the table and the rather disturbing old man, he wandered toward the front of the apartment, past a big old TV and some armchairs. On a side table he noticed several photos, silver-framed. They all showed a young girl, but she wasn't the one who had answered the door. They looked to be about the same age, but this one wore big clunky eyeglasses and she had a round, rather plain face.

After a rather awkward minute, a woman emerged from a back doorway, adjusting a headscarf. She wore a shapeless black dress, but Jack could see that she was plump. She gestured to the detectives to sit on a sofa, and then she perched on the edge of an armchair. She had big, doe-like eyes, high cheekbones, and full lips; Jack guessed that she had once been something of a beauty. Her niece stood next to her.

"Thank you for talking to us, Ms. Mamund," Jack said. "Or is it Mrs. Hasni?"

The girl responded. "She doesn't speak any English." Jack turned toward the old man, but she shook her head. "He doesn't either."

Jack frowned: the last thing he wanted was to put a little girl in the middle of a case involving murder and terrorism, but he seemed to have little choice. "What's your name?" he asked her.

"Raani."

"Well, Raani: Do you think you could maybe help us out by translating what your auntie says? That means—"

"I know what 'translating' means," she said with a touch of pride, and Jack guessed that she did pretty well with her homework.

"That's great. Thank you. Could you ask her when was the last time she saw Nadim Hasni?"

The girl did the honors.

Her aunt stiffened. She drew herself up, like a pigeon inflating its chest, and spoke rapidly in her foreign tongue.

The girl turned to Jack. "She says not for more than a year."

Jack tugged at his earlobe. Nadim's ex-wife had clearly said more than that, and he wished he could have understood it all. Despite her dumpy surroundings, the woman had an imperious air, as if she were some foreign princess being interviewed by low-caste inferiors.

"Does she know where he might be right now?"

Again, the translation and the rapid, bitter answer.

The girl shook her head.

"What did she say?" Jack asked.

The girl wrinkled her nose. "She doesn't care where he is or what he's doing, as long as he pays the . . . um . . ."

"Alimony?"

"Yes."

Jack regarded the scowling woman. He thought of the early days of his own divorce, of the tornado of feelings that had whirled inside of him back then: fierce anger and resentment, inextricably bound to remnants of true love. Christ, what a mess romance could be! He saw it all the time at work: people shot, stabbed, beaten, and battered, all in the name of disappointed love.

Richie reached into his jacket pocket and pulled out a photo of Robert Brasciak. "Ask her if she's ever seen this man."

The woman showed no signs of recognition. She shook her head.

"And you?" Richie asked the girl.

She shook her head too.

Jack nodded toward the old man. "What about him?"

The girl shook her head. "He never leaves the house."

Jack thought for a moment. "All right. Ask her if she saw any signs of erratic behavior in Nadim." He squinted. "That means—"

"I know what 'erratic' means. We had it in my spelling bee." She translated for her aunt.

Another angry outburst.

The girl frowned. "She says yes, of course. That he was a crazy man."

"How?"

"He was very nervous. He got angry for no reason. He couldn't sleep."

"Was he always like that, or was there something that made him change?"

The girl translated and Jack watched something flit across the woman's face. It was so brief that anyone but a trained interviewer might well have missed it. But Ghizala Mamund just shrugged and muttered briefly.

"Who knows what made him so? It was the will of Allah."

Jack stared at her. "If he was crazy, why did you marry him?"

During the translation, the woman squirmed. "He was not always like that. He was different when I met him."

"When did he start to change?"

It was interesting, not speaking the woman's tongue. That left Jack free to focus on her body language, the tone of her voice. And she sounded more anxious now than angry.

The girl turned to the detectives. "She says she doesn't want to talk anymore."

Jack wasn't ready to let it go. "Tell her that this is very important."

A brief exchange. "She must start cooking dinner."

Jack frowned. "Tell her that if she won't talk to us, we might have to bring her down to the police station."

The woman's haughty attitude crumpled; she looked like she might even cry. She finally said something in a faint little voice.

"He changed three years ago."

Jack stayed still, careful not to spook the woman. "Did something happen at that time?"

The woman pressed a hand to her mouth and mumbled something.

"That was . . ." The girl lowered her voice. "That was when Enny died."

Jack sat up a little straighter. "Who was Enny?"

After the translation into Urdu, Ghizala pressed a hand to her mouth. Her response was barely audible.

"She doesn't want to talk anymore."

Jack had a sudden inspiration. "'Enny'? Is that a girl?"

The niece nodded, sad-faced.

"The girl in those pictures?" Jack said, pointing to the side table. "Was she their daughter? Ghizala and Nadim's?"

Again the girl nodded.

"How old was she?"

"Eleven."

Jack glanced at Richie. What if Robert Brasciak had had something to do with the girl's death, and Hasni had wanted revenge? Maybe Brasciak had killed the girl in a car accident or something? But then, why wait three years to kill him? Perhaps Hasni had nursed a powerful grudge, and then a chance encounter in the deli had led to the killing?

"How did she die?"

Raani answered; she sounded somber, older than her years. "She was sick. Pneumonia. It happened very fast."

Jack slumped back. So much for *that* theory. He sighed. "Ask her if she has any idea where Nadim might be. Any idea at all."

Ghizala Mamund shook her head and muttered.

"She doesn't know anything about his life now and doesn't want to know."

Richie sat forward. "Ask her who he might be hanging out with."

This time the woman almost spat her answer: "*Koora!*"

"What does that mean?"

"It means garbage," the girl said. "Low people."

Jack wondered what the word might be for *terrorists*. He stood up and moved in front of the woman. "Ask her—"

The two detectives were startled by a loud sound from the rear of the room. The old man had slammed his hand down on the table. He stood up now and said something angry.

"That's enough," the girl translated. "He would like for you to leave."

"PNEUMONIA IS NOT A motive," Richie said as the two detectives got in their car and drove away.

"For killing some stranger in a deli? Not exactly. But I can imagine that having his kid die suddenly might make a guy a bit emotionally disturbed."

They chewed on that silently for a minute—detectives, yes, but also fathers.

"That must be some damn tough stuff to deal with in a marriage," Jack added, thinking of the bitterness in Ghizala's face.

"I don't like to think about it."

Jack stared out the windshield as they drove out of Jackson Heights. It was amazing, the sea of different faces here. He pulled over outside a Starbucks so Richie could run in to take a piss; Jack noticed that the counter girl was wearing an Arab headscarf. On the road again, they passed a shop selling international phone cards, and another one advertising global money transfers. Jack thought about phone calls and cash flowing back and forth from overseas, and about all the talk he'd heard of terrorist cells, camouflaged and imbedded in the fabric of daily American life. If Nadim Hasni was a hidden time bomb, evidently he had started to go off early.

They passed an Indian bakery, a taqueria, a Tibetan restaurant. Jack couldn't help thinking of his near-fiancée, how she would have liked this area. Michelle had always pushed him to try new food, expand his boundaries, step outside his comfort zone. Sometimes he'd felt irked by that, but mostly he had been grateful. He traveled all over the city and dealt with all kinds of people, but she had shown him that his view of the world could still be a bit limited. (Though what could you expect from the son of a Red Hook longshoreman?) If Michelle were here right now, she'd lead him into some exotic store or restaurant, laughing at his befuddled expressions. He'd pretend to be annoyed, but deep down he wouldn't mind.

Christ, he thought to himself—here he was, years later, still mooning about his lost love. Why? He remembered his urgent dream the other night. One thing you could say about the threat of terrorism: it had a wondrous power to focus the mind (and heart). If there was an attack now, the first thing he'd want would be to make sure his son was okay, but the second would be to find Michelle. He hated to admit it, but even after their disastrous parting, after what she had done, he still loved her. A lot of time had gone by. Maybe she wasn't with that other guy anymore. Maybe she regretted her affair. What if she wanted him back?

A car horn jolted him and he realized that he was cruising along the busy Brooklyn-Queens Expressway. "Wow," he said. He glanced at his partner. "You ever have this thing where you're driving and you have no memory of the last mile or so?"

Richie's eyes widened. "You're telling me this now? Christ—maybe *I* should drive."

Both men fell silent for a moment, but then Jack's partner spoke again.

"You know, here we are, looking for a guy who's supposed to be a terrorist. Don't you think we should be taking part in big task force meetings and stuff? Shouldn't there be briefings and meetings with NYPD brass, and crap like that?"

Jack shrugged. "We're only on this case because of the homicide. The terrorist part is Homeland Security's thing. And maybe the FBI. They don't want us involved, unless we can help find Hasni." He sighed. "I suppose I can understand. If we'd been following a case for a while, I wouldn't want some feds coming in and screwing everything up."

He drove on. There was something small and odd tugging at his subconscious, some little detail that he might have missed, but he couldn't figure out what it was. He sighed and let it go; it would come to him eventually, maybe later tonight, as he was drifting off to sleep.

They were going over the Kosciuszko Bridge now, that connected Queens to Brooklyn. To the west, a sort of grim visual pun: the bristly gray tombstones of Calvary Cemetery in the foreground, superimposed against the bristly gray skyscrapers of Manhattan in the distance.

A FEW MINUTES AFTER he dropped Richie off at the Seven-oh house, Jack's cell phone trilled. He fished it out of the cup holder and flipped it open with one hand.

"Leightner. Who's this?"

"It's Brent Charlson."

Jack's eyebrows went up. "How do you like that? We were just talking about you."

"*We* who?"

"Just me and my partner."

"Are you having any luck?"

"Nope. Not really."

"All right. I was just checking in."

Jack was about to sign off, but his partner's question came to mind. "You know, Richie was wondering: how come we're not being invited to any meetings on this? I mean, you must be coordinating with people, right? FBI, joint task forces, whatever?"

"That's right: we're working very closely with the FBI."

There was a short pause. "Do you know where I am right now, detective?"

"Of course I don't."

"I'll tell you: I'm in Hoboken, outside a storage facility. Inside, we've got a unit under surveillance. It was rented out by Nadim Hasni and his pals on December fifteenth. Does that date mean anything to you?"

"No. Why?"

"Remember what I told you about that Iranian ship getting hijacked with the radioactive cargo? That happened three days later, on December eighteenth. Now let me ask you, if you were transporting some radioactive material into New York, and you needed some time to build it into a bomb, where would you put it? Your apartment? Somebody else's apartment? In 'ninety-three, they worked out of a storage unit. In Jersey City."

Jack pressed the phone more tightly to his ear. "Did you look inside? What's in there?"

"*Nothing*, detective. They've been renting the unit for four months now, with nothing in it. Now why would they do that?"

Jack chewed on the question for a moment. "Because they're waiting for another shipment?"

"That seems like the best bet. This is not just some abstract plan. These guys are ready to move. Now, *you* can see how serious this is, and *I* certainly can. Why can't your partner?"

"I don't know," Jack said, feeling torn between Richie Powker, whom he was getting to know and like, and this relative stranger.

"I'll tell you what," Charlson said. "Why don't you ask Detective Powker about his wife?"

CHAPTER SEVENTEEN

Jack sputtered. "What the hell is that supposed to mean?"

"Ask *him*," Charlson said. "I've gotta run. One of Hasni's buddies just showed up here."

The line went dead.

Jack pulled over to the side of Coney Island Avenue and sat there for a moment, troubled and confused. What could Richie Powker's wife have to do with anything? He was about to turn around and head back to the Seven-oh when his phone trilled again.

"Jack? It's Larry."

"What's up?" Jack said, rather coldly. He was not very impressed with his old friend at the moment.

"Look," Cosenza said. "I'm sorry about what happened the last time you were here."

"I told you: don't worry about it."

"Come on, Jack—how long have we been friends? I've been feeling bad about not helping you out, and now maybe I can."

Jack perked up. "What's new? You want me to come over to the funeral home?"

Larry's voice sounded tight. "No. Don't do that. Just listen.

I've got a guy I did a favor for. A couple years ago his grandson got killed by a car, a hit-and-run over on Hamilton Avenue. I can't say I like the old man, but the grandson was a decent kid. He worked for me a while back, a part-time job, after school. When I heard about the accident, I did the embalming for free."

Jack squinted. "Okay—but what does this have to do with me?"

"This guy, the grandfather, he said he owed me a favor. And he, uh, he was *connected*. And he used to know your old man. Listen—you got a pencil?"

JUST AN HOUR, JACK told himself. Even though his shift had ended, he knew he needed to press on with the search for Nadim Hasni. And he needed to have a talk with his partner about Brent Charlson's mysterious implication. But for now, he finally had a lead on what might have really happened to his brother, and the urge to pursue it was just too great.

Brooklyn's Third Avenue looked grubby in the late afternoon sun. It was a long corridor of automotive repair shops, quick-oil-change drive-throughs, and sidewalk fix-a-flat joints, punctuated by strip clubs and XXX video shops that had been forced to this out-of-the-way stretch by city zoning changes. The avenue lay under the shadow of the Gowanus Expressway, which ran above it on stilts out toward Bay Ridge.

The area had always had its seedy side. The drive took Jack back in time to when his mother used to send him out to the bars to find his father and bring him home. If the long-shoremen weren't drinking after work in Red Hook, they some-times hung out on this side of the harbor, along with the ship machinists and welders and pipefitters. Hard workers and hard drinkers; their bars were rough. Jack remembered a joint on Thirty-ninth Street run by a transvestite named Queenie, and a place on Second or Third Ave. where the Norwegian riggers and seamen gathered. (They were known as *squareheads,* and their nights out involved a predictable three-step process: they would drink themselves silly, then they would dance to the jukebox, and then they would beat the crap out of each other.)

These were general memories, but right now Jack was pointed toward one very specific date. If he had been asked what was going on in the world during most years of his life, he might have been hard-pressed to answer, but 1965 was crammed with memorable events. There was the World's Fair in Flushing Meadows, and the Beatles' concert at Shea Stadium, and Malcolm X getting whacked up in Washington Heights. Civil rights activists got sprayed with fire hoses down in Selma, college kids burned draft cards in Berkeley, and Watts went up in flames. An astronaut took the first walk out into the black void of space, and the first U.S. combat troops sailed off to Vietnam.

For one fifteen-year-old from Brooklyn, the end of the year brought three significant events.

In October, Sandy Koufax of the L.A. (formerly Brooklyn) Dodgers decided not to pitch in Game One of the World Series because it fell on a Jewish high holy day. He took a lot of flak for that stand, but then went on to win the Series and the MVP award. A Jewish hero! That meant a lot to a kid in a rough neighborhood who was kind of small and had foreign parents and frequently got called a kike.

One November evening, just after John Lindsay became mayor, a partial electrical blackout spread across much of the five boroughs. Not a very big deal, not like the wild night to come when the lights went out in '77, but it taught Jack a lot about how a city could bond together—or be just a heartbeat away from utter chaos.

But for Jack Leightner, 1965 was not the year of space-walks or riots, of World Series or World's Fairs.

It was the year his brother had been robbed of his young life.

EVEN THOUGH THE TREES were budding and the air warmed with the rich, loamy scent of spring, the old man had a blanket over his lap. He sat in a wheelchair in front of his little Bay Ridge row house, with a middle-aged black nurse standing behind. Across the street, in a modest green spot called Owl's Head Park, a barking Labrador retriever leapt up in the air to catch a Frisbee.

"Goddamn mutts," the man said as Jack walked up the sidewalk. "They shit all over the goddamn place." His face was gray and liver-spotted, with sunken cheeks. A bad toupee sat awkwardly on his head.

"Mr. Farro?"

Instead of answering, Orlando Farro twisted in his chair to scowl up at his nurse. "Ya see this, Shirley? This is what I'm reduced to. My own goddamn son can't even be bothered to visit, so I have to rely on *cops* for a social life."

"Thank you for seeing me," Jack said.

The man just waved a hand as if he was pushing away some unpleasant food.

"Should we go inside?" Jack figured the old Mob soldier would not want to be seen with him in public.

"Bah. Let's go to the park."

"You sure?"

Farro scoffed. "I don't give a crap who sees me talkin' ta you. What're they gonna do? Kill me? It'd be a goddamned blessing."

The nurse spoke up. "Shall I push you, Mr. Farro?" She

had a pleasant Caribbean accent and a placid face; already, Jack was able to guess that her job required plenty of patience.

"*Phfft*. The cop here looks strong enough—let *him* push me. My tax dollars at work." Farro chuckled at his own joke, but the laugh cost him: he sputtered and wheezed.

Jack looked at the nurse. "Uh, I need to speak to Mr. Farro in private, but maybe you could follow us?" The old geezer looked like he might kick the bucket at any second.

The woman shrugged. "As you wish."

Jack took her place behind the wheelchair, and then he pushed the old man out across the street. The area was quiet and unassuming and working-class, two-story brick row houses with aluminum awnings over their front doors and American flags flying over postage-stamp lawns. Once it had been mostly Italian and Irish, but now Jack noticed Asians and Arabs walking by. Farro lived on the edge of the neighborhood, right near the harbor. Down at the end of his street, as if framed in a picture window, cars whizzed past on the Belt Parkway, and then—just beyond—stretched the great expanse of water.

The park was just a few square blocks. To the east, kids' high-pitched voices drifted across from a busy playground; Jack pushed the old man west, past a row of some of the grandest old trees he had seen in Brooklyn, and then he turned onto a curving asphalt path leading up the park's big hill. It was quite a tableau, Jack mused: a Russian-Jewish-American cop pushing an old Sicilian-American mobster, trailed at a distance of thirty yards by a Caribbean-American woman. As they made their way up to the crest of the hill, the sounds of the neighborhood—birds chittering, cars roaring along the parkway, the *ponk!* of a baseball hit by an aluminum bat—faded away, leaving a kind of dignified hush.

After a couple of silent minutes, they came to the peak

and Jack pushed the chair over to a bench, which offered a spectacular view of New York Harbor. The nurse sat several benches down, out of earshot.

Jack took a moment to look around. To the south, the Brooklyn tower of the Verrazano Bridge rose up over the houses of Bay Ridge like a giant blue clothespin. Across the harbor he saw the wooded outline of Staten Island, and then—to its right—the docks and loading cranes of Bayonne, New Jersey. Gazing north, he saw Governors Island out in the middle of the water, and then—just past it—the tip of lower Manhattan. He couldn't help remembering Brent Charlson's story about a hijacked freighter emitting deadly radioactivity, and a chill went up his spine as he imagined such a ship sliding into the harbor.

He glanced northeast, toward the peninsula of Red Hook, where he had been born, where his father had worked the docks, and where his younger brother had been slain. With any luck, this old man sitting next to him was about to say something about that.

"It's goin' the wrong way," Orlando Farro muttered instead, and Jack was confused for a moment, until he followed the man's gaze out toward the center of the slate-blue harbor, where a huge red freighter, loaded down with big cargo containers, like a pile of multicolored bricks, was wending its way toward the Jersey docks.

Jack knew just what the man meant. When he had been little, the Hook had been one of the busiest shipping destinations in the country. A longshoreman like Jack's father could find all the work he'd ever want, and the neighborhood had been an incredibly lively place. Then, in the late fifties, the whole industry changed. Where once the stevedores had hauled cargo up out of the ships' holds with brute muscle, now the goods were packed in giant metal containers. All it took was one guy sitting up in the cabin of a crane to swing them up out of the ship and onto the bed of a waiting truck or railroad train. And there was much more room for trucks and trains on the Jersey shore, so most of the industry had shifted across the harbor. Pretty soon, hard-laboring men like Jack's father were scrambling for scraps.

At Jack's side, Orlando Farro squirmed for a more comfortable position. "I hate this goddamn chair." He looked up. "Did you know that I used to be a Golden Gloves champ? I was ranked number three in the city back in 'thirty-nine. And now? I'm *shrinking*, and I cough my guts up, and I can't control my goddamn bowels. This is what old age will do to ya."

Jack felt a twinge of sympathy for the old man, so anxious to demonstrate that he had once been someone else, someone *more*. But he wasn't here to feel sorry for some thug. "I understand you knew my father. What can you tell me about him?"

The old man frowned. "You ever hear a saying, 'Be careful what you wish for'?"

Jack ignored the question. "I don't know how much Larry told you."

"He said you want to know what happened to your brother. Terrible thing." Farro squirmed in his chair again. "I loved ta fight. I was in the citywide championships in 'forty-one."

Jack resisted the urge to grab the old man and shake him, to demand the identity of the person behind his brother's killing. Take it slow, he told himself. Treat this like a professional interview. "What happened with my brother . . . I always thought it was just a random mugging."

Farro shrugged. "That was a long time ago. Maybe it's best to just let sleeping—"

Jack held up a hand. "I just wanna know what happened.

I'm not looking to stir up any trouble." The lie came easily, though what he really wanted was to find the perpetrator and beat his face to a bloody pulp. "So you knew my father?"

"I knew him," Farro said. "He was one tough bastard."

Jack nodded. The old man had been—like Jack himself—rather small, but he carried himself like a giant, with a cocky, rolling swagger. A handsome man in a rather crude way, Maxim Leightner had confronted the world with one eye squinting and a hand-rolled cigarette perched on his lower lip. Jack could picture him now, sitting in their kitchen eating soup, sucking the marrow out of an ox shoulder and eating garlic cloves like peanuts.

"He was one hell of a worker," Farro said. "Nobody earned a paycheck more than that crazy Russkie." The old man snorted. "He didn't have to work so hard."

Jack turned sharply. "What do you mean?"

Farro shrugged. "A guy like that, he could'a just worked for us."

Jack's face tightened. "Did he ever?"

"Ever what?"

"Do any work for you?" Jack already had a low enough opinion of his father, and he hardly wanted to abase it further—but he had to ask.

Farro didn't respond.

"I have a memory," Jack said slowly. "I don't know what it means. I know that when I was older, a teenager, my father didn't, ah, didn't want anything to do with . . . the, uh, people who ran the neighborhood." He felt like he was tiptoeing through a minefield, trying not to offend the old mobster before the man could tell him what he needed to know. "But there were a few times when I was little, I remember getting up late at night and seeing him get into a car filled with men. It would drive away, and he wouldn't come back until the morning. He would never talk about where he'd been."

Orlando Farro nodded. "You saw that, huh? I was drivin' that car."

Jack's heartbeat quickened. "Can you tell me where you were going?"

Farro shrugged. "Sure. We went down ta Philly."

Jack considered that info. Philadelphia was about eighty miles from NYC; he imagined his father headed down the Jersey Turnpike in the middle of the night, then cruising back in the wee morning hours. "What was going on down there? What did you need him for?"

Farro made a face. "Ya know, I hear you're a squeaky clean cop. Why the hell do you wanna know about this?"

Jack stared at him. "Do you have any brothers?"

Farro nodded gravely. "Yeah. I had one, real proud like you. He didn't want nothin' to do with our thing. A lotta good it did him, being such an upright citizen—he died on Guadalcanal back in 'forty-two."

"I'm sorry," Jack said. It was weird to feel any kinship with this old mobster. An airplane slowly ripped the sky overhead, and a breeze ruffled some daffodils next to the bench. "*So*—what was going on in Philly?"

Farro shrugged again. "We had some people down there we needed to do business with. Some Russkies. Only thing was, none of us spoke the lingo."

"You needed my father to translate?"

"That's right."

"This business," Jack said, stomach sinking. "What did it involve?"

"Narcotics," Farro said. "Child prostitution. A little rubout, when someone was givin' us trouble."

Jack winced, but then the old man laughed. "I'm bustin' yer balls, kid. It was just a crew down there that used ta hijack some trucks. Furs, cigarettes, crap like that. We'd sell the goods up here in the city. Your old man helped us out now and then."

Jack sat thinking for a moment. "I can't really imagine it. I remember him being pretty uptight about . . . you people."

Farro shrugged. "Hey, the work down the docks was drying up. And he had a couple'a young mouths to feed . . ."

That got under Jack's skin. Stay on track, he told himself. "Something changed, though. . . . Did he do something that pissed somebody off?"

Farro hacked up some nasty phlegm and spit it on the sidewalk. "What I heard, he decided he was too good for us. Didn't want to get his precious hands dirty no more."

"What do you mean, 'you heard'? Weren't you there?"

Farro took out a handkerchief and dabbed at his mouth.

"I was away at that pernt. I went up to Ossining for a few years back in 'sixty-four." Ossining, an hour north of the city, was home to Sing Sing Prison. The mobster turned to Jack. "So now what? You sorry you asked about all this shit? It doesn't exactly make you feel proud of your old poppy now, does it?"

Jack sat thinking for a minute, watching a little toddler chase after an anxious-looking dachshund, reaching out to try to pull the dog's tail. It seemed logical that the thug who had hired his father would be the man who'd want to teach him a lesson, if he stopped playing ball.

"This crew you had traveling down to Philly," he said carefully. "Was it a Joe Gallo thing?"

The old man scoffed. "Nah. Our little operation would'a just been peanuts for him."

"Who then? Who ran the operation?"

Orlando Farro didn't answer. He just made a pained face.

"It's ancient history," Jack said. "Just tell me who it was."

The old man moaned and pressed a hand to his stomach. Jack realized that his bowels were acting up.

"Listen," Farro said, squirming. "I think I already repaid my favor to Cosenza." He turned and looked over his shoulder for his nurse.

"*Please,*" Jack said. "Whoever it was, he probably died a long time ago . . ."

The old mobster grimaced; he looked like he was about to weep from frustration and shame. "It was Frank Raucci, goddamnit! And last I heard, he was plenty alive and kickin'." He cried out, "Shirley! I need you! Take me home!"

The nurse rushed over and began to wheel the man away. Farro looked over his shoulder and offered one bitter parting comment. "For chrissakes, Leightner, don't get old!"

Raucci. Jack frowned; he couldn't remember the thug from his childhood. Well, at least he had a name to work with.

He stood up and headed down the path toward his car. Right now, he needed to keep moving forward on the Nadim Hasni case. He was off duty, but that didn't matter: the possible consequences of not catching this suspect were more drastic than he liked to contemplate.

The first stop was the Homicide Task Force, to see if any of his contacts had come up with more information about Hasni. He found a new fax in his in-box. Sitting at his desk in the crowded detectives' squad room, he read it with mounting excitement. He made a couple of calls, and then he dialed Richie Powker. "You still at the Seven-oh? Something very interesting just came in. Hold tight—I'll be right over."

"I'M GLAD YOU'RE STILL here," he told his partner as he hurried into the squad room, bearing a manila folder.

"Whaddaya got? Richie asked. The Seven-oh detective was sitting amidst a mess of case files, message slips, and half-eaten food.

"When we were running Nadim Hasni's name through the computer the other day, I called someone I know over at the Department of Finance." Jack sat down next to his partner's desk, opened his folder, and took out several sheets of paper. "She faxed me these this afternoon. For the past couple years, Hasni has paid regular taxes for his car-service driving, but his income went way down in 2001 and 2002. Here's the weird thing: there's a period where he seems to go completely off the record: no taxes taken out, no paychecks at all."

Richie ran a hand through his thatch of red hair. "From when to when?"

"Mid-October 2001 to April of 2002."

The Seven-oh detective squinted. "I wonder when his daughter died? Maybe he just didn't feel up to going to work."

Jack shook his head. "I looked it up. She did die during that time, but not until March of 2002."

Richie thought for a moment. "Who knows? Maybe the guy was just driving for somebody who let him work off the books."

"Maybe—but notice that he went off the radar just after Nine-eleven."

Richie frowned. "Do you think he might have gone out of the country? Maybe to some training camp in Afghanistan or something? Isn't that what these guys do?"

"That doesn't seem like a very good time for a Pakistani terrorist to go traveling overseas by plane. I checked with Customs anyhow: there's no record of him flying anywhere. Unless he had a fake passport . . . But take a look at this." Jack flipped through the papers and held one up. "Just for the hell of it, I asked my friend to look up our *victim's* tax records. Robert Brasciak took in regular pay from his job at R. J. Stanley for the last couple of years. 'Go back a little,' I told her. It turns out that there's also a complete hole in Brasciak's records, from early October 2001 to April of 2002. Coincidence?"

Richie scrutinized the paper.

Jack's gaze drifted around the squad room. Now that his excitement about the new information had leveled off, he had time to think—and to remember. He looked at his partner.

Richie glanced up. "What?"

"Nothing."

"You've got this weird look on your face."

Jack sighed. "I got a phone call from our pal Charlson a couple hours ago. He wanted to check in, see how we were doing."

Richie shrugged. "Okay . . . So?"

Jack frowned. "Listen, I have no idea what this means, but he, ah, he said I should ask you about your wife."

Richie stared in disbelief, and then he shook his head and looked away. After a few seconds, he turned back and spoke in a low voice. "Her name is Amina. She was born in Pakistan."

Jack scratched his cheek. "And you didn't mention this?" He had heard his partner briefly refer to his wife a couple of times but had imagined some red-haired, doughy white woman.

"Mention it? Why should I?" Richie's voice started to rise—he glanced around the squad room, then lowered his voice again. "She's *American*. She's a goddamn citizen. Why should I have to mention her? I'm married to a Pakistani-American and that means I support terrorists or something?"

"*Easy*. No one is saying that."

"Charlson is, apparently."

Jack shrugged. "It's just ... *interesting* that you didn't bring it up."

Richie gripped the arms of his chair. "What am I supposed to do, *apologize*? I lived through Nine-eleven in New York City. I heard what people were saying. What my fellow *cops* were saying. *Towelheads. Sand niggers. We should go over there and bomb those fuckers and turn their countries into parking lots.* My wife had to live through that, people giving her dirty looks on the subway, making nasty comments. There were ignorant bastards around here beating up *Sikhs,* just because they wore turbans. What do you think all that did to my *kids*?"

"All right," Jack said. "I'm certainly not accusing you of anything. Or your wife. It's just ... Charlson seems to be saying that you might be a little less than *gung-ho* about this case."

His partner stared in disbelief again and gestured at the paperwork in front of him. "What do you think I'm doing right now, on my own time?! I'm a *cop,* Jack. True blue. And a native New Yorker. I love this goddamn city. You think I'm not gonna work to track down some asshole who wants to blow it up?"

Jack held up his hands in apology. "I don't think that at all. Look, I'm sorry. Let's just forget about it, okay?" He stood up. "Listen: I've got a court appearance tomorrow morning, but after lunch I'll come by here and we'll work on this together, okay?"

Richie scowled. "That fed can kiss my ass."

CHAPTER EIGHTEEN

Near sunset, Nadim Hasni paused after he rounded the corner onto his home block.

He looked carefully up and down the street. His gaze darted from sight to sight: a couple of little Pakistani children bouncing a ball outside the big twenty-four-hour Laundromat in the middle of the block; a cat poised halfway up the mottled trunk of an old sycamore tree. Nervous, Nadim lit a cigarette. He heard a skittering noise right behind him and his heart almost leapt out of his chest. He whirled around, only to see a squirrel dart behind a couple of trash cans.

Nadim pressed a hand to his chest and waited for his heart rate to slow. Anyone else might have attributed such jitters to the shock of having recently killed a man, but Nadim knew that he couldn't rely on such an obvious explanation. The truth was that he'd been having problems with his nerves for a long time now. He wondered if he was going mad.

Two lanky Pakistani teenagers walked toward him, both raptly listening to little earphones. Nadim wondered if they would startle when they saw him, if they would shout *Murderer!* and run, but they moved blithely past, slouching like true

American teens. He looked away and spotted an old black man sitting on his front porch, staring idly into the distance. Again, Nadim wondered if this neighbor would jump up at the sight of him, but the man gazed right through him. It seemed that word of the murder had not gotten out—or at least that he himself was still anonymous and invisible, as usual. Just another Pak car-service driver, like a thousand others.

He smoked the rest of his cigarette, watching the block. After a couple more tense minutes, he had to conclude that the block looked as it always did: a modest series of row houses in Kensington, Brooklyn. Concrete stoops, aluminum-sided houses, cheap cars in the driveways. But there had been a time when he would have marveled to think that he might ever live on such a respectable street. Back when he had first come to America, when he had been forced to sleep on couches in the homes of distant relatives, in dingy old brick apartment buildings whose hallways smelled of stale sweat and cat piss.

Nadim looked down. His heart rate had slowed, but his hands were trembling. He crushed his cigarette underfoot, took a deep breath, and moved on down the sidewalk. As he neared his apartment, he paused to look again for any sign that he was being followed. Nothing. He exhaled. It seemed impossible, given how the police always found the culprits quickly on the TV crime shows, but maybe he had come out of that deli the other day unobserved.

He walked around a battered white contractor's van parked in front of the house and gingerly moved up the concrete driveway, past the sign in the middle of the lawn: DR. TEKCHAND PARKASH, ADOLESCENT GYNECOLOGY. The doctor, a Hindu from a little town outside Delhi, kept to himself, which suited Nadim just fine; he came and went to his basement apartment from a separate door on the side of the house, so he didn't have to find out why on earth adolescent girls might be in need of such treatment.

He continued up the driveway, then paused to dig in his pockets. He caught his reflection in the glass outer door: he looked exhausted and disheveled. With difficulty, he managed to locate his keys. After he pulled the key ring out, he accidentally dropped it on the asphalt. As he bent down to pick it up, he heard a sharp *thwack* overhead. A chunk of brick fell at his feet and some crumbs of it landed on his hair. He looked up, dazed with lack of sleep—had it fallen off the top of the building? He didn't see anything up there. Out of the corner of his eye he saw a stranger moving up the driveway toward him, a stern fellow with severely short hair, holding up a long, thin wrapped bundle. Farther off, he saw the back door of the contractor's van hanging open in the street. A flash and a muffled sound came out of the front of the bundle and then Nadim heard another *thwack* on the wall next to him.

He glanced wildly around, but there were no neighbors in sight to help him. He scrambled to his feet and bolted, his chest gripped by an icy band of fear.

He heard shouting behind him, several voices, but he didn't look back, just sprinted up the driveway and veered around the little freestanding garage at the back of the house. There was a narrow space between the weathered gray wall and a chain-link fence; he hurtled into it, squeezed past some prickly yellow-budding shrubs, and burst out into a neighbor's backyard. He banged into a pole, part of a child's swing set, and careened around the side of that house, through another side passage, and out onto the next block.

To his right, the contractor's van came screeching around the corner. Nadim turned left and ran. He was soon gasping for breath—he cursed his smoking habit—and realized that he could never outrun the onrushing vehicle. Impulsively he veered again, vaulted a low fence, dodged around another aluminum-sided house, through another yard, around another house.

He felt a painful stitch in his side. There was no way he could maintain this pace. He paused, desperate, to think. At first he wanted to run toward one of the bigger avenues, where other people would be around. Surely his pursuers wouldn't dare shoot him in public. On the other hand, strangers might block his way . . .

He heard shouting behind the last house and he staggered off again—and that's when inspiration struck. He recognized this block: he had been walking Enny home from school one day when they heard a cat's pitiful mewing. He had wanted to go on home, but Enny had tugged at his hand. "Abbu, something is wrong." They stopped and listened more carefully. And they traced the persistent sound to the side of a nearby house: it was coming from beneath a pair of heavy metal storm doors. Nadim was never thrilled about contacting random American strangers—who knew how they would react to his brown face?—but he had walked back around to the front porch, gone up, and rung the bell. No answer. He returned to the storm doors. Hoping that he wouldn't get mistaken for a burglar, he bent down and discovered that they were not locked, and his daughter had looked so proud of him as he lifted out the bedraggled cat.

Panting now, he scanned the surrounding homes. Which had it been? They looked identical, made of pale yellow brick. He struggled to recall. The right side of the street—the house had definitely been on the right. He ran across. The first few houses had driveways, but no storm doors at the side. He ran on. *Yes!* Halfway down the next driveway, he could see a pair of black metal storm doors outside the basement. He rushed up the asphalt, bent down, and yanked on the right one. It didn't budge. He tried the other. Locked also. He straightened up, frantic. The house had a little window above the storm doors, and he had a flash of memory: a crystal pendant, a little angel, hanging behind the glass, sparkling in the sun. But there was no pendant here. In the distance, he heard screeching tires.

He couldn't run back to the street, so he dashed up the driveway, careened around the rear of the house, and down into the next driveway, where he found another set of storm doors. He skidded to a stop and looked up at the window: there was the angel! He bent down and lifted up with all his strength. The heavy metal squealed and complained, but it rose as he straightened up. Some concrete steps led down into the darkness from which he had freed the cat. He ducked inside, pulled the door down after himself, then caught its full weight at the last minute so it wouldn't slam.

He was in pitch blackness now. He sat on one of the steps, not knowing what lay below, struggling to quiet his raspy breath. He listened, every nerve straining outward. He heard a car engine revving, and shouting, and he crouched down, wincing, prepared to be discovered and yanked back up into the fading light. He had nothing to fight back with, nothing but his bare hands.

And then . . . the car sounds receded, and the shouting. He sat there in the dark, not daring to believe his luck. It had been brought to him, he realized, by his daughter. By Enny, his own little angel.

The darkness began to weigh on him, though. He started to tremble. Soon he was overcome by a screamingly powerful desire to lift the door, to emerge back into the air and light, but he knew it wasn't safe. Not yet.

The seconds ticked by and he began to sweat profusely, and then to shake as if overcome by fever.

CHAPTER NINETEEN

Jack Leightner was a humble man, but there was one thing that he felt was a bit beneath him: riding the subway. A homicide detective spent a good part of his life in cars, crisscrossing the borough, chasing after suspects, arriving at crime scenes like the cavalry coming over a hill. You didn't worry much about parking, and certainly not about getting tickets. But this morning he had to testify in a Manhattan courtroom, down near City Hall, and he'd hardly be the only one with an official parking permit on his dash, so he decided to just bite the bullet and ride the train.

As it went over the Manhattan Bridge, he opened his briefcase and reread his case file. Trials took a long time to wend their way through New York City's overloaded court system, but this case was particularly old. The defendant, a forty-five-year-old male with severe anger-management issues, had killed his wife in a fit of jealous rage. Then, overcome by remorse, he had jumped in his car, sped away, and decided to kill himself by careening into the side of a gasoline truck parked at a service station (no doubt imagining the massive fireball you always saw in such situations on TV). But the truck had not blown up—the car had wedged itself underneath the fuel tank, and the killer broke most of the bones in his body. He had ended up in the infirmary at Rikers Island for almost a year. Jack was thankful for his detailed notes.

Bright sun poured through the train's windows and he glanced down at the broad East River, and the pewter harbor, and then the skyscrapers of downtown Manhattan came into view. And then, of course, he was thinking about terrorism and the Hasni investigation. Frowning, he forced his attention back to the papers spread out on his lap; if he couldn't focus, the trial of this other killer might well go off track. But he looked up: *there it was again,* the fleeting sense that he was missing some simple but crucial detail in the Hasni investigation, something that had been in front of his face all along.

At his stop, along with a throng of fellow riders, he pushed out the door past a tide of rude city dwellers pressing into the car, and then he strode toward the exit. The fluorescent lights gleamed against the sides of the white-tiled tunnel, and hundreds of New Yorkers threaded their way past each other on the crowded platform. Jack noticed that half of them carried shopping bags or briefcases or knapsacks, and again he couldn't help thinking of terrorists, of the coordinated series of explosions that had rocked a number of commuter trains in Madrid the year before, killing almost two hundred. He couldn't remember if the bombers had blown themselves up, but there certainly seemed to be no lack of fanatics around the world who would. As a detective, Jack had seen hundreds of killers motivated by rage, fear, or greed, but it still seemed hard to believe that human beings might commit mass murder and simultaneous suicide, driven just by politics or religious devotion. It was even more incredible that they could believe that such a horrible act might get them into any reasonable heaven.

* * *

BY LUNCHTIME, HE WAS back on his home turf in Brooklyn. He arrived five minutes before his son, at their usual spot, a coffee shop on Atlantic Avenue.

On a number of previous occasions he had been caught up in work and rushed in late, or had even forgotten their appointments, and he knew that the kid registered every disappointment in a mental ledger, a stack of little resentments perched atop the great fat letdown of his parents' divorce. Luckily, though, he'd had the foresight to set the alarm in his cell phone. And he swore to himself that when his son arrived, he would forget about everything else and pay total attention to the kid.

The waitress brought him a cup of coffee, and he stared at the luncheonette's back wall, which was covered with nets and plastic fish, in keeping with the general Greek theme. He mused about this morning's perp who had lost his marbles and bludgeoned his wife, and about terrorists, and about a long-ago murder in Red Hook.

His son slid into the booth, startling him.

"Wow," Ben said, "you actually beat me here! That's gotta be a record."

Jack decided to ignore the slight snark and accept the acknowledgment. "You want some coffee or something?"

Ben picked up a menu. "Let me think about it for a sec."

Jack watched his son consider his choices. The kid was several inches taller than his old man. He wore a red flannel shirt; he looked rather gaunt in it, but he might have put on a couple of pounds since their last get-together. Jack noticed that his son's skin seemed to be clearing up and he was glad for that; the mid-twenties were already a pretty self-conscious age, but Ben's acne had burdened the kid with extra shyness.

Jack's mind began to drift again. Don't think about Nadim

Hasni, he told himself. Or Frank Raucci. Think about your son, right here in front of you. "D'you know what you want?" he asked, then turned to look for the waitress. "I'm just gonna get a cheeseburger." He turned back to Ben. "So—are you eating meat these days, or are you a veggie again?" Ben tended to fluctuate between the two, and to get annoyed if Jack couldn't remember his latest stance.

The kid started to answer, but Jack sat bolt upright. *Remembering.*

He jumped up. "Listen: I've just gotta do something real quick. I'll be back in two minutes, I swear."

Ben's face settled into its customary pout, but Jack was already on his way out of the coffee shop. Out on the sidewalk, he glanced up and down the avenue, then turned down the cross street. Up ahead, on the next corner, he spotted a deli and broke into a trot.

He hurried in between several ranks of brightly colored floral bouquets, barely acknowledged the nod of the Korean proprietor, and moved into one of the aisles, scanning the products arrayed there. *No.* He turned a corner and came up the other aisle. *There!* He stared at a row of cans of baked beans, the same brand that Nadim Hasni had used to crush the head of Robert Brasciak. Jack could picture the original clearly in his mind. Not the label with the green stripe, like those on the left. Not the vegetarian variety, but the ones on the right, with the blue stripe. He reached out, picked up a can, and turned it so he could see the list of contents.

And there it was.

Jack returned to the luncheonette and his son but spent the rest of their lunch in a bit of a daze. What was a radical Islamic fundamentalist, a Muslim fanatic, doing shopping for a dinner that contained a substantial helping of *pork?*

* * *

THERE WAS A SILENCE on the other end of the line, and then Brent Charlson finally spoke.

"Let me get this straight: we're in the middle of investigating a major threat to national security and you want to talk to me about the ingredients in a *can of beans?*"

Jack looked out the windshield of his car, still parked on busy Smith Street, outside the diner. "These guys, these terrorists, they're supposed to be fundamentalist Islamic—"

"So he was shopping for a neighbor! So what?! Is that your idea of detective work?"

"I'm just looking at the evidence."

"You don't *know* the evidence, detective, not even a tenth of it. You're not in the middle of this investigation. We already have enough rock solid information to put these guys away for life."

"Why don't you, then?"

Charlson's voice rose. *"Why don't we?* Because we want to make sure we get the whole goddamn cell, that's why. And this ridiculous beans nonsense is a great example of why we didn't bring the NYPD into this in the first place. This isn't amateur hour."

"All I'm saying, is it possible that Nadim Hasni is not really a part of the group?"

"Oh, I see," Charlson said, voice dripping with irony. "Maybe he's just an innocent bystander who got caught up in this case by accident?"

"I don't know."

"Aren't you forgetting one little detail? The man has already murdered someone in cold blood. What kind of goddamn beans he was buying doesn't alter that fact!"

"Okay, but—"

"You know what I'm looking at right this moment, detective? I'm in my office, staring at a confidential memo from the NSA. You know what 'NSA' stands for?"

Jack knew full well, but he was so irritated by the condescension in the fed's voice that he didn't bother to reply. "What does it say?"

"I'll tell you: it says there's been a considerable spike this week in intercepted international chatter. It says they recognized a number of coded words, like 'New York' and 'April' and 'Semtech'. That's a plastic explosive."

Again with the condescension. "Okay, but I was just—"

"Do I need to draw you a fucking picture? All right, I *will:* the next time I see you, I'm going to show you surveillance photographs of Nadim Hasni welcoming other members of the terrorist cell into his own goddamn apartment. And I'll show you some recent big wire transfers of cash that just came in from Pakistan. But right now, detective, you're wasting my time, and every second in this case is precious. So get off the phone and go take care of your own business."

Jack started to say something else, but his phone went dead. He sat there in his car and resolved to double his efforts on the case.

LATER THAT AFTERNOON, even Richie Powker was not terribly impressed by Jack's baked bean theory.

The squad room was busy: phones ringing, radios squawking, some detective in the corner having a heated phone argument with what sounded like her daughter or son. Jack watched as a couple of beefy white detectives marched in, herding a handcuffed, fairly harmless-looking Hispanic teen. The kid wore a profound look of despair: he'd probably gotten caught doing something stupid, and now the consequences—which he had previously ignored—were staring him smack in his young mook face.

Richie leaned forward in his overburdened chair. "I don't like this Charlson guy," he said to Jack. "I don't like feds in general. They didn't work the real evidence they had before Nine-eleven, and then they went and made up stuff so they could go into Iraq. Not to mention that this particular bastard is implying some nasty crap about me and my wife." He frowned. "But even *I* have to admit that this beans thing seems a little thin. Maybe Hasni *was* just doing some shopping as a favor to a neighbor. Or maybe he's not a religious nut—maybe he just likes blowing shit up."

The Seven-oh detective squared one of the piles of paperwork on his desk, a lost cause. "I still think that fed is an asshole. But you know what? Even if he's a total clown, that's all the more reason why you and I need to be on our best game. We both lived through Nine-eleven here. And we know these terrorist bastards are out there."

Jack nodded somberly. He straightened up and pulled his chair closer to his partner's desk. "Anything new on the ATM front?"

As they would with any fugitive, the detectives had tracked down Nadim Hasni's bank accounts and asked to be informed about any automatic-teller transactions. (They wouldn't get the info in time to catch him at any particular branch, but at least a recent withdrawal could tell them that their suspect was still in town—and several might indicate that he was hiding out in a particular neighborhood.)

Richie shook his head. "*Nada.* The guy worked in a cash business and I bet he had some dough squirreled away."

Jack sighed. These days, only the dumbest perps didn't

watch enough cop shows on TV to know that they shouldn't use their debit or credit cards when on the lam.

Richie laced his hands behind his head. "So what do you want to do next?"

Jack frowned. "I wanna put the bastard's picture on the front page of the *Daily News* and the *Post*. I wanna go interview every one of his car-service buddies. And I wanna give every cop in the city his goddamn photo."

Richie snorted. "Our buddy Charlson would love that."

Jack glanced at the clock on the squad room wall: their shift had ended half an hour ago. He shook his head. "I'll be damned if I'm gonna just go home and watch TV. How about we drive back over to Jackson Heights and take another crack at Hasni's wife? I mean, at least *I'll* go—I know you've got a wife of your own to get home to . . ."

Richie stood up and grabbed his car keys. "We're trying to protect the city from a radiation bomb. I don't think my wife is gonna complain."

AND SO THEY SET off to re-interview Nadim Hasni's ex. Or, at least, they made it to Queens . . .

"*I'll* drive," Richie said, pointedly referring to Jack's spacey command of the steering wheel during their last trip to the neighboring borough.

Jack was happy to give in. He found a toothpick in the pocket of his sports jacket and chewed all the mint out of it as his partner steered toward the Brooklyn-Queens Expressway. Over the Kosciuszko Bridge they went, past the backdrop of little gravestones and big skyscrapers, Jack absorbed in thinking about Hasni and Charlson. And about an old man sitting in a wheelchair on a hill in Bay Ridge.

Despite the expressway's notorious problems (frequent mysterious traffic jams; potholes the size of meteor craters), they reached Queens in excellent time and got off the highway just a few blocks from Ghizala Mamund's apartment. As always, Jack was impressed by the foreignness of the neighborhood. New York City had a number of these little compact transplants from other worlds: Little Korea on Thirty-second Street in Manhattan, Little Brazil in the Forties . . . Somewhere, undoubtedly, there must be a Little Burkina Faso and a Little Iceland. Despite the vastness of the city, people liked to clump together with their own, often spending most of their lives within a familiar quarter-mile. Jack gazed at the scenery as they cruised down Thirty-seventh Avenue; the passing faces growing browner, the clothing more colorful . . .

"Stop the car!" Jack blurted. "Be subtle!"

"What the hell?" Richie was puzzled, but he managed to pull over without too much fuss.

"Back there," Jack said, looking into the side mirror. "In front of the bakery with the green-and-white awning. You're not gonna believe this!"

Richie stared up at the rearview mirror. "You think it's possible?"

They had spent a lot of time studying the driver's license photo. And now Nadim Hasni, or a young brown-skinned guy who looked one hell of a lot like him, was standing outside the shop, wearing bleached jeans and a navy blue tracksuit jacket. He held a paper bag in one hand and peered up and down the street like an anxious bird. In fact, after Jack's decades of police work on city streets, those nervous head motions had drawn his attention before he even registered the man's face.

Hasni walked away from them, disappeared from view behind a newsstand, then reappeared. He paused for a moment on the next corner, looked right, then turned left, out of sight.

Jack was already out of the car. "Drive around!" he urged his partner through the open window. "Come down the block and close him off!"

He was in pursuit before Richie had time to hit the gas.

NADIM PAUSED AS HE came out of the bakery with his brown paper bag. A serving of *rasmalai*—he could already taste the sweet cheese balls floating in their soothing cream.

That childhood favorite seemed particularly appealing at this stressful time, but it was actually the need for cigarettes that had driven him out of hiding. For the past day he had been holed up in Malik's little fourth-floor walk-up two blocks away. Last night, the young stud had gone out to a nightclub. "Come with me," Malik had urged, but Nadim said that his stomach didn't feel well. And it didn't: he had spent a good part of the afternoon in the bathroom retching, and then he had tried to sleep, but he was still trembling too hard. Thank God he managed to calm down a bit before his friend came home—Malik still didn't know anything about the incident in the deli or the subsequent attempt on Nadim's own life. As Malik dressed for his date, Nadim anxiously watched the TV news, but there was nothing about the man in the deli or about any kind of manhunt for his killer. Very puzzling. At least no one had trailed him here to Jackson Heights. Not yet, anyhow . . . He had not taken any chances today, though, and stayed inside. But he had smoked his last cigarette while watching the news. All day long, the need for a smoke had gripped him, like a big fist, squeezing. He knew Malik didn't smoke, but he hoped that one of the other two roommates did. He had ransacked their tiny bedrooms, had scrounged under the piles of magazines and random detritus in the messy little common room...No cigarettes, anywhere. Nadim held out for as long as he could. What had he read somewhere? Nicotine was more addictive than heroin.

I'll just step out for a second, he finally told himself. *I'll be very careful.* He peered out the front window for a full fifteen minutes, scanning the street below. Nothing suspicious. No vans in sight. Wary, he edged out the front door, ready to duck back at the first sign of anything suspicious. Quiet. He allowed himself to exhale. And he had set off down the block, without incident. Turned onto Thirty-seventh Avenue: no problem. Stopped at a deli and bought his smokes. He turned to go back to Malik's, then realized that he was starving. Malik's bachelor refrigerator was empty.

With his stomach so upset, Nadim figured that there was only one thing he might be able to keep down: a helping of *rasmalai*. And Kabir's Bakery was just a half block down... After the harrowing past few days he could really use a bit of a treat.

Now he stepped out onto the sidewalk, feeling like a successful secret agent. He had completed his stealth mission: cigarettes in his breast pocket, his dinner in his hand. Enough tempting fate, though: it was time to hurry back to Malik's, to his safe hiding place.

He set off, savoring the fresh air outside and the gorgeous spring afternoon. The new-leafed trees along the avenue provided some shade from the bright sun; their dappled shadows danced on the sidewalk. Nadim reached the corner of Seventy-fourth Street, glanced right, and panicked. Just what he needed today: his wife—his ex-wife—was standing right there on the opposite corner! She was looking down, thankfully—digging for something in her ever-bulging leather purse, a cheap

Gucci knockoff she had bought one time for ten dollars on Canal Street, stupidly convinced that she had scored a miraculous bargain. Yes, it was definitely Ghizala, under those dowdy clothes: her doe eyes, those plush lips that had once driven him wild. Amazing to think how she had once made his heart swell with love.

It certainly wasn't love that swelled his heart right now—it was anger, a raw surge of grievance and resentment, and maybe even another rash impulse toward homicide. He felt it wash over him, a scalding red wave, but all of his common sense was not carried away. That was the last thing he needed right now: another killing. The plan would be ruined for sure.

He turned quickly, in the opposite direction, down Seventy-fourth Street, into the heart of Little India.

JACK WAS THIRTY YARDS behind, running.

He forced himself to slow down as he rounded the corner onto busy Seventy-fourth Street. The sidewalks were thronged with shoppers, which was good, providing him with cover, but he wished this was a street in midtown Manhattan, where a white man in a sports jacket and tie could blend in. He was blitzed by distractions as he moved down the packed shopping street: a heap of battery-powered, arm-waving baby dolls on a card table outside a gift shop, a couple of women in dazzling orange and purple saris strolling hand in hand down the middle of the crowded sidewalk. He kept his eyes fixed on the back of Nadim Hasni's blue jacket.

He glanced up ahead, hoping to see Richie Powker maneuvering toward him through the crowds. Should they grab Hasni now, bring him in for the Brasciak murder? Or should he call Brent Charlson first? He had promised to do so, but he didn't dare take his eyes off his quarry long enough to find Charlson's number. His heart was racing—it was one thing to be chasing a murder suspect, but now he was after someone who was also plotting another vicious, depraved terrorist attack on the citizens of New York.

Down the block, Hasni stumbled against something and then regained his balance.

Two men carrying a big cardboard box suddenly emerged from a store and stepped in front of Jack. Cursing under his breath, he veered around them.

SEEING HIS EX-WIFE AGAIN stirred up so many powerful emotions at once that they threatened to overwhelm Nadim. He needed to escape, immediately. Random faces, garish colors, dazzling glints of light—they streamed past him in a blur as he plunged off through the Little India crowds.

He could forgive Ghizala, he thought, for so many things. He could forgive the way she had represented herself when they had first met, when she was on her trip back to see relatives in Pakistan and she had seemed to him, a poor student in Karachi, like such a glamorous woman, come from America, where—she said—her father owned a prosperous business. He could forgive the way she had looked back then, so beautiful, like the ripe, curvy star of some Bollywood movie. He could forgive the way she had captured his heart, had drawn him to this foreign country with tales about her ambitions to become a fashion designer, about the job her father would give him, about the rich life they would build together in her fancy New York home. He could forgive the discovery, once he arrived here, that she lived in a small, dumpy apartment, that the old man was something of a charlatan, with only a part-interest in a tiny newsstand, that Nadim would have to work like a dog to support them, that Ghizala's ambitions were just pipe dreams, that she really just wanted to sit on the couch all day watching soap operas, growing plumper by the month. She had never bothered to go to fashion school, even though he offered to pay; worst of all, she had never troubled herself to learn any English, the language of her adopted country. And though he could, perhaps, forgive all the rest, because she had given him the greatest gift in his life, his beautiful Enny, he could never forgive her that. Because when Enny had fallen ill that fateful night, and he had been away, Ghizala had not been able to place a simple phone call for help. (If she had just known enough to call 911, even if she couldn't speak, they might at least have sent someone to check!) And he could never forgive her smug old father, who must have sat there at the kitchen table, stupid hand cupped around his stupid cigarette, unable to do anything while, in the next room, Enny lay wheezing for breath. Just *pneumonia*! It would have been so simple to save her! And he could never, never, never forgive Ghizala because she had waited three weeks before she dared to come see him and tell him that his daughter was gone.

Now he threaded blindly through the crowds, not seeing anything but his daughter's anguished face. He knocked into an old woman's shopping cart, almost fell over it, and snapped to. Was Ghizala still behind him? Had she crossed the street? He couldn't bear to look at her—instead, he veered to the right.

UP AHEAD, NADIM HASNI had vanished. Completely, as if a giant hand had reached down from the sky and snatched him up. Desperate, Jack scanned the sidewalk, the street, the opposite sidewalk. He looked ahead and saw Richie Powker striding toward him through the crowds. The Seven-oh detective

gave a quizzical look and Jack raised his hands, utterly mysti-
fied.

The two cops met in the middle of the block.

"Damnit!" Jack muttered. "I was right on him. Somebody
blocked my view for a second, and then . . . I don't know." He
walked forward a few yards to where he had last seen their
suspect, and his heart sank. On the right, its entrance partially
blocked by a Dumpster, a little alley led in toward the center of
the block. He turned to his partner: "Go around! Meet me on
the other side!" He ran into the alley, reaching into his sports
jacket for his gun. He had no idea if his suspect might be armed.
So far, the man had only used a can of beans—but he had
proved that he was ready to kill.

Breathless, Jack reached the end of the alley. He slowed,
then stepped out into a cross lane. He glanced left: a dead end
maybe thirty yards down. He glanced right: another dead end a
few yards the other way. This wasn't a throughway, just a place
for a few shopkeepers to park their cars. And there was no sight
of Hasni.

Hypervigilant, he walked along the cross lane on both
sides, holding up his gun with one hand while he tried the back
doors of the buildings. All locked. There was no other possible
exit—except for one spot, where a walled section of rough plywood marked some kind of construction site. The walls were
maybe ten feet tall, too high for a man to jump. The wood was
roughly joined; Jack glanced through a gap into a muddy vacant lot, where a building on the other side of the block might
have been demolished to make way for new construction. But
the gap was only two or three inches wide, too small for a man
to squeeze through.

As he came back through the alley, he took out his cell
phone, looked up a number in its address book, and called Brent

Charlson. He wasn't looking forward to admitting that he had let their mutual suspect escape.

"You sure it was him?" Charlson asked after Jack explained the situation.

"Pretty sure," Jack replied, glad the fed couldn't see his sheepish expression.

"Did he see you?"

"I don't think so," Jack answered, though he had to wonder why—if not—the suspect had bothered to disappear.

"All right," Charlson said briskly. "We'll be right over. If you spot him again, don't try to engage."

Jack walked around the block, every sense alert for any sign of Hasni, and finally met up with his partner on the other side, outside the construction site.

"This looks like the only way out," Richie said.

Jack nodded, then frowned. "I just called Charlson."

"What'd he say?"

Jack shrugged. "He said, 'Stay out of the way'—they'll be right over."

Richie's face tightened. "Let's go back and find this bastard first."

Jack nodded and they set off again, returning to Seventy-fourth Street, stopping to check in every store and restaurant along the way.

THE DOORWAY ON THE right led up a flight of stairs. Nadim jogged up them and found himself in a big showroom full of female mannequins dressed in bright saris—sky blue, magenta, yellow, bedecked with rhinestones, swirling with beadwork—arrayed around the room like a mute chorus, staring at him. A bored-looking woman stood up from behind a counter. "May I help you?"

"Just looking." Nadim walked around for a moment, touching the sleeve of a dress now and then as if he was shopping for a present. He glanced at his watch, wondering how long he could stay up here without making the shopgirl nervous.

He looked toward the back: a mirrored alcove. He wandered over, hoping for a back exit, but there wasn't one.

"Are you looking for anything in particular?" the woman called out. "Something for a special occasion?"

Nadim shook his head nervously. "I'm waiting for my wife."

Indeed he was: waiting for his wife to go on her way, so he could get the hell out of here.

After another minute he could see that he was wearing out his welcome and he felt foolish. His ex had probably already waddled off down Thirty-seventh Avenue and he was just being paranoid. It was time to go back to Malik's now, to enjoy his *rasmalai*, and to rest.

"Thank you," he told the shopgirl, and then he descended the dim staircase, walking toward the bright rectangle of sunlight below. He came out onto the sidewalk again, only to find Ghizala walking straight toward him, just a few yards away.

He saw his own surprise mirrored on her face, which then bloomed into alarm.

The surprise he might have expected, but the alarm was something else. She glanced wildly around, as if looking for something. For someone? She seemed scared—it occurred to him that maybe someone had warned her about him. Was she hoping to spot a policeman, ready to shout *Murderer*?

He spun around and noticed a small alleyway; coming the other way, he hadn't seen it because it was partially obscured by a Dumpster. Without waiting for her to say anything, he veered into the shaded little lane and ran.

Thirty yards down, he glanced right, glanced left, and realized his mistake. Panting, he searched for a means of escape. He tried every door he could see, but every damned one was locked. He ran over to the wall of plywood. Wheezing with exertion and fear, he grabbed the edge of a sheet, felt a splinter jab into the palm of his left hand, planted a foot on a neighboring board, and yanked back with all his might. With a screech of nails pulling out of wood, the board gave way a bit, and Nadim fell back. He jumped back up, then found that he was just able to squeeze through the widened gap between the boards. He stumbled thirty yards through a rubble-filled dirt lot, found a dead-bolted door on the far side, threw the bolt back, then lurched through, out onto the other side of the block, where he almost crashed into a couple of squat little *desi* women. He straightened up, brushed at a torn spot on his jeans, then limped off down Seventy-third Street.

At the next corner, he walked into the shadows beneath the train tracks, darted through traffic to cross Roosevelt Avenue, and plunged into the subway station. Two minutes later he was sitting up in the window seat of an F train, gazing out on a jumbled panorama of Jackson Heights, leaving Little India and Ghizala and his safe hiding place all behind.

CHAPTER TWENTY

Jack Leightner was not a violent man. He could hardly remember the last time he so dearly wanted to punch someone in the face.

Of course, he knew cops who liked to throw their weight around. Guys who went on the job tended to be beefy, athletic types, the kind who had learned early on to hold their own in playground fights or street brawls. But he was on the smaller side, and so he'd learned to rely on his wits. As a cop, he solved his cases through superior reasoning and solid investigation.

Which was why he was so riled up now, as he sat at the far end of the bar in dim Monsalvo's, nursing a beer and his wounded pride. He recalled how—a couple hours before—Brent Charlson and his team had roared into Queens in their shiny goddamn van.

Jack would have loved to be able to tell the man that he had picked up Nadim Hasni's trail again, but no such luck.

At first, the fed had been all business. "Where was he when you lost him? What was he wearing? Where was he when you first saw him?"

Jack did his best to ignore the sting of the first question.

He explained how he had returned to the alley and discovered the freshly opened gap in the plywood. He watched as Charlson dispatched his team to the hunt. Without their bulky radiation suits, the men looked lean and muscled, with the intense, unnerving focus of Navy SEALs or Green Berets.

Jack crossed his arms. "No radiation gear today?"

Charlson ignored the question. "Thank you, detective. We'll take it from here."

Jack frowned. "Why don't we split up the area? My partner and I can keep searching along Seventy-fourth Street."

Charlson didn't even acknowledge the suggestion; he just watched his men fan out down the street.

"*Look*," Jack said. "This is our case too. Let's work together."

Charlson barely bothered to conceal his contempt, as if he was speaking to some rookie just out of the Academy—a rookie who had just botched his first case. "You've done enough, detective. Why don't you worry about your other investigations?"

The fed walked away.

"Another Bud?"

Jack looked up at Pat Senior, who was wiping down the bar with a rag that smelled of bleach. He sighed. "I guess so."

MEN WITHOUT WOMEN. THAT seemed to be the theme of the bar tonight.

There was ancient Tommy McKettrie, who had practically moved into Monsalvo's upon the death last year of his beloved wife of fifty-seven years. And there was young Mike Faurer, racked with guilt and regret, who came to Monsalvo's to avoid his wife of only a year. "I don't know what I was thinkin'," he kept moaning. Jukebox songs wafted around in the dim neon light: crooned odes to perfect loves, loves sorely missed.

Four beers later, the music had picked up, something bright and feisty with an accordion in it, and Jack was transported back to Prospect Park, a warm summer night, a concert in the bandshell, an unfamiliar kind of music. "What *is* this?" he had asked. "It's Zydeco," Michelle Wilber answered. It was their first time together, a blind date, and he remembered watching her walk up to him, and feeling as if he'd won a jackpot. They had eaten some tasty Southern fried chicken and drunk a few beers, and she'd even got him up and dancing.

He missed her. He missed having a reason to look forward to time off; he missed brushing his teeth with her and joking around at bedtime; he missed making love to her; and he missed having something in his life besides work.

A new tune from the juke, a slow dance. A voice poured out of the dusty speakers above the bar, feisty, smoky, inimitable. Brenda Lee, "I'm Sorry." What if Michelle could ever bring herself to say those words? What if she knocked on his door late tonight and asked him to forgive her? What then? Was there any way, after what she'd done, that he could find such mercy in his heart?

He ordered another beer and sipped it, stirred by old memories.

Finally, he got up and went over to the phone booth at the back of the room. Sat down and pulled the accordion door shut. Took out his cell phone. He snorted: he was sitting in a phone booth using a cell phone. His fingers felt clumsy on the tiny buttons, but he found the one for the address book. Sure, enough, Michelle was still in it.

He was just about to dial her number, but then—through the glass door—he heard some peppy old doo-wop song on the jukebox and he thought of Petey, singing "Help Me, Rhonda" that tragic morning so long ago. Jack had never liked the Beach Boys, himself—they were so sparkling clean, so college, so California. What did they have to do with a poor kid from Red Hook, Brooklyn? But Petey liked the blond surfers.

Jack shriveled, there in the phone booth. He remembered how popular Petey had been, good at sports, blessed with his looks, attractive to the girls. He had loved the kid, Lord knows he had, but at that moment when his brother dropped wounded to the sidewalk, there had been a tiny part of him that was glad to see his competition fall. And what kind of a person could even think such a thing? How could he ever make up for it?

He closed his phone and pressed his forehead against the cool glass door. What was he doing? His brother's murderer was within reach, and he was worrying about a goddamn exgirlfriend?

He opened his phone again but called Information instead. He said a name out loud, talking into a computer, into a hole. What had happened to human beings, for chrissake?

After a moment, an actual woman's voice came on. "I have two Frank Raucci's in Brooklyn, sir. One in Mill Basin and one in Carroll Gardens."

"Gimme the one in Carroll Gardens."

Now he had the number. He had told himself that he would come armed with research, that he would find out whatever he could about the man first. To hell with that—he would poke another stick into the hive. He punched in the number.

"Hello?" A crusty old man's voice.

"Is this Frank Raucci?"

"Who wants to know?"

"Are you the Frank Raucci that used to work out of Red Hook?"

"Who the hell is this?"

That was enough. Jack clicked his phone shut, yanked open the phone booth door, and pulled out his car keys.

THE HOUSE WAS STUCK in a time warp. Unlike many of the other homes in Carroll Gardens, brownstones that had been rehabbed and sandblasted and made fit for swanky new owners, Raucci's place was straight out of the fifties, part of a stretch of modest row houses with striped aluminum awnings and flights of stairs rising up from the sidewalk like airplane boarding steps to the second floor, where each house had a little porch where the owners could sit in Bermuda shorts and wife beater T-shirts in the summertime, drinking beer and gazing down on the passersby.

To Jack's surprise, a petite teenage girl answered the door. She wore a pink tank top and had braces on her teeth.

"Is Frank Raucci in?"

"Grandpa!" the girl called out over her shoulder, then disappeared inside, letting the screen door slam.

A few seconds later an old man shuffled into view behind the screen, holding something black in one hand: Jack stared to make sure it wasn't a gun. No—just a TV remote. Raucci wore a faded plaid shirt and stared out through thick eyeglasses; beneath them, one of his eyes was clouded over, milky-white. His cheeks were gaunt and his gap-toothed mouth hung slackly open. He looked to be near ninety.

"You know who I am?" Jack said, standing on the little porch.

"If you're selling something, I ain't buyin'. Wait—did you just call me and hang up?"

"I'm Max Leightner's son. And Petey Leightner's brother."

The old man squinted. "John, right? No: *Jackie.* You're the cop."

Jack ignored the comment. "You went down to Philly with my old man. And then he wouldn't work for you anymore."

Raucci frowned. "That's ancient history. Why the hell are you botherin' me now?"

"Am I?" Jack said. "Am I bothering you?" He pictured his brother Petey lying on a Red Hook sidewalk, staring at his hand covered in blood. "Why'd you do it? Why'd you have him killed?"

"What?" the old man sputtered. "Are you crazy? Have *who* killed?"

Jack's voice rose. "You think you're safe now? Don't you know there's no statute of limitations on murder?"

Raucci's face tightened. "You better get the hell away from my house, cop."

"What, you were afraid to go after my father? So you picked on a helpless thirteen-year-old kid? Did that make you feel like a big—"

A voice rose up from the dark sidewalk. "Is that you, Leightner? Whaddaya think you're doin'?"

Jack turned. It took him a moment to make out the face below: John Carpsio Jr., emperor of the dumpy social club on Smith Street. The mobster was standing there with a tiny sparrow of an old woman gripping his elbow. Carpsio turned to her. "Ma, go on home. I'll be there in a minute."

The woman's voice was tremulous. "Is everything okay, Johnnie?"

"Sure, Ma. Everything's fine. Now go on."

The little woman tottered off.

Carpsio stared up out of the dark. "Are you on duty,

Leightner? Is this official business? Not for nothin', but if it isn't, you might wanna call it a night."

"You think I'm scared of you scum?" Jack had dealt with plenty of thugs in his day, and he wasn't about to be intimidated now.

Raucci pushed his screen door open. "Get outta here, you punk!"

Carpsio came up the steps. He laid a hand on Jack's shoulder, and Jack was tempted to spin around and take a swing at him, but the mobster spoke calmly, in a low voice. *"Think about this*, Leightner. Do you really want to make a scene out here, put your job on the line?"

It was exasperating, how the criminal mistakenly thought Jack had once done him a favor, how he seemed to think they shared some kind of bond. But while Jack would never have backed down due to a threat of violence, Carpsio's even tone got through to him. He wasn't afraid of personal harm, but he *was* concerned about keeping his job.

With fists still clenched, he turned, stepped around the mobster, and stalked off.

MICHELLE CAME TO HIM once more that night, in his dreams. He was thrilled to see her, but again she was hurrying ahead of a terrible dark cloud, a swift-moving storm that threatened to devour their whole city.

CHAPTER TWENTY-ONE

"Just give me a few hours."

"Take a break," replied Sergeant Stephen Tanney. "Enjoy your days off."

"Come on. This is not exactly an ordinary case." Jack was sitting at his kitchen table, groggy from a night of poor sleep. He noticed that his bare feet were sticking to the linoleum: time to mop.

"I understand that, Leightner. But we've had word from above to not interfere with this one."

"You realize what's at stake here?"

"Of course I do. And Charlson has promised to work closely with the FBI and the JTTF." The Joint Terrorist Task Force, which included a new post-9/11 unit of the NYPD. "They don't need Homicide on this one. So we'll see you Monday."

The sergeant was fond of an obnoxious saying: "There are two kinds of problems in this world: the *my problems* and the *not my problems*." Jack could actually hear the relief in his boss's voice: if something bad went down here, it wouldn't be Tanney's responsibility. He grimaced, struggling to come up with a better argument.

"I know you want to help out," Tanney said. "But they're

on it. And we'll be available in a support capacity. I've let them know how to reach me twenty-four/seven if anything new arises."

Wonderful, Jack managed not to say. *I can't tell you how much better that makes me feel.* "All right. I'll be in on Monday."

He hung up, wondering how much investigation he could get away with on his own.

As he pulled a mop out of the kitchen closet, the memory of what he had done the previous night rose up like a bubble of indigestion. Oh well, at least it was obvious that Frank Raucci had not called in to gripe. The Mob avoided contact with the NYPD like vampires shunned garlic. And if they got *really* pissed off, they certainly wouldn't bother with any official complaint. It was rare for them to stir up scrutiny by messing directly with a cop—but not unheard of.

As Jack mopped the kitchen floor, he remembered how Michelle had enjoyed teasing him about being a neat freak. He should have explained it to her: putting things in order at home gave him some little relief from the appalling disorder he saw at work every day.

There were a lot of things he should have talked with her about, instead of playing the stoic cop all the time. But would that have made the difference, if he had talked more? He frowned: maybe her new lover had been more exciting in bed. He'd always thought he did okay in that department, but who knew? If the guy was younger, maybe he'd learned some new tricks from reading those new magazines about men's health and grooming and crap. Maybe they had discovered some new female erogenous zone in the past few years. It happened. When he was young, who talked about all this G-spot stuff? Back then, foreplay was some flowers and a nice dinner in an Italian restaurant.

He vacuumed the front room. Forty-eight hours to kill. He wondered what Brent Charlson was up to this morning, wondered if the man and his squad were getting any closer to shutting down the terrorist cell. He thought about how the feds had mismanaged their confidential informants before the 1993 Trade Center bombing and that hardly boosted his confidence—not to mention the way that warning signs had cropped up in the first few months of 2001, picked up by field agents for the three-letter outfits, only to be ignored at the national headquarters. He sat down and reorganized the papers on his desk.

He looked at his watch. The day was crawling, and he hated to think about how he was going to make the time pass during the next two evenings. He thought about calling Michelle again, but then scowled: *to hell with her.* There was no reason he couldn't find someone else. For months now, his son had been urging him to try online dating. Jack liked the way computers helped out at work, the way you could search databases so easily or find common elements in different cases, but he didn't like to use the things at home. Old dog, new tricks. He glanced at his watch again, then gave up and turned on his computer. What was the name of that dating service his son had recommended? He finally remembered it, then called up the Web site. It asked him for some basic info: his gender, zip code, what age range he was looking for.

He sighed. If he entered anything, he was probably gonna get bombarded by spam. He was tempted to just turn off the computer, but he heard his son's voice in his head. *Dad! Just give it a try! What do you have to lose?* My dignity, he muttered. Not to mention my self-respect. But he entered the info, including the age range. He went with women close to his own age; he knew he could have gone for perky tits and wrinkle-free skin, like a lot of guys, but he wasn't interested in dating someone who had never heard of Brenda Lee. Or the Beatles.

A column of women's faces came up onscreen.

Christ, it was like a precinct mug-shot book. Not that these women looked like the usual scarred, dented, snaggle-toothed bunch. No, at most, these would be misdemeanor criminals: bad check passing, DWIs, maybe possession of a controlled substance. He scrolled down a bit . . . yikes: this one had definite serial killer potential. He kept going: so many hopeful faces, so many forced smiles, these women posing in their bridesmaid dresses or their ski jackets, holding their beloved little dogs. His heart sank lower with every face. *I'm too old for this,* he kept repeating to himself. His marriage had been pretty rocky, but at least it had saved him from ever having to date again. Or so he had been foolish enough to believe.

He looked at all the eager faces. What was wrong with them, that they couldn't get a date the old-fashioned way? After a moment of reflection, he realized how uncharitable he was being. After all, *he* was hardly awash in offers. No, this was just what people did these days: they met in "cyberspace." It was normal.

He turned his computer off. Some other time.

He went into his bedroom to get dressed. As he was picking out some clothes, he glanced over at the bed. He could picture Michelle so clearly, sitting up on her side of it, deep into some book, her brown hair draped over her shoulders, her face so serious as she read, her silky nightgown giving him a tantalizing hint of her lovely breasts.

He stared at his cell phone, seized by the urge to call her. But he had no idea what he might say.

He dropped the shirt and slacks he'd picked out and traded them in for a T-shirt and some shorts.

He went for a long run in Prospect Park.

MR. GARDNER WAS A reliable source of company whenever Jack needed one; his elderly landlord never had other plans.

After he managed to kill most of the day with stocking his refrigerator, picking up some dry-cleaning, and doing other errands he didn't have time for during his workweek, he picked up a pizza and a six-pack and went upstairs for a visit.

He knocked on the door but heard no answer. After a moment, he knocked again; Mr. Gardner had grown hard of hearing in his old age. Jack felt a sudden bad premonition and opened the door without invitation, remembering the morning, four years before, when he had found his landlord lying on his kitchen floor, felled by a stroke.

The apartment was dark. "Mr. G?" he called out, heart sinking. No answer. He made his way down the hall by touch, until he came to the front room. He reached up, found the pull chain for the overhead light (three delicate antique globes), and found the old man sitting in his battered recliner over by the front window, staring down at the street.

Mr. G turned in his chair. "That you, Jackie? Is Mrs. Kornfeld all right?" Their elderly neighbor across the street.

"I don't know. Why?"

"The last couple'a nights, I ain't seen no lights on over there."

Jack shrugged. "I don't know."

They sat and ate the pizza and drank their beers. For once, Jack was eager to talk; he had been thinking about calling Michelle all day, and he wanted some advice. But now, as he chewed his pizza, he considered the photo of Mrs. Gardner resting on top of the TV. The old woman had been very nice; Jack had only known her for a short time because she had passed away soon after he moved in. He remembered that she was always baking something; he could never stop by to pay the rent without sitting down for a slice of her lemon poppyseed cake or some warm cookies.

He couldn't see asking Mr. G for advice about forgiveness for a cheating lover. The old man and his wife had been happily married for almost sixty years, and Mr. G was hardly a worldly character; he tended to change the channels when anything remotely sexy came on TV. *Did your wife ever cheat on you?* No, his landlord would hardly react well to such a question.

Who else could he talk to? Not Ben. His son seemed to blame him for Michelle's departure, and he wasn't anxious to open that can of worms. Someone on his squad at work? He liked his colleagues except for his boss, and he might have raised the matter if he was sitting in a car with one of them, staking out a suspect's residence, but he couldn't see calling out of the blue. Richie Powker, maybe? No, he barely knew the guy—and Powker seemed happily married too.

Who would know something about this situation?

Inspiration struck. Jack finished his beer and turned to his landlord. "I gotta go. I'll check on Mrs. Kornfeld in the morning, okay?"

Mr. G nodded, then turned back to his vigil at the window.

CHAPTER TWENTY-TWO

Tonight, the downstairs door was open. As Jack tromped up the staircase, which smelled faintly of incense, and also of feet—a bunch of shoes were lined up on the upper landing—he glanced at his watch: five minutes to nine.

He entered the Dhammapada Buddhist Center and was about to call out, but something warned him not to, which was lucky, because as he came into the big main room he found about fifteen people sitting on cushions on the floor, facing away from him, in absolute silence. In front of them, sitting on a raised little platform, sat the woman he had come to see. Tenzin Pemo, the center's director, was a little middle-aged Caucasian nun with a rather mannish face. She wore wine-and-orange-colored robes, and sat cross-legged with her hands linked in front of her. She didn't see him because her eyes were closed.

Jack considered sneaking away, but nobody was paying the slightest attention to him. It was hard to tell much from behind about the people sitting facing the nun, but a few things were obvious: none of them were Asian, they all wore normal street clothes, and they were of varied ages. No one was saying anything; they were meditating. It looked awfully dull. They just sat there.

Jack stood in the rear, wondering how long it might go on. He glanced around; the room was pretty spare. Next to the nun sat a little table with some bright flowers in a vase; behind her were some elaborate pictures of the Buddha. Out in the street below, a car passed by thumping rap music; nobody stirred. Jack was restless, but he figured he'd wait. A few minutes later he noticed that the calm in the room seemed to be contagious; he was okay with standing there, and was even tempted to sit down.

Tenzin Pemo began to speak, though she didn't open her eyes. "We'll close with a brief *metta* meditation," she said in her British accent. "May all living beings be happy. May all living beings be free of suffering. May all live in security and peace. Let no one do harm. Let no one, out of anger or ill will, wish anyone harm."

The little nun went silent for another minute, then shifted on her cushion. "And now, slowly, we can open our eyes."

After a moment, the room began to rustle with movement, then people started getting up, stowing their cushions in a corner of the room, and chatting with each other. Jack didn't look out of place—they were a bunch of mostly middle-aged white people, like him—but he felt conspicuous nonetheless, and he waited in the back until he caught the nun's eye. She finished talking to one of her congregation, then strode over to say hello.

"Good evening, sister." He frowned: "Is that right? I never know what to call you."

"You can call me whatever you like, but just don't call me late for dinner."

The little nun looked very serious, and Jack blinked,

unsure of how to react, until he remembered her wry sense of humor. "It's been a while," he said. "How have you been?"

"Very good, detective. And yourself?" She gazed up at him with her clear blue eyes and he felt as if she was seeing right into him.

"Would, uh, would you have a few minutes to talk?"

"Is this official business?"

"Not really. No."

She smiled. "I'll just be a minute."

After the last of her little group left, she returned to Jack and gestured toward her office in the back. "Would you like to sit down?"

He shifted from foot to foot. "Would it be okay if we took a little drive instead?"

"Certainly. I'm still in your debt, you know."

He brushed away the suggestion; he hadn't done much for her young bottle thrower, but the prosecutor had agreed to a charge of manslaughter instead of premeditated murder.

Downstairs, out on the dark street where the death had taken place, they settled into Jack's car.

"How's the kid doing?" he asked. "You still visiting him?"

The nun pulled the seat belt across her robes and sighed. "Yes. It's incredible to me that the state can think that there might be any possible positive outcome from imprisoning a child in a place like that."

Jack didn't answer. His job was to arrest the guilty; what happened to them after that was more than he could worry about. He smiled. "Have you converted him yet?"

Tenzin Pemo smoothed her robes. "We don't proselytize, detective. Anyway, he seems quite content being a Baptist. I just go so that he has someone to talk to now and then. And I bring him comic books."

Jack smiled: it was pretty weird to think about, a white British Buddhist nun bringing a black Baptist kid from Flatbush comic books in Juvie. He turned on Flatbush Avenue and drove north, instinctively heading for the waterfront, where he and the nun had last discussed his personal affairs—in the midst of their official business, he had somehow ended up telling her about his girlfriend's abrupt departure.

They made small talk until they reached the neighborhood between the Brooklyn and Manhattan bridges, a quiet area of big old factory buildings that were being converted into condos and co-ops. Jack parked and they walked through the dark echoing streets until they came to a little park next to the East River. High above them, a subway train thundered over the Manhattan Bridge, which was strung with white beads of light. Across the river, the glowing office towers of Manhattan rose into the darkness.

"I hope this isn't too personal," Jack said. He cleared his throat.

The little nun strolled along with her hands clasped behind her back. "What's on your mind?"

"The first time we came down here, you told me a story about how you became a nun."

Tenzin Pemo nodded and waited for him to say more.

"You told me about how your husband was cheating and left you for that other woman."

"That's right," she said simply. This was one of the things he appreciated about her: she seemed to take everything in stride, without getting huffy or passing judgment.

He took off his sports jacket and slung it over his shoulder. It wasn't that the night was so warm, but he was starting to sweat. "I was wondering something. After that happened, and you became a nun and all . . . Were you able to forgive him?"

She gazed up at him calmly. They were walking along an asphalt path above a little riverside beach layered with pebbles, which shone faintly under the park's streetlamps.

"I don't mind discussing my marriage," she said. "Not at all. But I don't think you're asking me this out of some casual interest."

Jack chewed his bottom lip. "No, I guess not. Do you remember what I told you about my fiancée? I mean, the woman I asked to be my fiancée?"

The little nun nodded. "She left rather suddenly, as I recall."

Jack looked down at the sidewalk, embarrassed. "I've been thinking about calling her up again. And, uh, about this whole forgiveness deal."

Tenzin Pemo thought for a minute. "If you called her, what would you expect to get out of it?"

Jack pulled back. "*Get out of it?* What do you mean?"

"What would you hope to achieve? Would you just want to forgive her for her sake, or would you be hoping she might respond in a certain way?"

There it was again: that sense that she was able to look right into him. He sighed. "I dunno." Yet when he looked into his heart of hearts, he could see that in fact he did; he hoped Michelle might apologize, and couldn't help fantasizing that she might want to come back.

"Forgiveness is an interesting beast," said Tenzin Pemo. "It's not really something we can do in hopes of a certain result. What would happen if you forgave her but she refused to admit any wrongdoing? Or if she told you that she was still in love with that other man?"

Jack's face tightened.

"Would your forgiveness be a failure then?"

He didn't answer. The conversation wasn't going the way he'd hoped.

"Here's a thought: What if you forgave her but didn't tell her?"

Jack squinted. "What good would that do?"

Tenzin Pemo shrugged. "It might help *you*. We tend to think of forgiveness as something we do for someone else. But you're the one who's been carrying around the burden of what happened between the two of you. Wouldn't it feel good to set it down?"

"What about you?" Jack said. "Did you forgive your husband? I mean, that was pretty awful, what he did."

"I forgave him," she said simply. "He was just a human being, not thinking very carefully about what he was doing. And things ended up for the better, anyhow. We had a not very interesting marriage, and I had a not very interesting life, and now I do. I get to meet all sorts of intriguing people, including even the occasional homicide detective. I was a big fan of Agatha Christie, you know."

Jack smiled. He couldn't really see the nun as a big reader of mystery novels. But then, he hadn't seen her as a former wife either.

A couple of blond teens on skateboards came *click-clacking* into the park, swooping in and out of the circles of light cast by its streetlamps. Jack watched them round the bend of a hill. Finally, still looking away from the nun, he said in a small, tight voice, "I'm not really sure I want to forgive her."

"Do you think that forgiveness means that you would have to excuse what she did? That you'd be giving up your right to say that it was wrong? Because it doesn't, you know. It just means that you acknowledge that she's a human being, and you can forgive her for her mistakes. Maybe you could let go of a bit of your anger about what happened."

He thought about that. Because he *was* still angry. Sometimes, anyhow. When he wasn't just sad or mooning over what he and Michelle had had together.

"It's a funny thing, anger," the nun said. "Someone once said that it's like a poison we drink, believing it will cause someone else to suffer."

They had walked all the way around the little park and were almost back out on the street.

Jack stopped. "Well—do you think I should try calling her? I mean, do you think that would be a mistake?"

Tenzin Pemo shrugged. "What do you have to lose?"

More pain, if she blows me off again.

He pulled his car keys from his pocket. "I'll think about it."

CHAPTER TWENTY-THREE

He spent half the night rolling around thinking about it. He woke up without any better idea of what to do. Now he had a whole second day to keep chasing the thought, like a lab rat on a treadmill. He took a long shower and let the water drum down on his stubborn noggin. It occurred to him that he was probably just thinking about Michelle as a substitute for worrying about more pressing matters, but it seemed like the more he tried to let her go, the more the idea of making the call obsessed him.

By early afternoon, he was pacing his apartment like a mangy lion at the zoo. He went out and got into his car. Where to? He considered for a minute, then turned the key in the ignition.

HE CIRCLED NADIM HASNI'S block twice, searching for surveillance vehicles. There wasn't a single van on the block. The second time he went slow enough so that he could see into every parked car. Nothing. Unless Brent Charlson and his crew had found some empty apartment nearby, he couldn't see how they might be operating a stakeout.

He parked twenty yards up the block and then walked

over to the house. There was the sign on the lawn: DR. TEK-CHAND PARKASH, ADOLESCENT GYNECOLOGY. Yikes. Jack walked up onto the stoop. Only two doorbells: one for the doctor's office, and one that just said T.P. He walked back to the sidewalk, then looked up the driveway.

Another entrance. He pinched his lower lip, musing. Officially speaking, he would need a warrant to enter. If he didn't have the warrant, he might still be able to get inside, but any evidence he found could be compromised in court. But he assumed that Charlson and his crew had already gone over the place. So it wasn't evidence that he wanted, so much as a simple clue to Hasni's whereabouts. He pondered what to do; he wasn't a bureaucratic stickler, but once you started playing around with the law, you found yourself on a slippery slope.

And then, from fifteen yards away, something caught his eye. He glanced around to see if any neighbors might be watching, then hurried up the drive.

There, on the wall of the house just next to the door: a missing chunk of brick. And *there:* a furrow across several other bricks. He had seen a lot of crime scenes in his day, and many such traces. A couple of bullets had passed this way.

He looked sharply around, then walked back down the driveway and peered at the edges of the little lawn, hoping to find a shell casing or two. Nothing.

He went back to his car and sat there, musing. Someone had fired a gun in Nadim Hasni's driveway. At Hasni? Or had Hasni shot at someone else?

He felt a gray weight of suspicion rise in his chest. Maybe Brent Charlson and his men had decided to take justice into their own hands. Rather than letting the court system have a chance to free their terrorist, why not just take him out? Such things were not unheard of. Covert missions. Black ops. There were certainly people in the upper reaches of the government who would argue that in the War on Terror any means of eradicating terrorist threats were justified.

He was startled by a sudden rap on his window. He looked out at a stern, crew-cut young man with a soldier's stiff bearing. One of Charlson's guys; Jack recognized him from the recent hunt in Jackson Heights.

He rolled down his window.

"Mr. Leightner?" the man said. He held up a cell phone. "My boss would like a word."

BRENT CHARLSON'S VOICE. THE irate grandfather. "What the hell do you think you're doing?"

"I'm looking for our suspect."

"The house is under surveillance, Leightner. We've got it covered."

"We need to work together on—"

"*We* don't need to do anything, detective. *You* need to butt out of this case and let us handle it."

"Are you trying to say that the NYPD is not competent to handle our share of this case?" Make him spell it out, the arrogant bastard.

"I'm not trying to say anything: I let you do the talking. And so you have, with that ridiculous baked bean bullshit, and the way you screwed up a simple surveillance the other day in the very first minutes."

Jack's face burned; he looked out the windshield and was glad to see that Charlson's man was staring manfully off into the distance.

"Yeah," he responded. "Like *you guys* are doing such an excellent job of tracking this suspect. Aren't you forgetting something? *I'm* the one who found him."

"All right, kudos then. Good for you: you found him. Now for chrissakes, give it a rest! I don't pop up in the middle of your cases and try to run the show."

"You could've at least told me about the ballistics traces in the driveway."

"What? What the hell are you talking about now?"

"I was just there; I saw them. Is Hasni gone? Did you guys take him out?"

"Have you completely lost your mind? Look—I don't know what you're going on about, but I'll have my guys check it out. In the meantime, you need to just butt the hell out of my case."

"It's not just your case. We've got a murder that happened in the middle of south Brooklyn, and that makes it an NYPD matter."

"So what—you close one piddling little homicide but screw up an entire national terrorism investigation? Is that what you want? Now what do I need to do? Go to your bosses and tell them you're interfering? Make them yank your goddamn chain?"

Jack scowled. "Yeah, why don't you try that? In the meantime, I'm gonna keep doing my job. That's what I get paid for. And after I find Hasni and we talk to him about our homicide for a day or two, maybe I'll give you a call." He hung up, then reached the phone out the window and dropped it on the grass. He started his car and zoomed away, leaving Charlson's man staring after him.

Two blocks away, he came to a red light. He slammed his hand on the dashboard in frustration. *Little fed prick. Nobody talks to an NYPD detective like that. Nobody.*

By the time he reached home, he had managed to calm down. It was stupid and pointless: two grown men, both on the same team, squabbling over jurisdiction like dogs over a bone, while a team of terrorists were getting ready to move against their city. *Someone needs to be the grown-up here,* he thought. He was going to have to stop letting the fed get under his skin. Nadim Hasni might have a real weapon now. Someone was going to have to find him very soon. As to who actually made the collar, and who got the credit, that didn't matter one damn bit.

HE WAS PARKING THE car when his cell phone trilled. He glanced down at the caller ID: Larry Cosenza.

"Christ, what did you do?" the funeral-home owner said.

For a second Jack was discombobulated: How on earth could Larry know that he'd just tangled with a Homeland Security agent? Then he remembered the scene in Carroll Gardens two nights back.

"I guess word travels fast," he said.

"What, do you think Raucci told me directly? Is that what you think, that I'm in cahoots with these guys?"

"Whoa," Jack said. "I know how things work in the neighborhood. Somebody was looking out their window or sitting on their front porch. And they told someone, who told someone."

"That's right. So now the word is out that there's a rogue cop on the loose, going around threatening old men. Is that what you want?"

Jack leaned back in his seat and sighed. At this point, he just wanted to go upstairs and watch soap operas all afternoon with Mr. Gardner. Or maybe scrub his bathroom tiles. He could hardly remember two less relaxing days off.

"What did I tell you?" Larry continued. "I'd love nothing better than to be able to say that the days of these wiseguys are over around here, but you read the papers. Hell, you're a cop—you know what still goes on. Don't go pushing these guys around unless you've got a rock-solid case! I would hate to see something happen to you."

Jack was about to sputter, to ask if Cosenza was making some kind of veiled threat, but he had the wisdom to shut up. His old friend wasn't the problem. Larry just lived in the neighborhood. He made a living for his family. For a fee, he'd put anyone in the ground, be they wiseguy or cop.

Jack was tired. He just wanted to go inside and lie down. "You're right," he said. "I'll take it easy. And Larry?"

"What?"

"Thanks for the advice."

CHAPTER TWENTY-FOUR

The walrus swam forward until its great mustached face was just a few inches from Nadim's own. It hung there, in the bright blue depths, weightless in the water, buoyant as a huge ungainly angel, though its face was mournful, with the sadness of all trapped animals. They had a moment together, the human and the beast, staring into each other's eyes, and then the gray boulder swirled off toward the other side of its tank.

Nadim shivered, though it was actually rather warm in the aquarium's dark viewing room. He took out his wallet and squinted at its contents: only twenty-seven dollars left. He had been crazy, spending money on the admission fee; who knew how long he might have to make the rest last? He couldn't go back to his apartment, couldn't return to Jackson Heights. If he tried to pick up shifts from some new car service, the owner would want references, and then what would his old boss say? *Yes, Nadim was an excellent driver but unreliable. And then there's the little matter of the police coming around and asking why he killed a man . . .*

Despite its briny, rather rank smell, Nadim could normally find a certain measure of peace in the aquarium, staring into the tanks at the seals and manta rays gliding through their worlds. And pausing, of course, to watch the jellyfish, those pulsing, shimmering umbrellas of light. But now he shoved his trembling hands into his pockets. He remembered how he used to feel when he drank too many cups of coffee to make it through a long driving shift. This was like that, but triple—as if he couldn't stand being inside his own skin. He watched the walrus swimming round and round in a circle, in its underwater cage, where the scenery never varied, where nothing new and good could ever happen to it. He wondered if it wondered how its natural free life had shrunk down to this.

Blue shadows rippled across the walls. Nadim's thoughts turned, as they always did here, to his daughter. To Enny's face, round, bespectacled, beaming with pride as she helped him wash the town car on a Sunday afternoon. She would lecture him if they didn't get every square inch sparkling clean. He remembered one time when he had interrupted her instructions by spraying her with the hose. He had expected her to giggle, but she had broken into tears. His heart ached for her: she didn't seem to know how to play, to be a young girl, to have spontaneous fun. Maybe it was because of her utterly humorless, falsely pious mother and grandfather, or the way the other children teased her—maybe Nadim had unintentionally echoed their unkindness. He wished he could apologize, could hold her close.

He thought of his daughter and of the soapy car, and that got him considering the future of the plan. Maybe he couldn't contribute his fair share of the necessary money, but he could still offer his skill. They would need drivers, that was certain. He had not counted on such a direct role, not the way he'd laid it out in his mind, but that was when things were simpler, when he wasn't on the run. But maybe, if he could just stay out of trouble for a few weeks, things would calm down again, and he could rejoin the others and help make the plan happen. He could do his part.

A mother wandered into the dark room with two small children in tow, and again Nadim's thoughts returned to his daughter. To Enny's face shining in the light of her bedside lamp, as he read her favorite story. What was it that Heer had cried out when her beloved Ranjha was taken? "Oh, Lord, destroy this town and these cruel people so that justice may be done!"

And the evildoers paid for their wrongs as they writhed in the flames.

Perhaps his wife had been right after all.

Perhaps it truly was the will of Allah.

CHAPTER TWENTY-FIVE

Despite all of his worries and whirling thoughts—or perhaps because they had just plumb tired him out—Jack enjoyed a night of deep, restful sleep. Before heading out for work the next morning, he remembered that he had forgotten to deliver a message to his landlord.

The old man was upstairs having breakfast, made for him by his home aide, a pleasant Jamaican woman.

"You want some eggs?" Mr. G asked when Jack popped his head in.

"Thanks, but I'm off to work. How are you doing, Thea?"

The aide smiled. "Just fine, Mr. Jack. Thanks for asking."

Jack turned back to his landlord. "I just wanted to tell you that I checked on Mrs. Kornfeld yesterday. She's fine; the lights were off the other night because she was down in Cape May visiting her niece."

Mr. G stared up through his Coke-bottle-thick glasses. "That's good to know. We old folks gotta look out for each other." He dug a fork unsteadily into his plate of eggs.

"You sleep okay?" Jack asked.

Mr. G nodded. "Not too good. I guess we're birds of a feather, huh?"

Jack gave him a quizzical look. "What do you mean?"

Mr. G shrugged. "I was lookin' out the window. I seen you down there, workin' on your car so late."

Jack frowned. Had the old man been dreaming? Or maybe he hadn't been wearing his glasses?

"I was wonderin' why you couldn't fix it in the A.M.," Mr. G added. "I thought that was kinda funny, why you were out workin' under it in the middle a' the night."

Jack stared at the old man. His blood went cold.

THE BOMB SQUAD CREW cordoned off the block at both ends, evacuated all the neighbors, and then sent a little robot rolling under the undercarriage of Jack's car. After it sent them a closed-circuit video report, they were able to jack up the vehicle and take care of business.

When they were done, the sergeant in charge, a slim man with a professional mechanic's aura of quiet confidence, came over to speak to Jack, where he was standing on the other side of the unit's armored truck.

"I'll tell ya," the man said, shaking his head: "You are one lucky cop. The second the ignition went on, your ride would have been history."

Jack frowned; his ride would hardly have been the only thing that became history. "Did you get any prints or anything?"

The sergeant shook his head. "This was a pro job."

Jack lowered his voice. "Did you recognize the M.O.? I have reason to believe that this could be a Mob thing."

"We'll look into it. It's not often we get to see a Mob package in one piece."

Jack turned. Beyond the yellow tape, he saw Mr. Gardner and Thea, and Mrs. Kornfeld in a faded bathrobe, and a group of other neighbors standing around, looking anxiously on. Jack imagined the fierce whirlwind that had almost just incinerated him, and which would probably have blown out the windows of their quiet homes. Such a peaceful neighborhood, so sheltered.

Not anymore.

"I'M GONNA NEED SOME very direct answers here. No pussyfooting around."

Jack nodded somberly at Lieutenant Frank Cardulli. He wasn't thrilled to be on the hot seat but was immensely grateful that Sergeant Tanney was out working a fresh double murder in East New York. The thought of having to deal with his immediate supervisor today was more than he could bear.

"Did you make any direct threats against this Raucci character?"

Jack strained to recall his beer-soaked recent night in Carroll Gardens. "I don't think so." Cardulli's thick eyebrows rose. "No, sir, definitely not. I just mentioned that there's no statute of limitations on murder. That was just pointing out the law, right?"

The lieutenant didn't even begin to look relieved. "Were there any witnesses?"

Jack sighed. "Yeah. Another mobster. John Carpsio Junior."

"Wasn't that the guy who tipped you off about that case a couple years back?"

Jack nodded.

"And what was he doing there?"

Jack shrugged. "Just passing by. I guess he lives in the neighborhood."

Cardulli sat back, steepled his hands together, and turned toward the window of his office. He stared out for a couple of minutes, then turned back, shaking his head. "I really wish you had come to me when you first got this information about your brother. We're not vigilantes here. We don't operate on our own."

Jack nodded. "I know that. I was just hoping to get some information first, to see if I could find any grounds to turn this into a real investigation."

Cardulli snorted. "Well, I guess we've got grounds now." He ran a hand across his face. "I'll talk to the chief of detectives and to DCPI, see if we can't keep a lid on this for now."

Jack tried not to squirm in his chair. "Can we bring Raucci in?"

Cardulli shrugged. "We can extend the invitation. And then he's gonna go to his lawyer, and his lawyer is gonna advise him not to cooperate. And then, of course, he'll refuse to talk."

WEIRDLY, THAT WASN'T HOW it played out. Raucci did go to his lawyer, and his lawyer undoubtedly advised his client to stay mum—and there was no legal way to order him in, short of an arrest, which wasn't going to happen without any concrete evidence—but after an uncomfortably long wait out in the task force squad room, Cardulli called Jack back into the office.

"I just got off the phone with Raucci's attorney," he said. "You're not gonna believe this: for once in the history of the planet, we've got a mobster who's actually willing to talk without the pressure of an indictment. But he's got an unusual request."

CHAPTER TWENTY-SIX

"There he is," Jack said, squinting through the binoculars against the glare of the afternoon sun. He turned to Lieutenant Cardulli in the driver's seat.

"We've got you covered," his boss replied. "Go see what this bastard has to say."

Jack nodded, then stepped out of the car. Behind him, the Shore Parkway thrummed with early rush-hour traffic; ahead, a fishing pier stretched several hundred yards into New York Harbor. Out in the open like this, he felt seriously exposed, but there was one thing you could say about the NYPD: like any large bureaucracy, it had its share of inefficiencies and inanities, yet when it came to the attempted murder of a member of service, it didn't fool around. Behind Cardulli sat two other cars, both RMPs containing highly capable-looking uniforms. It seemed hugely unlikely that a mobster would issue such a public invitation to a cop, then try to bump him off, but there was no point in taking chances.

Jack pulled on his sports jacket; it was always cooler by the shore, with sea breezes sweeping in off the harbor. As he walked out onto the broad concrete pier, the traffic noise behind him faded away, leaving the sound of seagulls cawing overhead and the cable for a flagpole pinging against the hollow metal. As Jack walked forward, a man sitting on a bench stood up, a big bruiser with deep-set eyes and a face the color of liverwurst. One of Frank Raucci's crew, evidently. Jack glanced behind him: the NYPD vehicles seemed a long ways away. The muscle gave Jack a quick but thorough pat down, checking for a wire; not finding one, he nodded and sat back down. Next to him, a little sign read DO NOT CUT BAIT ON BENCHES OR PICNIC TABLES.

Jack walked on, out into the harbor, under the vast blue plain of sky, toward a lone figure standing out at the end of the pier. He understood Frank Raucci's stipulation that he wouldn't talk on record—the last thing any mobster wanted was to have proof lying around that he had cooperated with the NYPD—but he couldn't understand why the man had insisted that they meet at this isolated but still public spot.

Jack passed several fishermen; none of them looked suspicious. A wrinkled old Asian man reeling in his line, a couple of Hispanic homeboys joking around as they baited their hooks. The concrete was spattered with seagull shit. Ahead, a big green brass torch rose up in the middle of the concrete. As he drew closer, Jack was able to read the inscription around the monument's base: BROOKLYN REMEMBERS . . . FOR THOSE LOST ON SEPTEMBER 11, 2001. He glanced to the north, across the broad harbor. Who could ever have imagined that the Empire State Building would once again rule that distant skyline—that those brash usurpers, the twin towers, might simply disappear?

Out at the end of the pier, free as a bird in the bright sunshine of a glorious spring day, stood the man who had likely ordered the killing of Petey Leightner. And ordered a bomb placed under Jack's car. Jack felt a fury rising in him but tamped it down. He was a professional, and he wasn't about to give this thug the slightest excuse to skate from the murder charges he so richly deserved.

The gap-toothed old man rested both hands on a cane and squinted up into the sun as Jack approached. Jack thought of the mafiosi he had seen around as a kid, who prided themselves on their sharp hand-tailored suits and their impeccable Italian shoes; he compared them to this one-eyed old-timer, who wore ancient white loafers, Sansabelt poly slacks, and a beige jacket from the seventies, with epaulets and too many pockets.

"Thanks for comin'," Raucci said.

Jack, expecting a mobster's usual sarcasm, was taken aback. "You must be pretty disappointed to see me standing here in one piece."

"You got the wrong idea about me, Leightner."

Jack snorted. "I don't think so. I know exactly what kind of creep you are."

The old man frowned. Clearly, he wasn't used to being talked to with such disrespect—but he didn't rise to the bait. Instead, he turned, hooked his cane on the railing, grasped the metal with gnarled hands, and stared out at the vast silvery plain of the harbor. The breeze ruffled his wispy white hair.

Jack edged closer. "So what do you have to say that you didn't already try to say the other night?"

Raucci shook his head. "Other than you comin' around my house like that, I got no problem with you."

"I know about you. About your crew, about what happened down in Philly." Of course, Jack didn't know much about it at all, but it was always good to start an interrogation at least pretending that you held some cards.

Raucci waved a liver-spotted hand. "That's ancient history."

Jack gritted his teeth. If he heard that damned phrase

once more, he wasn't going to be responsible for his actions. "I know how you hired Darnel Teague. I know all about you."

The old man gave him a look over his shoulder. "You know *nothin'*."

Jack made a face. "What the hell are we doing here? You're just wasting—"

Raucci held up a hand. "Here's an idea, cop: How about you just shut up for a minute? You've got everything ass-backwards."

Jack was about to argue but held his tongue. He wouldn't have gotten far as a detective if he didn't know that you learned more from listening than from talking.

Raucci turned back to the harbor and pointed just to the left of the Statue of Liberty, toward the distant Jersey docks bristling with loading cranes. "Lemme tell ya about me and your old man."

"THE DAY WAS APRIL twenty-four, Nineteen forty-three. We were workin' the docks over there in Jersey City, loadin' a ship called the *El Estero*, a freighter out of Panama."

"You and my father?" Jack asked.

The old man frowned. "Don't innerupt. Yeah, me and your pop. We were fillin' the holds with bombs."

That, of course, reminded Jack of the purpose of his visit, but he decided to wait and see where the story was going.

"The ship was bound for what they called the European theater." Raucci shook his head in wonder. "God, you should'a seen it! We'd come up on deck for a break, and this whole god-damn harbor was crammed with warships, ready to go give them Nazis a serious ass-kickin'—if the U-boats didn't get 'em first."

He patted his shirt pocket, pulled out a pack of cigarettes, offered them to Jack, then lit one up. "See what I'm doin' right now? I would'a had my tail thrown right off the job for this. We were bein' watched over by these pimple-faced Coast Guard knuckleheads in what they called the Explosives Loading Detail. We couldn't smoke, couldn't wear boots with nails in 'em, got a lot of guff if we overloaded a cargo sling. Nobody griped, though: we had more than two and a half million pounds a' munitions sittin' under us, from small arms ammo to half-ton blockbusters. And the three ships next to us were filled up too, not to mention all the railroad cars next to the docks.

"In case the point was lost on any clown who still wanted to sneak a smoke, the Coasties made sure to tell us about what happened in Halifax back durin' W.W. One. You know about that? No? I'll tell ya: a munitions ship smacked into another ship in the harbor. That explosion killed more than fifteen hunnert people. It sent goddamned *railroad cars* flyin' in the air. And that was just Nova Scotia; it didn't take a rocket scientist to see how much worse things would'a got if somethin' like that happened here. If a nail in somebody's boot sparked some gasoline fumes, say, and one ship went up, and then the other ships went *kablooey* . . . Did I mention that one'a the biggest oil refineries in the U.S. was right next door? The shock wave would'a taken out Jersey City, and Bayonne and Hoboken, and it would'a smashed out across the harbor, rippin' through the convoy like the worst hurricane ever, and flattened the north end of Staten Island over there, and knocked down half'a downtown Manhattan. As if that wasn't bad enough, all'a them bombs would never have made it over to our boys in Europe, and then who knows what would'a happened with the whole goddamned war . . ."

Raucci paused to take a drag off his cigarette, then heaved up a rattly cough. "So anyhow . . . The convoy was leavin' the next morning, and ours was the last ship to be loaded, and we were fillin' up the last hold. The next day was Easter, and I'll tell you this: we were ready for a coupl'a days of rest. We went up on deck for an afternoon break, and I was lookin' across the harbor at Red Hook over there, and I could practically smell my mother's basil lamb roast.

"Our foreman called out, 'We're in the homestretch, fellas,' and down we went, back into the number two hold. That was a weird, grim scene down there, I'll tell ya. On a normal job you would'a had guys goofin' around, but a munitions ship is the most dangerous thing in the world; it doesn't make ya feel much like jokin'. The cargo was almost up to the ceilin'. See, first the carpenters lay down some wooden flooring, and then we'd load in the bombs, real careful, with chocks between 'em to keep 'em from rollin' around once they hit the high seas. Then another layer a' wood, another layer a' bombs . . . That was some hard goddamn work.

"What? Yer givin' me the fish eye here. You don't think I pulled my weight? Okay, so I admit I wouldn't'a been doin' any heavy liftin' if this was Red Hook and a normal ship. I would'a been takin' care'a business for the old guys. But ever since that goddamn Mussolini brought It'ly into the war on the Axis side, we Italians over here had to work double hard to prove we weren't collaborators or spies. So yeah, Frankie Raucci got his hands dirty, loadin' bombs that might be used against Milan or Rome. And I was glad to do it, 'cause the Nazis sure as hell didn't care where we Allies originally came from. Every month, another shipment of Red Hook boys came home in pine boxes."

Jack squinted. "Is, uh . . . is my father in this story somewhere?"

Raucci stubbed out his cigarette on the concrete of the

pier. "Young people these days, so impatient! Anyways, down in the holds it wasn't about where your people came from, it was about how hard you worked. And on that score, I have to hand it to your old man: he wasn't the friendliest bastard in the world, but he worked as hard as two men.

"So there we are, I'm down there wipin' the sweat out of my eyes, waitin' for the dinner break, and I hear somebody say, 'You smell somethin'?' And I sniff the air, and there's *smoke*. And I'm standin' near a bulkhead, and I reach out and touch it, and I snatch my hand back: it's *hot*.

"Our foreman turns to me. 'Raucci! Go out and see what the hell's goin' on.' So I walk between the bombs and go out in the passageway. There's definitely smoke out there, thick and horrible smellin'. Burnin' oil. And my heart goes up into my t'roat, and I run for the engine room. As I step over the hatchway, I see open flames flickerin' away in the back. I damn near shit my pants. An engineer is runnin' around sprayin' a fire extinguisher, but it don't do no good. Suddenly, oil on the bilge water beneath the gratings goes *whoosh*! To tell ya the truth, I'm panicking now, but I grab a fire extinguisher and try to get in there to help, but within five seconds I'm down on my knees, on account'a all the smoke. I try to get up again, but the heat and all is squeezin' the air out of my lungs. And I fall down, and I'm lyin' there on the hot metal floor, waitin' for the ship to blast into hellfire and damnation. Ya know what was my last thought? I'm prayin', *Please God, don't let the shock wave reach Red Hook and my mother.*

"And then, all of a sudden, I'm movin'. I feel an arm around my chest, and I'm bein' dragged through all the smoke, outta that blazin' engine room. And I feel myself lifted up onto somebody's shoulder, and I see a little spot'a daylight up top, and I'm thinkin,' *I died and an angel is carryin' me to heaven.* But it wasn't an angel; it was your old man, that little Russkie prick. And he dumps me on deck, and we're both gaspin' for air, and then he turns around and he goes back in.

"He brought the engineer and another guy up, before he passed out himself."

Jack stared across the harbor, dazed, struggling to reconcile this heroic Maxim Leightner with his own memories of the man. "And then what happened?"

"We couldn't put the damned fire out. We had some pumps on the dock, but there wasn't much water comin' out of 'em—it was like tryin' to piss on the flames. We would'a just scuttled the ship right there, but we couldn't get to the seacocks because they were in the engine room."

Jack pictured the roaring flames, the men frantically darting through the greasy smoke.

"Lemme tell ya," Raucci said. "If the *El Estero* had gone up, it would'a been the biggest disaster in all of human history."

"Why didn't it?"

The old mobster snorted. "There was no love lost between us stevedores and them young Coasties, but I gotta give 'em this: they put up a hell of a fight that day. Most of 'em were already a couple'a miles away, in their barracks, shining their shoes and getting ready to go on leave. When the alarm sounded, their commander asked for volunteers. Them kids knew damned well what could happen, but they jumped on a truck and came haulin' ass back to the pier. And a couple'a New York fireboats came runnin' up too."

Raucci's voice caught, and Jack was astonished to see that his good eye was wet. "I had never seen nothin' like that, and the only other time I seen it since was on Nine-eleven. When everybody else was runnin' away, those boys ran right toward the trouble."

"Did they put the fire out then?"

Raucci shook his head. "They ordered all us longshoremen off the ship, and then the fireboats tried to pump as much water as they could up onto the fire. And still the goddamn flames were winnin'. Finally, the Coastie commander decided that the only thing they could do was to tow the ship away from the pier and out into the harbor, and fill 'er with water and sink her before she could go up. A couple'a tugs showed up, and those brave goddamned bastards towed the *El Estero* out and to the south." He pointed across the water. "As they went, there were still firemen on her deck, with their goddamn boots sizzlin' on the metal. And there was guys down in the holds, feeling for hot spots so they could tell the others where to put their hoses. Can you imagine that? Before they got on the ship, they threw their wallets to the guys on shore, 'cause they figured they probably weren't comin' back."

Raucci pointed again. "The tugs hauled the ship out by Robbins Reef there, and for two hours the fireboats kept pumpin' her with water. She started listin' to starboard. Then, around nine o'clock, we was watchin' from the docks, we saw a flash of light and heard a couple'a explosions, but the old gal finally went down. It took a while for all the fires to go out, even underwater; we could see this ghosty glow comin' up from the bottom of the harbor, out there in the night." He nodded, remembering. "We didn't lose a single goddamn man."

Jack blinked, awestruck. "I can't believe this isn't in every history book."

Raucci shrugged. "Ya gotta remember: this was the middle of the war. There were a couple'a little stories in the papers, but I guess the Navy didn't want word getting around that the whole port was so vulner'ble. After the war, there was a parade in Bayonne for the firemen and the Coasties, but those guys never really got their due. Goddamned heroes, every one of 'em."

The old man hocked up some phlegm, then spit it out onto the water. "Anyhow, the point here is simple: I didn't have no beef with your old man."

Jack frowned, thinking about his father, such a riddle. Loving one moment, brutal the next. A drunk, a criminal, a hero. A proud man, and stubborn, ashamed of what he had turned to in order to feed his family. "He was helping you, down in Philly, and then he stopped. Weren't you pissed off?"

Raucci shrugged. "We were makin' some good money down there, I'll give you that. Some of the other guys were sore, but I let it go. That Russian bastard saved my life, and I never forgot it. I tole the guys: you mess with Leightner, you mess with me."

Jack grimaced. "So they hired some punks to mess with me and my brother instead."

Raucci's face closed up. "I don't know nothin' about it."

"Come on," Jack said. "You knew they were angry at my father. And they got his son killed."

Raucci made a pained face. "I wanted to do somethin' about what happened to your brother, but we, ah, we had an organization, see? The bosses were not too happy about what went down, but they decided to let it go. You weren't even Italian."

Jack clenched his fists. "Who were the guys that were riled up at my father?"

Frank Raucci ran a hand over his mouth. "Listen, Leightner: we got a little thing you might've heard of. A code. Now, I just explained to you why I would never hurt your old man. And why I had nothin' to do with that crap under your car. But that's as far as I'm gonna go."

The old man waved at his muscle man, who came lumbering up like a big rhinoceros. And as much as Jack pestered him as he shuffled off down the pier, Raucci refused to say another word. When they reached the shore, the mobster climbed into his car and his soldier started the engine.

Jack stood at the edge of the pier, watching them zoom off down the parkway, marveling about his father and wondering how he was ever going to discover who had really been behind Petey's killing. And who had the sheer gall to plant a bomb beneath an NYPD detective's car.

CHAPTER TWENTY-SEVEN

"I need to go in alone," Jack said to Lieutenant Cardulli. "He won't talk if he sees all of us on his doorstep." They were parked up the street from Orlando Farro's Bay Ridge home; Jack liked to keep a low profile, but with this security retinue he moved with all the subtlety of a Mack truck.

"You sure you'll be okay in there?"

Jack snorted. "The guy's in a wheelchair and he's about two hundred years old. I'll be fine."

The Caribbean nurse answered the door. *Shirley.* She let him right in, which he found surprising: Why hadn't she asked her boss first if it was okay?

"He's not having a very good day," she said, and he noticed that she looked considerably less placid than the last time he had seen her. In fact, her statement clearly translated to *We're* not having a good day. "He's like an old TV set," she said over her shoulder as she led him down a hallway inside the musty house. "He goes in and out."

Jack soon discovered what she meant. He found Orlando Farro sitting in a gloomy living room, watching the local news on TV. The old man was bald as a cue ball; when he saw that he had a visitor, he gave a quick panicked glance at his hair-piece, which bristled on top of the old TV like a sleeping musk-rat. *Ah, vanity.* Then he turned to Jack with a befuddled air. "Who the hell are you?"

"We talked the other day, Mr. Farro. Up in the park."

The room smelled sour, like a bathroom in a dive bar. In a corner, several gold statues glinted in the flickering light of the television: boxers, raising their dukes. A bunch of old photos decorated the walls above them: Jack recognized a young Farro, in his Golden Gloves days.

The old man looked anxious. He raised a remote control with effort, as if it weighed a lot, and turned down the TV's volume. "You're with Social Services?"

"No," Jack said, as gently as he could. "I'm Max Leightner's son."

Farro tilted his head back for a better look. "Oh yeah, the cop. Did ya miss me?" His sharp laugh turned into a coughing jag.

Jack waited it out. "Would you mind if I sit down?"

The old mobster waved a hand. *Suit yourself.*

Jack sat on the edge of a plastic-covered sofa; it squeaked as he adjusted his weight. "I talked to Frank Raucci," he said.

"Oh yeah? How is the old bastard?"

"It's been a while since you've seen him?"

Farro snorted. "I'm retired, kid. And I don't hang around the Hook no more."

"I was thinking about my father. Maybe it wasn't any of your crew who were mad at him. Maybe he did something to piss the Russians off, down there in Philly?"

Farro shook his head. "Your old man and the Russkies got along swell. Thick as thieves—ain't that the expression?"

"Did he get along with everybody on your crew? I mean, Frank Raucci's crew?"

"I thought you talked to Frank. Didn't he tell you?"

Jack kept his expression flat, as if he were about to make a poker bluff. "He told me that my father had a big problem with someone on your crew that went to Philly." This was in direct contradiction to the speculation he had just raised about the Russians, but the old man didn't blink or make any move to disagree. "Raucci said it wasn't him," Jack continued. "He said that either you were lying or that you were just a useless old geezer, gone senile." He didn't feel good about baiting the old man, but then, he couldn't forget that this was a Mob thug sitting in front of him.

Farro's face clouded up. "I never said that, that it was him that had the beef with Max."

"That's what you told me. Don't you remember? Maybe Frank was right about you and your memory."

The old man's face contorted. "Why the hell would I say that, if Sally Ducks was—"

"Who?"

The old man had enough sense left to realize how he'd been played; he glared at Jack. "Fuck off, cop!"

"We can discuss this down at the station house, if you want."

The old mobster didn't fall for the idle threat. "Shirley!" he shouted. "Bring me the phone." He glared at Jack. "You wanna talk, talk to my lawyer. But first, get the hell outta my house."

Jack almost felt sorry for him, the old Golden Gloves champ, taken in by such a weak fake right.

* * *

"WELL?" LIEUTENANT CARDULLI SAID as Jack got back in the car. "Did you find anything out?"

Jack shook his head. "Nope. Total waste of time."

He was acutely aware of the weight of his service revolver in its shoulder holster, pressing against the side of his chest.

CHAPTER TWENTY-EIGHT

Jack peered past the curtains at the front of his apartment and looked to the left, at the squad car sitting a ways down the block, under a streetlamp. A couple of patrol guys from the local precinct house. Jack had tried to veto the idea, but his bosses insisted. He had asked the uniforms to at least not park right in front of the house, so as not to alarm Mr. G.

He stared down at his desk, at the unregistered snubnose .38 Special he had just pulled out of the back of his closet, and then he picked up his phone. One of the patrol guys out front had given him his cell number; Jack dialed it now. "You guys wanna come in and use the can? I'm about to go to sleep."

He met them at the front door. The evening outside was humid and breezy, with intimations of a coming storm; the air was cool against his bare ankles, under his bathrobe.

The uniforms both took the opportunity to relieve themselves before their long boring night ahead. Jack yawned as they trooped out again. "G'night, fellas."

He turned off the light, then peered out the window. As soon as the young cops settled back into their car, he went into his bedroom and got dressed again, finishing with a windbreaker to hide his shoulder holster.

Leaving the lights off, he slipped out the back door into his landlord's little garden plot. He edged around the tiny lawn in the middle, thankful there was no moon out, and clambered over the back chain-link fence into his neighbor's yard. As he crossed the garden there, he tripped over something—a hoe left lying in the soil—and ended up on his hands and knees. Smothering a curse, he got up, found the latch for the side gate, and came out into a driveway on the other side of the block.

He was thinking about a case he'd worked a short while back, a suspected double rapist and strangler who had managed to avoid a similar police stakeout, sneaking out of his own home late one night. Jack thought of what that man had done, and what Jack was about to do, and it wasn't just the soil on his hands that left him feeling dirty.

HE GOT OUT OF the taxi two blocks away from his destination. In case anyone might think to check the logbook, later.

Sally Ducks. The name sounded silly, as Mob nicknames often did, but there was nothing amusing about the origin of this one: legend had it that back in the late sixties one Salvatore Buonfiglia had executed three members of a rival family in the kitchen of a Rockaway Beach summer bungalow, lining them up on their knees. "I'm putting all my ducks in a row," he had supposedly announced before cold-bloodedly pumping a round from a .44 Magnum into each man's forehead, denying them even the tiny mercy of a shot from behind.

So Jack had learned earlier, when he made a long-distance call to Lou Caprioni, an old friend from the Brooklyn D.A.'s office who had long since retired to San Diego. Caprioni was in his seventies now, but he had made a distinguished career out of prosecuting Mob cases.

"Why are you asking about this guy?" he'd said.

"The name just came up in a case I'm working on and I wondered who he was. Any chance there was more than one guy by that moniker?"

"Only one I ever heard of." Caprioni snorted. "Another guy would've needed some pretty big balls to use the same one."

"How come I've never heard of him?"

"Sally was never one of the flashy ones. After that thing in Rockaway where he made his bones, he did his best to fly under the radar. I always wished I could make a case against him, but he was shrewd. He had other people do his dirty work."

Like Darnel Teague, Jack thought. From what Caprioni said it sounded like Buonfiglia had not really started his rise to prominence until at least the late '60s—by which point Jack was gone from Red Hook, in the Army.

"Eventually," the prosecutor continued, "he became one of the real bosses in South Brooklyn, only you never saw his name in the papers."

"He still around?"

"Last I heard, but you know I retired back in 'ninety-three. He lived in Carroll Gardens. Sackett Street, if I remember right."

"So how's the weather where you are?" Jack said, doing his best to not sound too interested in the old mobster.

"It's already hot as hell. It's not really my kinda place, but my wife loves it. At least I can golf whenever I want."

They chatted for a minute more, then Jack said good-bye.

And now here he was, walking along Sackett Street in the dark. A stormy breeze was riffling the trees, turning the leaves upside down. The air felt heavy, expectant. It was late, with only an occasional dog walker out on the street. Jack's nerves were jangling. *Revenge*, somebody smart had once said, *is a dish best served cold.* He had had forty years to consider this wisdom.

He took out his cell phone and redialed the uniforms sitting outside his house. "Sorry to bother you guys. I thought I heard something in the back of the house. Would you mind taking a look, then calling me back?"

Setting up an alibi.

He stopped on the sidewalk, staring toward the north side of the street. Buonfiglia's house was certainly a shrewd choice. Most of the homes around here were three-story row houses, with tiny front yards wide open to the street, but the mobster's home could only be approached down a very narrow alley between two small apartment buildings; the house was actually in the center of the block. A twelve-foot-tall iron gate with a spiked top barred entrance to the alley from the sidewalk. The place looked damned near impregnable. There was an intercom, but how could he bluff his way in at this late hour?

As the storm came on, the treetops began bucking like the heads of wild horses. A few heavy raindrops spattered down, one of them hitting Jack's shoulder with considerable force. And then the sky broke open with a brilliant flash of light, followed closely by a stunning thunderclap. Jack stared through the gate, wondering what to do. The rain began to sheet down. He stood there for a minute, with his windbreaker tented over his head, getting soaked, until he saw a little Honda Civic come up the street and double-park in front of a brick building several doors down. A DOMINO'S PIZZA sign shone on the roof. A man jumped out, holding a pizza box, dashed up to the front door, and pressed the intercom. Jack came up behind him just as the customer buzzed the front door. He pulled out his car keys, as if they were keys to the building; the delivery guy held the door for him. "Thanks," Jack mumbled as he trotted around the man and up a staircase on the right side of the foyer, as if he knew exactly where he was going.

He tread softly as he came up the last flight of stairs, careful not to alert the top-floor residents. On the last landing, he gazed up at an iron ladder that led to a roof hatch. He could see a padlock on the hasp but couldn't tell, in the dim light, if it was locked. He started up the ladder but was only three rungs up when his cell phone vibrated. Impeccable timing. He held onto the ladder with one hand and pulled the phone out with the other.

"Detective? This is Tommy Searle." One of the cops outside his house. "We didn't see anything back there."

"Sorry to bother ya," Jack said softly, praying that the residents of the building's top floor were sound asleep. "G'night." He shoved the phone back into his pocket, then continued climbing. Thankfully, he discovered that—though the shackle was indeed looped through the hasp—the padlock was not fully closed.

The storm was still coming down heavy as he climbed up onto the tar roof. He wasn't happy to be drenched again, but he was grateful for the covering din of the raindrops on the rooftops and the crowns of the trees. He moved toward Salvatore Buonfiglia's house, stepping over thigh-high walls that divided the connected roofs of the intervening buildings. And then he came to a gap between two buildings, maybe four or five feet. He grimaced, then stepped up onto a parapet, took a deep breath, and jumped across the divide. He landed on the other roof and fell to his knees; the tar was sticky on his hands as he pushed off it and stood, sputtering rain away from his mouth.

He stepped carefully to the back of the roof and peered

down into a little courtyard surrounding Buonfiglia's house. He found a corroded fire escape and clambered down. As he eased past dark windows, he hoped the din of the storm would mask his progress, especially when he slipped on the wet metal passing the second floor and had to make a wild grab for the railing.

Finally, he dropped from the bottom of the fire escape. The balls of his feet stung as they hit the little concrete apron at the back of the building, which gave out onto a small yard in front of Buonfiglia's place. A couple of security floodlights above the eaves sparkled through the rain and reminded Jack of a legendary time in Red Hook. The Gallo brothers, engaged in a fierce war with their rival Carmine "the Snake" Persico, took to the mattresses one summer in their house on President Street, holing up with a bunch of fellow gang members and a cache of guns. They set up floodlights that glared around their house all night long, but their sleepless neighbors didn't dare complain.

Jack wondered how many *soldieri* the old mobster might have with him tonight. He drew the .38 snubbie from his holster and held it down by his leg as he darted across the yard, peered around the side of the house, and pressed up against a wall. He looked up and saw several windows on the different floors, all dark. Reconnoitering, he passed along the back of the house and came around the other side, which seemed to be some sort of enclosed sunporch. The big picture window there flickered with blue light. Jack risked a look up into the window and took in the scene: an old man, lying on a daybed, watching a massive old TV. He ducked back out of sight, then moved a few feet away from the base of the wall so he could see up the side of the house. All dark. He knelt there for a moment, considering his next move. Holding up the .38, he came back around to the rear of the house. A little porch, a back door. He glanced at his watch: almost midnight.

He took a couple of deep breaths to steady himself, then stepped up onto the porch and tried the doorknob. Miraculously, it turned freely in his hand. His heart was beating so hard that he actually worried about cardiac arrest; he couldn't help remembering how—years ago, on a dark summer night—he had been working a case and taken a bullet in his chest.

He bit his lower lip, extended the revolver in front of him, and carefully pushed the door open. He stepped inside, then took a moment for his eyes to adjust. He was in a dark kitchen that smelled of garlic and another, incongruous note: some kind of Mexican spice?

Outside, the rain ran in rippling sheets down the kitchen windows. Shoes squishing, Jack tiptoed across the linoleum floor, through a doorway, into a dark hall. He moved through another doorway on the right: a faint light glimmered on the surface of a dining table. He stepped carefully around it, past a china cabinet, and into a front parlor, looking intently for dark shapes sitting in the big armchairs there. Nobody. Water dripped into his eyes from his wet hair; he brushed it aside and came around into a little front hall, where he saw a staircase leading up into the dark. He ignored it for the moment, stepping through another dark doorway and another dark room: more furniture, unoccupied. Ahead, blue light flickered. Having circumnavigated the entire first floor, Jack edged up to the sunporch and dared another peek in. He was behind the old man and the daybed; the TV displayed a shopping channel, a bleached blonde holding up a glittering necklace. Jack noticed a big oxygen tank standing like an old World War II bomb next to the bed.

"That you, Maria?" the old man called out, lifting a bony hand; thin plastic tubes trailed from his wrist.

Jack moved across the room in two quick strides and jabbed the stubby barrel of the .38 against the man's head. "How many people in the house?"

The man sputtered. "Who the hell are you?"

Jack stepped around and saw that a thin plastic tube came up out of the oxygen tank and branched into the man's nostrils. He compared the face to the one photo he'd managed to find on the Internet, a black-and-white snapshot of Buonfiglia in a snazzy suit, standing behind mobster Paul Castellano. Jack recognized his thin lips, sad eyes, and bony nose, the profile of a corrupt Roman general. Now, with his sunken cheeks and emaciated body, he was just a shell of the man he'd been.

"Answer me or you're dead: how many people?"

The old man wheezed. "Just one. My night nurse, Maria. She's up on the third floor."

Jack bent down so the man could get a good look at his determined face. "If you're lying and you call for help, I'm gonna shoot you in the teeth."

The old man didn't look frightened, which made Jack nervous. "I'm a cop," he added. "I've got men outside, so don't try anything stupid."

"How the hell d'you get in here? Cops ain't allowed to go bustin' in somebody's house. You got a warrant?"

Jack held up the .38. "Right here."

Buonfiglia looked unimpressed. "You came alone. You know, you could'a just rang the doorbell, like a normal person."

Jack picked up the remote control and turned down the TV's volume a bit. (The noise gave him some cover, but it was too grating to talk about what he needed to talk about while listening to a plug for crappy jewelry.) He pulled a photo out of his pants pocket, a snapshot damp from the rain: a picture of himself and Petey, two kids making goofy faces for the camera as they stood, bony-chested, on the concrete deck of the Red Hook pool. "*Now* do you know who I am?"

The old man nodded. "Max Leightner's boy. I been expecting you."

"I *bet* you have," Jack replied, thinking of the bomb under his car.

The old man sighed. "I been waiting for you to show up on my doorstep for thirty years now. Ever since I heard you became a cop."

Jack pressed the .38 against the man's temple again. "Why is that? Why would I come looking for you?"

Buonfiglia's hands moved over the blanket that half-covered his wasted body.

Jack yanked it down. No gun.

The old man turned and stared out the window at the rain. "What happened, that was tragic. I'll tell ya, I feel real bad about it. That jig, he was just supposed to throw a scare into you, you and your brother."

Jack's eyebrows went up at this direct talk. (For once, no bullshit about *ancient history*.) "You don't deny that you hired him?"

Buonfiglia shrugged. "I got nothin' to hide. Sure, I hired him, but what happened wasn't my fault."

"Not your fault, huh? My father stopped translating for you—for that you robbed my brother of his whole life? Just because you were so worried about making a buck?"

The old man scowled. "You judge, but you don't know nothin' about it. It wasn't about the money—it wasn't so tough to find someone else who spoke Russian. It was the disrespect. When he quit, your old man said some stuff that he should never have got away with. We came to get him one night, and he was all drunk and he called us *thugs*, after we helped that bastard earn! That arrogant pinko—all of a sudden he's too good for us?"

Jack thought about his father's volatile moods, his stubborn pride. The man had paid his tributes to the union and the Mob but didn't hide his reluctance. And so—until he had taken on this translator role—the only jobs he had ever been given were donkey work. Max Leightner had done things his own way as much as possible, given the circumstances. For that, Jack had to offer some grudging respect—evidently, he had inherited the old man's stubborn nature.

Buonfiglia made a face as if he had just bitten into something foul. "I couldn't see why Frank didn't just take care of him right on the spot. Aside from the fact that lettin' somethin' like that go is bad for business, why the hell would he let anyone disrespect him like that?" The old man shook his head. "I could never understand it, that weakness. So I took care of it myself."

"You took care of it? You coward—you hired some kid to do your dirty work!"

Buonfiglia just wrinkled his nose. "*Please*. I wasn't gonna get my clothes dirty messin' with a coupl'a son-of-a-bitchin' punks."

Jack felt his rage come surging back. He pulled the trigger until the hammer cocked, but at the last second he reconsidered. Shooting the man would just call up a big homicide investigation. Fate had provided a much simpler solution.

He reached out his foot and stepped on the oxygen tube.

Within a few seconds, the old man was gasping; he tried to push the branched tubes deeper into his nostrils. In the morning, no one would know that it was not his illness that had carried the mobster away.

"You're a lying sack of shit," Jack said. "You handed that kid Teague a knife."

The old man wheezed, desperate now. "I never . . . tole him to use it. It was just . . . to scare you. I only—"

Jack stared down at the old man. He deserved to die. He had killed Petey, and then—decades later—he had tried to finish off Maxim Leightner's only surviving son. He had killed three men out in Rockaway Beach, and God only knew how many others. Now it was his turn.

Buonfiglia writhed on the bed, tortured for lack of air. He struggled to speak but couldn't. After a deeply satisfying minute, Jack took his foot off the oxygen tube—he would let the old man plead for his life, as some of his victims had pleaded, and then he would seal off the tube for good.

Buonfiglia lay back against his pillows for a moment, savoring the returned flow of oxygen into his wasted body. "You know," he finally rasped, "I talked to that jig Darnel again, after. He said one'a you kids called him a nigger. I guess that made him go a little crazy."

Jack turned away, determined not to let the old man see how this shot had struck home. Through the picture window, he watched the heavy rain fall through the floodlights' glare. More than anything, he had hoped this little talk might ease his mind about that long-ago encounter. But he couldn't deny the old man's point: if he had not acted so rashly, his brother might still be alive. Or maybe Darnel Teague would have stabbed him anyhow. There was no way of knowing. He realized that killing this withered shell of a man would never free him from the weight of that question.

He felt something go out of him. He turned back to the old man. "How come you don't have anybody guarding this place?"

"What for? I'm an old fuck. My enemies are all dead." Buonfiglia glanced at Jack's gun. "Most of 'em, anyhow."

"After last night, I'd have thought you'd want plenty of protection."

The old man gave him a quizzical look. "What happened last night?"

Jack felt his anger coming to a boil again. "Spare me the bullshit. You knew I was asking around. And you knew I was getting close."

Buonfiglia blinked. "I heard you was askin'. So what?"

"So you thought you'd take me out before I caught up with you."

The old man made a face. "I got no idea what you're talkin' about."

"Who'd you get to put the bomb under my car?"

Buonfiglia shook his head. "You lost me."

"Don't insult my intelligence."

Buonfiglia wheezed for a moment, inhaling his oxygen. "Why," he finally said, "would I bother to do any such thing? You cops are always goin' on about motives this, motives that. Okay, so what's mine?"

"You know damn well that there's no statute of limitations on murder."

Buonfiglia snorted. "Oh cop, cop, cop. First of all, I didn't murder your brother. I just wanted to scare him. Second, even if I had done the deed with my own hands, I got no reason to whack you now."

"Of course you do. Nobody wants to end up in prison."

Buonfiglia scoffed. He waved his frail hand, a gesture that took in the oxygen tank, the tubes in his wrist, the rows of pill bottles on a bedside table. "I got emphysema. I'm nothin' but a broken-down valise. The doctors give me three months, tops. You think the D.A.'s gonna take the time and money to prosecute somebody who's gonna kick before the case even gets to trial?"

Despite Jack's childhood memories of the immense power of the Mafia, despite Larry Cosenza's recent warnings, he was starting to sense that this man was like the Wizard of Oz— the biggest part of the mobster's power came from his fear-some reputation, even though he was now just this shriveled little bastard hidden away on a porch.

Buonfiglia scratched his caved-in chest. "Yeah, I knew you were comin.' But I had no reason to try and stop ya. I hope you don't take this the wrong way—I know what happened to your brother means a lot to you, an' I'm sorry about that. But I'm about to move into a hole in the ground, so your per-sonal troubles right now? They mean about as much to me as a mosquito on an elephant's ass. You wanna find out who tried to clip you? You're gonna have to look someplace else. Some-body's got a hard-on for ya, but it ain't me."

Jack stood there in the dark for a couple of minutes, lis-tening to the rain drumming on the roof of the porch.

The old man stared out the window too, musing. *"Our thing?* We're dinosaurs, cop. Pikers. Used to be, our guys could each pull one, maybe two hundred large a year—we thought that was a big deal. The other day, my grandson came to me, said he wanted to go into the family business. I tole him, Don't be an idiot, kid, this is the year of Our Lord two thousand an' five. You don't need a gun; get an MBA. Go work on Wall Street. You can rake in two, three mil' a year, and the feds won't give a flyin' fuck."

Jack looked around: the oxygen tank, the pills, the falling rain. He was tired, awful tired, and he had been robbed of the resolution he'd been hoping for. But at least he hadn't ruined his life's work by killing a man in cold blood—that was one thing he wouldn't have to live with. He didn't have to do anything now; time would soon have its way with Sally Ducks. He stood up and reholstered his .38.

The old man raised up a little from his pillow and smiled a feeble death's head smile. "Hey, cop? Thanks for stoppin' by."

CHAPTER TWENTY-NINE

The big dog lunged out of the doorway, snarling, jaws snapping, and Nadim scrambled backward, tripped, and dropped into a bottomless well. He was falling, falling, but then, somehow, he was rising, up toward a bright light . . .

He cocked a grainy eyelid open, saw slatted light coming down from overhead, and heard a scrabbling sound and a dog's sharp bark. He spat some sand from his mouth and rolled over; his whole body ached from the damp, cold night. Over his head, the underside of the Coney Island boardwalk stretched off into the distance, its diagonal wooden boards throwing herringbone patterns of brightness across the dim sand below. On the beach side, the sand rose to the level of the boardwalk; on the other side, a chain-link fence obscured by tall weeds created another wall, leaving this strange subterranean alley.

Overhead, a dog was scratching at the wood, as if digging down, trying to get to him. It couldn't reach him, but it might alert a passing policeman.

Heart thumping, Nadim got to his knees, grabbed the knapsack he had bought at a discount store the other day, and scuttled like a crab past decades of detritus: Styrofoam take-out containers, rotting remnants of beach towels, mounds of plastic water bottles, scraggly deflated condoms. Condoms! The thought of making love down here in this mess boggled his mind.

He edged around a little blue camping tent some homeless person had set up and put some distance between himself and the dog.

After fifty yards of scrambling through this gloomy underworld, he lay back with his head on his knapsack and caught his breath. He listened for the dog, but it had ceased its frantic yapping. Nadim pressed his forearm over his eyes, thinking about another barking dog, the one that had gotten him into this whole terrible mess in the first place.

IT WAS A SMALL German shepherd with sores on its flanks, and it lived its life, such as it was, in a tiny backyard next door to Nadim's former apartment in Kensington. It was left outside, day and night, through all but the very coldest times of the year. The dog went on frequent barking jags, upsetting neighbors all around, but the owner was a sour old Caucasian man who refused to listen to their complaints.

The dog affected the members of Nadim's household in different ways. His sanctimonious father-in-law didn't like it because he said it was *haraam*, unclean. Nadim resented the animal because he often worked nights and it roused him from his morning sleep. Enny, his dear little Enny, felt sorry for the imprisoned, unloved beast.

Nadim, still an alien in the eyes of the law, did his best to avoid any confrontation with white Americans, but finally his exhaustion and his daughter's pleas for compassion wore him down. He bought a box of chocolates as a gift, dressed up, and went next door to politely request that the neighbor bring the dog inside. The meeting did not go well.

"I put up with the smells of Injun food comin' out of your place, don't I?" snapped the man. "I put up with your goddamn kid laughin' over there all day, and I don't complain!"

Indian food. Laughing. Nadim did his best to keep his temper, and finally—gritting his teeth to avoid an outright altercation—he walked away. But he was branded as a trouble-maker. He would never call the police, but when other neighbors did, the old man shouted profanities across the fence at him. And then, just a few days after the terrible events of September 11, when the winds still carried a bitter burning smell across the East River to Brooklyn, a minor tragedy occurred in Kensington. The old man went out one morning and found his mistreated pet lying dead in his yard. Perhaps it had died of illness or of an overstressed heart. But nothing, nothing at all, would disabuse the old man of the notion that it had been poisoned by Nadim.

One week later, in the middle of a night off work, he woke to a pounding on his front door. Bleary-eyed, he opened it to find three men who identified themselves as federal agents. Without explanation, they grabbed his arms, pulled them behind his back, and handcuffed him.

Ghizala came to the bedroom door, saw what was happening, and shouted at the men, but one of them blocked her from coming out.

"Abbu?" Enny, in her pink pajamas, stood frightened at the entrance to the living room, where she slept on the couch. "What is happening?"

"It's okay," Nadim told her. "Go back to sleep."

He heard his daughter crying as he was dragged out of his home, still in his nightclothes.

"Why you are taking me?" Nadim said, his command of English failing him in his fear. "I do nothing!"

The men did not respond; they just hustled him out to the curb and shoved him into a waiting van.

"I have made application for green card!" he said. "My wife, American!"

The men wouldn't answer.

"I have papers!" Nadim cried. "Please! In my house!"

The van roared off into the night.

Nadim sat shaken, arms aching behind his back. His captors, stone-faced, avoided looking at him; after a couple of minutes of listening to his baffled pleas, one of them pulled some duct tape from the glove department, ripped off a section, and slapped it over Nadim's mouth.

He stared out the windshield at the red taillights glowing on the highway in front of the van. He was a professional driver and he could see where they were headed. Along the Prospect Expressway. Onto the Gowanus Expressway. Toward Sunset Park.

We will straighten this out, he told himself, struggling to calm his panicked heart. Ghizala will bring the immigration papers; these men will have to let me go.

BUT THEN THE HELL began.

Outside a big windowless building on a desolate stretch of Brooklyn's Second Avenue, a metal garage door slid up and the van screeched down a ramp. Nadim was yanked out into a bright basement parking lot where three new men were waiting. They wore brown pants and khaki shirts with epaulets, and they placed ankle restraints on him and marched him toward a doorway. One of the men stomped on the short chain that separated his ankle cuffs, and Nadim fell to the oily concrete.

"Get up, towelhead!"

Nadim stared up in incomprehension. The man, a big brute with a hard face and a strangely small mouth, grabbed his handcuffs and yanked him to his feet. Then, while the other two looked on, the man grabbed the back of Nadim's head and mashed his face against a concrete pillar.

"I have done nothing!" Nadim mumbled. "Please! My wife, American citizen!"

The big man grabbed the middle finger of Nadim's right hand and began to bend it back so far he feared it would snap.

"Please!" Nadim screamed.

"I had a cousin in the towers," the big man said. "I hope you're ready to feel some pain."

"I have done nothing!"

"Come on," one of the other men said to Nadim's tormentor. "We gotta get him up to the S.H.U."

AN ELEVATOR, BARRED GATES, stark hallways, a bare room containing only a doctor's examining chair and a weight scale.

The big man unlocked Nadim's cuffs and leg shackles.

"Clothes off!"

Nadim just stared at him.

The man slapped him in the face. "I said *clothes off.*"

Slowly, not believing what was happening to him, Nadim began to comply.

The big man walked over to the door and shouted down the corridor. "Hey, Laney, come check this out!"

Just as Nadim got fully naked, a plump female guard appeared in the doorway, looked at him, and laughed.

Burning with shame, Nadim covered his groin with his hands.

"No, *please*," he said. "I am Muslim."

The big man imitated him in a high-pitched voice. "'No! Please!'" He scowled. "I *know* you're a Muslim, you fuckin' terrorist! Hands at your sides. *Now.*"

UNDER THE CONEY ISLAND boardwalk, Nadim tried to rouse himself to go find a better hiding place, but he was just too tired. His head dropped back against the cool sand, and those dark months, from the end of 2001 into the spring of 2002, played out again inside his mind.

The first three days had passed in a terrible blur.

He had been thrust into a tiny cell that reminded him of the bathroom on the airplane that had brought him here from Pakistan: windowless, bare, smelly, with a sink and toilet of polished steel. He spent his first few minutes inside, still cuffed and shackled, calling out through a slot in the door.

"Please! I drive for car service! No terrorist!"

The door swung open, knocking him backward onto the floor. The big man with the small mouth entered. He stepped on Nadim's head and kept his foot there. "You need to understand something: you will speak only when spoken to. Or else I am gonna flush your towelhead down that fucking toilet, do you understand me?"

The foot left his head and Nadim looked up: the man's face was contorted with rage.

"Please!" Nadim cried. "I have done nothing." It was a misunderstanding. A simple case of mistaken identity. There was no reason for him to be here, swallowed up inside this windowless building, trapped inside this nightmare.

The big man knelt down and stared into Nadim's face. "We know all about you, Hajji. One of your neighbors turned you in."

Nadim thought of the dead dog and of its owner's hate-filled threats of revenge, and suddenly he understood why he was here.

Now he was *truly* frightened.

THE HOURS PASSED, BUT he didn't know how many—he hadn't seen a clock since he emerged from the van. He desperately wanted a cigarette, but he had no way to get one. After a while he needed to evacuate his bowels, but he noticed that there was no toilet paper in his cell, and so he refrained. He turned and lay down on his little metal bed; it was a bunk, but the upper berth was empty, with the mattress folded in half.

He expected that someone would show up at any minute and he would be able to explain about the neighbor and the dog, but no one came. Eventually, he curled up and tried to sleep, but the lights in the cell were so bright that they bored through his closed eyelids. He lay there and thought of his daughter, of her frightened face, and he prayed that his captors would let him call and tell her he was all right.

He would demand that they let him phone a lawyer. This was America, not some foreign dictatorship. He had rights. He had seen this on TV; everyone in America had rights.

But no one came.

Later, as he was finally dozing off, someone rapped on the door of his cell. Nadim jolted upright, but no one entered.

Again, he started to fall asleep; again someone banged on the door.

Hours passed.

Then days.

BRIGHT LIGHT, ALWAYS, AROUND the clock, glaring in his face when he tried to sleep. Sometimes, when he was mercifully able to drift off, he would be awakened by a barrage of recorded sound, booming along the corridor, angry songs with screaming voices and thundering electric guitars. Even without the aural assault, he wouldn't have been able to find deep sleep, racked as he was by the desire to smoke and tormented by thoughts of his worried daughter. No one would tell him what he was charged with, and he wasn't allowed to call a lawyer.

He was kept in his little cell twenty-three hours a day; the other hour he was escorted up to a little recreation area on the roof, where he could pace back and forth, alone. But there were other prisoners in the area they called the S.H.U.; sometimes Nadim could hear their voices. Egyptians. Turks. Yemenis. There was a fellow Pakistani from Sahiwal across the corridor; Nadim was not allowed to talk with anyone, but sometimes in the middle of the white nights they managed to exchange a few words. The other prisoner's name was Mahmood and he ran a little magazine stand on McDonald Avenue. As far as the man could tell, he had been detained because the FBI found it suspicious that he had been sending "too much money" to his brother in Karachi.

A sentry came by and ordered the men to be silent. The guards were angry—and confused, and scared. The sky had cracked open, that bright September morning, and their whole world had been shaken.

The one they called *Barshak*, though, and some of his colleagues, seemed neither confused nor scared. They appeared, in fact, almost glad about what had happened recently: it gave them a perfect excuse to vent some deep inner rage. Nadim remembered a vicious bully in his neighborhood when he was a child, and how Nadim had become expert at finding hiding places in order to avoid this boy. But now there was nowhere to hide.

He was surrounded by people, day in, day out, who wished him harm. He couldn't flee and he couldn't fight. (On his second day in here, he had resisted Barshak's rough handling. The result: another guard had been called in and they had taken turns grabbing one of Nadim's manacled arms and swinging him into a wall. This treatment achieved its purpose: he had been forced to realize the futility of fighting back.)

And so the pressure built, with no way to release it, like a tornado trapped inside his brain.

CHAPTER THIRTY

Even after a largely sleepless night, Jack was wired and eager for action. He would have gone to the park for a run, but he couldn't do that now, not with his security detail. Two new guys had replaced Tommy Searle and his partner; they were supposed to keep a protective eye on him until he went on duty. What were they gonna do, jog along beside him, like Secret Service guys forced to trot after the president out on his Texas ranch?

He was scheduled to work a four-to-midnight; he stayed home to think awhile. He was searching for the answers to several questions, but he had a feeling that he wasn't looking in the right place. He read the paper to try to give his restless mind a break. Then he paced around some more.

In the early afternoon, he called the lieutenant from the bomb squad. And then—though he hated to do it—he phoned Brent Charlson.

"Listen," he said, "I don't know if you heard about this, but somebody planted a bomb under my car the other night."

"My God!" the fed replied. "Do you know who did it?"

"I don't. I thought it was probably due to a Mafia thing I've been investigating, but I just talked to someone at the bomb squad and he said that the explosive they used was Semtech. I remembered that you said that you had intercepted chatter involving that word. And here I've been poking around, looking for this Hasni guy. So I'm wondering: Do you think maybe word could have gone out to his terrorist cell? That they might have targeted me?"

He was fully prepared for more scorn or at least impatience from the fed, but Charlson's reasonable, grandfatherly tone was back.

"I wouldn't be at all surprised, detective. We have reason to believe that the cell is directly connected to Al Qaeda. At the very least, they're part of a splinter group. Now, these people are highly motivated, highly organized, and they've already proven that they're willing to kill innocent bystanders. I don't see why murdering an NYPD detective would trouble them one bit. I'll be glad to look into this, to see if we've picked up any more chatter. I trust you're taking security measures?"

"Yeah. I've got a couple of uniforms watching my house."

"Good, good. Listen, I promise we're gonna roll up the whole gang very soon. In the meantime, I'd suggest you just go about your normal routine and stay away from these guys. Okay?"

"Thanks," Jack said. For once, he thought he might have even detected real comradeship in the fed's voice. If there was one bond that could unite all law enforcement officers, it was the risk of getting killed on the job. From all Jack's years as a cop, he knew that nothing could make you put aside petty differences faster than hearing a 10–13, a radio call about an officer in trouble.

On the other hand, someone had tried to kill him. And he had absolutely no intention of resting until he tracked that person down.

———

* * *

JACK'S SECURITY TEAM TRAILED him until he was safely inside the Seven-oh precinct house. The uniforms stopped in to the detectives' lounge for sodas, then bid him farewell until later that night.

He told his partner about the car bomb and about his suspicions.

"Christ!" Richie said. "Do you think I oughtta see about getting some security too?"

It sounded like a rather self-centered reaction, but Jack didn't hold it against his partner—the man had a wife and two kids to worry about. "I don't know," he replied. "But we should definitely watch each other's backs." He glanced around the Seven-oh squad room. A busy day, evidently: most of the other detectives were out. He noticed a bumper sticker on the side of the next desk: it read DON'T MAKE ME RELEASE THE FLYING MONKEYS!

He dug a pinkie in his ear. "I'm thinking about who we've interviewed: someone who might have sent a warning to Hasni or his buddies. The ex-wife? Not a likely prospect, I gotta admit—there was no love lost there. But if she heard from Hasni, she might have mentioned our visit."

Richie frowned. "And there was the car-service boss and the other drivers. And the shopkeepers along Coney Island Ave. I know your business card doesn't give your home address, but it would hardly take a genius to track you down."

Jack nodded. There was no shortage of candidates. He glanced at his partner's worried face and decided that it wasn't going to help anything if they were *both* freaked out. "Look at the bright side. It was probably just some Mob guy who thought I was getting too close. If that's the deal, you've got nothing to worry about."

Richie looked pained. "Hey, I'm not just thinking about *me* here!"

Jack nodded. "I know you're not. And I appreciate it." He sat up straight. "Let's focus on finding Hasni. I've been thinking about why he and Brasciak both disappeared from the tax rolls back in Two thousand one. Now why does someone go off the radar like that?" He ticked off possibilities on his fingers. "They've just gone out of town for a while. They got fired or laid off. They're out sick. Or they're in jail or upstate."

"I already checked with the Bureau of Prisons. They don't have a record of either guy being inside at that time."

Jack nodded. "I know. But it seems unlikely that two strangers left town at the same times, or got sick simultaneously, or something. And it seems like a very big coincidence that this happened right after Nine-eleven. So what else could have happened?"

Richie's face scrunched in thought.

"I was looking at the paper this morning," Jack continued. "I was reading about these 'black sites' where guys who got suspected of terrorism were flown to other countries. Or were held in secret detention."

Richie frowned. "I could see that with Hasni. But what about Brasciak?"

"I don't know." Jack frowned. "I think maybe I should give a call to a friend of mine in the FBI."

Richie's bushy eyebrows went up. "You've got a friend who's a Feeb?"

"Yeah, we worked together on a case out at Governors Island a while back." Agent Ray Hillhouse was a big African-American man. Like Jack—a Jew in the NYPD—he was a minority in his outfit; with that in common, maybe that's why they'd been able to skip the usual chest thumping and nonco-operation.

Richie frowned. "What about what Charlson said, how we aren't supposed to discuss this with anyone?"

If his landlord had not uttered a lucky warning, Jack knew that he would be in a thousand bloody pieces right now. "To hell with Charlson." He glanced around: there were a couple of other detectives in the room. "I'm gonna go outside and call my guy. I'll be right back."

The day was unsettled, warm and humid, a harbinger of the coming miserable New York summer. Jack watched a gaggle of young uniforms walk down the street—they all looked like they were about sixteen.

"How the hell have you been?" It was good to hear Ray Hillhouse's booming voice through the little phone. Jack pictured the man: heavyset, bespectacled, sporting an FBI windbreaker.

"Aside from the fact that I almost just got blown to bits, not too bad." He explained about the recent incident, then said, "Listen, have you got a couple of minutes? I need to talk to you about something, in complete and total confidence." Keeping his voice low and an eye on his surroundings, Jack laid out the whole saga of Nadim Hasni and Robert Brasciak. "So can you poke around?" he concluded. "But keep it really quiet?"

"No problem," his friend replied. "You know I don't specialize in counterterrorism, but I'll be glad to ask around. And lucky for you, I'm having a slow day around here—you're saving me from some really boring background checks. Why didn't you call before?"

Jack frowned. "Charlson made a huge deal about how I

wasn't supposed to discuss this with anyone, so as not to compromise his investigation. But if my life is at stake . . ."

"Say no more—I'm on it. I'll call you back as soon as I find anything."

When Jack returned to the squad room, Richie was eager to move. "So where do you wanna go with this today?"

Jack scratched his cheek. "I don't know. I've been thinking about Hasni's apartment. I'd love to get a look inside, but the feds are probably keeping an eye on it." He mused for a moment, then grinned. "But maybe we can take care of that."

"I ALMOST FEEL GUILTY about this," he said, half an hour later.

"You feel bad?" Richie said. "After the way that fed has treated us?"

"I said *almost.*"

Jack had called Charlson and told him that they had spotted Nadim Hasni again—back on Seventy-fourth Street in Jackson Heights. Then the two NYPD detectives sat in their car at the end of Hasni's block. A few seconds later a couple of crew-cut bozos hustled out of a house just down the way from the Pakistani's apartment, jumped into a car, and went racing off.

Three minutes later Jack and Richie were standing outside their suspect's front door. Luckily for the detectives, the landlord upstairs—the gynecologist—had handed over the keys without demanding to see a warrant. He had been more concerned about how he was going to collect the next month's rent.

Richie got his first look at the bullet traces. He scratched the back of his neck. "This doesn't play right to me. If Hasni was out here and he saw one of Charlson's guys breaking in, why would he shoot? You'd think he'd just hightail it the hell out of here."

Jack nodded. "I wondered the same thing. Maybe it was the feds who did the shooting. Maybe they like playing vigilante." He turned the key and gave his partner a wry look. "I'm glad we didn't have to break in. My lock-picking skills are rusty."

In they went.

Another lonely, low-ceilinged basement pad. This one was quite different from Brasciak's: it was dedicated, not to a bachelor's crude pleasures, but to the memory of one rather homely but sweet-looking little girl. Jack examined the snapshots on the fridge: the dead daughter blowing out birthday candles, standing in front of a seal pool at an aquarium, riding a bicycle, eating an ice cream cone on the Coney Island boardwalk. There were other photos of her scattered throughout the apartment, and drawings and paintings *by* her—she seemed to have a special fondness for fish and other aquatic creatures.

As Jack rummaged around, he couldn't help feeling a bit of sympathy for Nadim Hasni. Yeah, the guy had committed murder, but he also seemed to be a pretty loving dad. There were different ways of dealing with the death of a child: some people went through a period of mourning, then put the snapshots and photo albums away. Hasni, though, clearly wanted to keep his daughter's memory alive. The apartment was practically a shrine. And it had a strange frozen-in-time feel. Judging by the deli's surveillance video, Nadim Hasni had not set out to commit a homicide the other morning. He had gone out to work or to shop, leaving things in his place in a typical bachelor's jumble: dishes in the sink, open newspapers on the kitchen table, clothes scattered by the foot of the bed . . .

Jack's cell phone vibrated and he almost jumped. He looked down at the little blue screen: Brent Charlson.

The fed sounded breathless. "Where did you say you saw him?"

"I told you," Jack replied. "The corner of Seventy-fourth Street and Thirty-seventh Ave."

"Where are you guys now?"

"Driving around, looking for him."

The fed didn't say anything; he just growled and hung up.

Moving quickly, the detectives tromped from room to room, scanning opened mail, looking for a calendar or address book, checking for any possible indication of where their suspect might have gone to ground. It was highly doubtful that he would come back here, or return to Jackson Heights, or go back to his place of employment. And where was he sleeping?

No calendar or address book—maybe Charlson had taken them. The detectives kept on pawing through Hasni's belongings; they wouldn't have much time until the feds came back. It was not what they might have expected from the home of a fanatical terrorist. There wasn't a single picture of Osama bin Laden or anyone else who looked like a radical leader. There wasn't any religious imagery at all. Jack tried to remember: Was that a Muslim thing, that you weren't supposed to have pictures of God or his prophet? Either way, he realized that he hadn't even seen a copy of the Koran.

He sorted through a heap of stuff on a dresser in the bedroom: some coins (all U.S.), an electric bill, a couple of movie stubs (for Pakistani or Indian-sounding flicks), a receipt for a visit to the New York Aquarium. He held the latter up and gave it a good look. He had noticed several snapshots of the girl at an aquarium, and now he recognized it as the city's own. He went back into the kitchen. On the little dining table, buried under some bills and junk mail, he dug down for something he had glanced at ten minutes before. *There:* another aquarium receipt. Both were date stamped.

Jack called to his partner. Richie came in and he showed him what he'd found. "That's weird," Richie said. "Check this out." Jack followed his partner into the living room, where the detective rustled through a pile of papers on a side table and came up with another receipt.

Jack scanned it, then looked at his partner. "All these dates are fairly recent. You can tell from the snapshots that he liked going there with his daughter. But why would he still be going there now that she's gone? I mean, I could see him visiting once, maybe with a friend's family or something. But three recent trips?"

Richie squinted. "Maybe it's where he meets the other terrorists. Maybe they're planning something out there."

Jack considered that possibility. Coney Island was already open for the season. Each weekend, thousands of New Yorkers thronged the boardwalk and the beach. The place was known as America's Playground.

If the terrorists wanted to slaughter a lot of people and make a big political statement, it was hard to imagine a more effective setting.

He glanced at his watch: the aquarium was probably closed for the day. But tomorrow he and his partner would definitely pay it a visit.

CHAPTER THIRTY-ONE

Nadim sat in his hiding place under the boardwalk, finishing some french fries he had snuck out to purchase at Nathan's Famous hot dog stand. The hot greasy starch filled his stomach, which was good, because he was rapidly running out of cash.

He considered emerging back up into the sunlight. His cell phone battery had died and he needed to go up and find a pay phone, to assure Malik and Aarif and others that he was still totally committed to the plan—after all their preparation together, it would be terrible if they moved on it and left him out. But he thought of the police roaming around, and the men who had shot at him, and the effort it took to run, and he sank back onto the damp, smelly sand, drifting toward the hope of sleep. As usual, before he reached that oblivion, memories of his imprisonment arose, a salty, suffocating tide.

AFTER WHAT MIGHT HAVE been ten days in detention, or perhaps two weeks, during what might have been midday or the middle of the night, the door of his cell swung open and someone came in. He had pretended to be asleep on his bunk, but the intruder was not fooled; he dragged Nadim onto the floor, pushed him facedown, yanked his arms back, cuffed his wrists, and put on the ankle restraints. It was the guard they called Barshak.

The man stepped out and returned with a chair, which he placed in the middle of the cell. "Guess what, Hajji? You got a new visitor today. Now, you're gonna behave, or I'm gonna come back in here and play some football with your testicles."

Nadim lay limp. He had been forced to surrender all power over his own life, and this loss had taken its toll: he was lethargic and sad all the time, and he was fast losing weight inside his prison garb.

Now Barshak lifted him up by the armpits and slung him back onto his bunk. After the guard swaggered out, a new man entered the little cell, sat down, and placed something on the floor.

Nadim blinked, trying to see him clearly under the bright lights, but his vision had been suffering under the constant barrage of white. The stranger was surrounded by a golden nimbus.

As if reading his mind, the man began to speak. "Hello, Nadim. You may be wondering who I am. I'm going to tell you: I'm an angel." The man's voice had a flatness, a calm, even tone that might—under other circumstances—have felt reassuring. But Nadim just shivered; he had woken a number of times trembling with fever, and he wondered if he might be dreaming now.

"I'm an interesting angel," the man continued, "because you get to choose what kind I am. I can be your angel of mercy. I know you have a wife and a little daughter. I bet you'd like to see them again, and soon. I have the power to make that happen. *You* have the power to make it happen. You work with me, and I'll get you out of here.

"But if you don't do your part"—as the man shifted closer, the scraping of his chair on the floor set Nadim's teeth on edge—"I'll be the angel of your worst nightmare. Do you understand?" The man wore eyeglasses; they glinted in the harsh light.

Nadim nodded dully. He was starting to get a headache. Since the second day here, he had been interrogated several times a week, in the room with the doctor's examining table, with several men present, and a video camera. He hoped this might be the man who finally believed his story.

"There is a man in the other house," he said. "An old man. He does not like me. He has a dog. One time—"

The bright light overhead disappeared from the visitor's eyeglasses as he bent down to pick up the thing he had put on the floor: a manila folder. He lifted a paper out, held it up, and shook his head. "I've heard this silly story, Nadim. You keep this up and you're going to stay inside here for the rest of your life. Am I making myself clear?"

"I know America," Nadim ventured. "There is laws. I would like a lawyer."

The visitor stared at him. "Times changed a few weeks ago. You people changed them, with what you did downtown. So I'm making the laws now, and if you don't tell me who you're working with, I'm going to bury you alive. You'll never see your wife and daughter again."

Nadim was on the verge of tears. "I tell the truth. I tell you everything."

The man contemplated him for a moment. "I'm going to give you one last chance. Who are the other men in your group?"

Nadim remained silent.

The man bent down and carefully placed the paper back

in his file. He stood up, brushed his hands together, then moved to the door. He called out, then came back and sat again.

Barshak and one of his fellow bullies crowded into the cell. The other man carried a big black canvas bag. They shut the door behind them. Barshak knelt down and unzipped the bag.

"Now, Nadim," his angel said, "we're going to make you wish you had never been born."

CHAPTER THIRTY-TWO

The next day Jack called Ray Hillhouse again; he wanted to add a few more details about the Hasni case, and he gave the FBI man the rest of the lowdown as he drove south toward the shore with Richie Powker.

He hung up as he parked on Surf Avenue. Next to the aquarium, the old Cyclone roller-coaster was sending its cars full of screaming thrill seekers ripping and roaring around its bends. The wooden structure rattled as if at any second it might fly apart. Jack remembered riding it once with Michelle; she had talked him into it, his only time since he was a kid. He recalled that first hill, which made you think, *Gee, this isn't so high*—and then all of a sudden you were in absolute freefall, terrified for your life.

He glanced up and down the avenue, which even this early in the season was packed with couples and families strolling along, eating cotton candy and hot dogs, enjoying the weather. One block over ran the boardwalk, and then the Coney Island beach. What would the ocean breezes do to radiation particles, he found himself wondering, chilled by the thought: Sweep them out to sea or blow them back along the crowded shore?

"Two adults?" said the girl behind the ticket window, a nervous-looking kid with straggly blond hair and braces on her teeth. "That'll be, um, twenty-six dollars?"

Jack flashed his badge. "We're with the NYPD."

The girl looked confused. "Okay, but . . . um . . . I think I'm still supposed to charge you?"

Richie stepped forward impatiently. "Listen, sugar, we're on a case."

"It's my first week," the girl said. "I think I better call my supervisor?"

Jack imagined a terrorist meeting wrapping up inside while he and his partner haggled over admission fees. Maybe the plotters were arranging the next attempt on his own life. He pulled out his wallet and paid the money.

They strode past the first big coral-filled tank, where a trio of silvery fish as flat as dinner plates slid past the glass, and then a big manta ray winged by. The aquarium was not heavy on security. Around the bend, looking for someone to talk to, the detectives came upon a squat little Hispanic woman in a janitor's blue dress. Jack pulled out his photo of Nadim Hasni. "Excuse me, ma'am, do you recognize this person?"

"No speak English," the woman said. Jack tried again in his limited Spanish, but the woman just shrugged.

They found a bona fide security guard, a lanky, bored-looking young guy, at the doorway to the aquarium's central courtyard.

The guard shrugged too. "We get hundreds of people through here every day. I only look at 'em if they're bangin' on the glass or throwing popcorn at the penguins."

The detectives stepped out into the courtyard and strode past the outdoor seal tank, the walrus tank, and the penguin tank, stopping to question every employee they saw. No results,

until they went down a flight of stairs into the dark below-
surface viewing rooms, where they found a stocky young
security guard who looked like she took her job very seriously.
"Lemme see that," she said, snatching up the photo and holding it up under a dim spotlight. She tapped the picture. "Yup.
I think I seen this one. He comes in now and then."

Jack could feel his heartbeat picking up.

"Was he with some other guys?" Richie said. "Pakistanis,
maybe? Or Arabs?"

The guard shook her head. "Nope. He's a loner."

"When was the last time you saw him?"

"You know what? I think he was in earlier."

"Today?"

She nodded.

Jack and Richie exchanged an excited glance.

"Where did you see him?"

"Across the way, in the jellyfish rooms. He'll spend an
hour in there, easy. That's why I recognized him."

"Could he be in there now?"

The woman shrugged. "It's possible. I been workin' in
here for the last hour."

Instinctively, Jack patted his service revolver. "Where
is it?"

The woman pointed. "Go up, then straight across the
courtyard."

Jack started to move, but then he turned back. "Was he
carrying anything? A bag or a knapsack?" He had no idea how
big a dirty bomb might be, but he knew that the Madrid subway bombers had carried their explosives in knapsacks.

The guard frowned, trying to remember. "I think he had
a knapsack." She nodded. "Yeah, definitely."

Grim-faced, Jack and Richie took the stairs up two at a

time and jogged across the outdoor space, trying not to draw attention as they wove through knots of visitors who were eating snacks from the café or showing their kids the dolphin and shark toys they'd just purchased in the gift shop.

They burst into the building across the way, pulling out their pistols as they tried to adjust their eyes to the darkness. But there was no one remotely Pakistani or Arab-looking anywhere in the galleries. Nor in the rest of the aquarium, as the detectives rushed on, through the shark exhibits and back past the fish and the rays.

And then they were out on the Coney boardwalk, scratching their heads and wondering where their suspect might have gone.

NADIM HASNI WAS JUST two hundred yards away, beneath the boardwalk's gray planks.

He sat in that dim alley and listened to people above screaming as they rode the rides, and he began to tremble. He lay back, dug his fingertips into the cool, densely packed sand, and tried in vain to push another screaming out of his head.

After the first few weeks in detention, totally cut off from the outside world, Nadim had finally been told that he would be allowed one phone call to an attorney per week. They gave him a list of lawyers, and he waited eagerly for his chance. At last, they led him to a phone and he called the first number on the list. It was out of service. He tried to explain, but they just led him back to his cell. "Next week, Hajji, next week."

A week later, he found a lawyer who agreed to come for a visit, but the man seemed cowed by Nadim's captors. He listened to Nadim's complaints about his mistreatment, then asked for proof. And what could Nadim say? He had no lasting bruises—none on the outside, at any rate. The lawyer promised to see what he could do, but three months later Nadim was still inside, and beginning to lose all hope. He had been able to receive several visits from Ghizala, but they hardly helped: all the damned woman could talk about was the bills they owed and the rent they needed to pay; she spoke with a tone of annoyance that suggested that he had gotten himself incarcerated just to inconvenience her. It got to a point where he could only tolerate her visits because she brought him news of Enny. (They had agreed that it would be wrong to bring the child here, for her to see her father like this; instead, they made up a story about him going back to Pakistan to help an ailing relative.)

And then, one time, he had heard things from the cell across the way. It had probably been late at night. (He could never be sure, with the endless summer inside the S.H.U. But there were few staff around, so Nadim figured the others had gone home for the day.) All he knew was that this was the time when Barshak and the older man, the interrogator who held the guard's leash, liked to do their dirty work. He could hear their voices through the slot in his door: the interrogator's eerily calm tone; Barshak's ugly snarl. And he could hear Mahmood, his fellow Pakistani, begging and pleading as they did bad things to him.

Mahmood's voice rose to a scream; Nadim huddled on his bunk and covered his ears, but it didn't help. He got up, walked to the door, and listened, praying for his neighbor in this godforsaken place. Mahmood screamed again, then fell silent. After a pause, Nadim heard the interrogator's voice, more urgent than usual. Then Barshak's voice, less confident. Nadim pressed his ear against the cool metal of his door. A muffled sound of something heavy being moved around . . .

A couple of minutes later, Nadim heard the door across the way opening and closing. He was just turning to go back to his bunk when he heard a key turning in his own lock. He scrambled back into bed, but it was too late. The interrogator came in, followed by Barshak, who closed the door and then stood in front of it, arms limp at his sides, looking oddly subdued and pale.

The interrogator seemed shaken too. He looked at Nadim, then stepped forward with a strange tentativeness. He did something he had never done before; he sat on the edge of Nadim's bunk, which made Nadim want to press himself into the far corner.

"You want to get out of here, right, Nadim? You want to see your wife and daughter?"

Nadim nodded, scared and unsure of where this might be going.

"I want you to know that I believe you. I believe your story about the dog and the neighbor, and I believe you're innocent. I'm going to help you get out of here. It may take a while, but I can make it happen."

The interrogator leaned into the shadow under the bunk. "Listen to me very carefully, Nadim. I'm going to help you, but you have to help me. There's been an accident. Now, very soon some people are going to come in here and ask you if you've heard anything. And you're going to tell them that you didn't, that you were sound asleep. This is very important. Do you understand?"

Nadim just stared.

The interrogator scowled. "We don't have much time. Let me put this more clearly. You can say you were sleeping, and I'll get you out of here. Or you can talk about what you might have heard tonight, in which case you will *never* see the light of day again. We'll transfer you to someplace much worse than this, and your wife and daughter will never hear from you again. Tell me that you understand."

Nadim finally spoke, the words coming rusty out of his mouth. "I . . . I understand. I am sleeping. I hear nothing."

The interrogator reached out to pat his shoulder and Nadim had to struggle not to flinch. "Good boy. Now just hold tight. It might take me a little while, but I promise I'll get you out of here." He stood up and then he and Barshak walked out.

Half an hour later, out in the hallway, a guard making his nightly rounds shouted for assistance.

An hour later, two official, very worried-looking strangers came to Nadim's cell to question him. It seemed that a prisoner across the way had somehow managed to hang himself.

"I hear nothing," Nadim told them. "I am sleeping."

For a while after, he lived in two states of mind: guilt, over the way he had helped cover up the killing, but also hope, that he would soon see his Enny again.

And then, shortly thereafter, he saw his wife in the visiting room, and her face immediately told him that something was terribly wrong. After he managed to get the story out of her, the story of how his daughter had died, he shouted for the guards to take her away.

He couldn't remember the next week at all. He fell into a dark pit. He couldn't eat. He couldn't sleep. They strapped him to his bunk because he kept banging his own head into the wall.

He emerged out of that dark place into a strange, light-headed mind of disbelief. He was still here. He could feel the breath in his lungs, the metal of his bed, cool to his touch. So Enny must still be out there, still alive. She would go to college and he would take her picture as she threw her graduation cap up in the air, just like he'd seen in American movies. There was a whole future that they were supposed to live together. She would have children of her own, and then he would grow old and pass away, leaving her, grieving, behind. He yearned to be in her presence again, to talk with her about any silly little thing. It seemed impossible, a profound violation of the fundamental laws of physics: there was no way that life could move forward, that everyone could still go about their business, while his daughter suddenly disappeared, leaving a girl-sized hole in the world. His wife must be mistaken. Perhaps she had gone mad.

A month later, Nadim got his release from detention. He never knew if the interrogator had arranged it or if the others had simply gotten tired of listening to his story about the neighbor and the dog.

He visited Enny's grave, and the reality sank in. He recited the *Salat al-Janazah*, and then he managed to find a new place to live, on his own, in Brooklyn, because he couldn't stand to see his wife's face. He would never forgive her. Never. As he would never forgive the men who had kept him imprisoned while his daughter was dying.

He moved into his new basement apartment and found another car-service job. Occasionally he thought of trying to report what had happened inside the detention center, but he was afraid that no one would believe him or that the interrogator would make good on his ominous threats. So he kept the man's secret, and went about his daily business, but he was like the walking dead.

By 2004 he had begun to recover, but then the news came out about what had happened in the prison at Abu Ghraib, and the terrible photographs, and Nadim began to suffer nightmares again and sweats and shakes.

And then, one morning last week, he had rounded a corner in a little local deli and saw the big man who had roared with laughter as he slammed Nadim into walls.

Now he rolled over and moaned at what he had done.

But it was not too late. He could still move on with his life—and with the plan. He needed to go out right now and find a phone booth, and call the others to reassure them that he was still just as committed as ever. He snatched up his knapsack, rose to his feet, and headed for a gap in the chain-link fence.

"YOU WANNA GO BACK to the Seven-oh house?" asked Richie Powker.

"I don't know," Jack said. After the big adrenaline rush of thinking they were right on top of their suspect in the aquarium, he felt deflated and tired.

Richie took a bite of a corn dog he had just purchased from a boardwalk concession stand, two hundred yards west of the aquarium exit.

"You know," Jack said, "I think you're the first person I've ever seen eat one of those things."

Throngs of New Yorkers strolled past, an incredible parade of people whose ancestors had come from Africa and Puerto Rico and Scotland and Trinidad and Poland, all drawn here by dreams of a new life. Jack looked up and watched the giant green-and-orange Wonder Wheel spin slowly overhead, the cars swinging as they traveled up into the sky. Out on the water, a cruise ship slid along the horizon. He didn't want the trip out here to be a total waste of time, so he pulled the photo of Nadim Hasni out of his pocket. "Why don't we ask around, check if anybody's seen our guy?"

"He could be anywhere by now," Richie cautioned. "He could've hopped the F train back to Midwood, or Jackson Heights, or God knows where."

Jack nodded. "I know. But he was here today, and that's the only actual lead we've got."

THE NINTH STEP | 251

"I'm with ya."

Jack appreciated his partner's willingness to follow through.

Richie tossed his corn dog stick into a trash barrel and they set out. They tried the vendors in the fried clam stalls, who answered with the hard suspicion of lifelong shore vets. They tried the tough boardwalk watering holes, Ruby's and Cha-Cha's, where grizzled old-timers were already settled at the outdoor picnic tables. Striking out, the detectives questioned random passersby.

Sighing in frustration, Jack turned at one point and caught someone looking at him. A deeply tanned thirtyish guy with a lean, athletic air; he seemed familiar, but Jack couldn't place him.

"Hey, partner?"

Richie was calling him; when he glanced back, the stranger had disappeared into the river of people cruising the boardwalk.

"You wanna try Brighton Beach?"

Jack shook his head. That neighborhood was just a few minutes down the boardwalk, but it was a very white (Russian) world.

The detectives moved deeper into the Coney amusement area. A few yards down the boardwalk, they could hear the resort's most unusual and nutty attraction before it came into view. An incredibly raspy amplified voice stopped passing tourists in their tracks. "Step right up, folks, and shoot a live human target! You shoot him; he can't shoot back!"

Between two low brick buildings that housed a bar and a concession stand stretched a banner that read SHOOT THE FREAK. Below it, the public could stare down off the boardwalk into a vacant lot that held an odd array of abandoned refrigerators, trash barrels, and mannequin heads. This jumbled landscape was home to the Freak, who was actually just a teenager wearing a visored helmet and an armor of dirty football pads. He dodged back and forth, taunting the spectators, which might not have seemed like such a good idea, given that the amusement's operator, a bald mountain of a man wearing a headset microphone, was renting some of them high-powered rifles. Luckily for the Freak, the only ammo was paintballs, which *thwocked* against his armor and coated the whole attraction with a wild palette of Day-Glo splatters.

The kid took advantage of a short cease-fire between customers to lift his visor and wipe his sweaty face. He looked about seventeen. His pay probably wasn't great, but at least he wasn't stuck behind some fast-food counter. Talk about weird jobs: the kid was a scapegoat, the daily target of hundreds of people's life frustrations. *You shoot him; he can't shoot back!*

As a homicide cop, Jack was hardly thrilled with the idea of anyone offering training in how to shoot unarmed people, but as a lifelong New Yorker he knew that a contained dose of unruliness and "danger" was essential to Coney's character. New York's working class spent dull days as bus drivers or supermarket cashiers; on nights and weekends, they needed to bust loose a little.

But the two detectives were far from busting loose; in fact, they were seriously flagging. They were about to leave when Jack spotted a couple of local patrol cops cruising along in an NYPD beach buggy. The driver was a stout, muscular young black woman; her partner, a white guy, also looked like a serious weightlifter. (Maybe they worked out together.) Jack waved them down and flashed his badge. "How you doin'? We're working a homicide and we're on the lookout for a suspect." He held up the photo.

Confronted by two senior detectives, including a member of the elite Homicide squad, the two cops in the buggy straightened up from their relaxed slouch. The uniform riding shotgun lifted up his wraparound blue shades, then nodded, excited. "I think I rousted this guy from a bench along here a few days ago. I was workin' a double—it would'a been right around sunrise. He was conked out and I told him to move along."

"You sure it was him?"

The uniform nodded. "Pretty sure. He seemed kind of disoriented when I woke him up, but he wasn't making any trouble, so I left."

"Did you see where he went?"

The uniform shook his head.

Jack scratched the back of his neck, glanced up and down the boardwalk, and turned to his partner. "Our guy can't go home. He might have been staying in Jackson Heights, but after we chased him, he wouldn't feel safe there." His eyes narrowed. "Maybe he's crashing out here."

Richie frowned. "If I was on the lam, with hardly any money, where would *I* hide?" That was a big part of the job: trying to think like a perp.

Jack considered the matter. It would seem, in such a big city, that it would be easy to find a place to sleep, but if you were forced onto the streets, the options were actually few. If you were just homeless, there were church steps and a few other possibilities, but if you needed to hide, there were eight million potential spotters walking around. Coney Island had more than its share of skels and dopers, but at night they probably ended up in city shelters or low-rent SROs.

He turned back to the uniforms. "You guys know the area better than us, so why don't we split up? You two"—he pointed to Richie and the male uniform—"can look through Astroland,

and we'll check around the Wonder Wheel." His colleagues started to move, but Jack held up a hand. "There's just one thing." Gingerly, he explained to the two young cops about the possible radiation risk. "You up for this?"

The uniforms gave each other a look, then nodded gravely. Jack felt for them: they probably spent most of their time dealing with pickpockets or drunk-and-disorderlies, but suddenly they had been dropped into the middle of a bizarre and potentially life-threatening terrorism case.

"He'll probably be carrying a knapsack," Jack concluded. "If you spot him, don't approach. We'd better call for backup before we go in for the arrest."

CHAPTER THIRTY-THREE

The first pay phone had no dial tone. The second didn't even have a receiver, just a couple of wires sprouting from the end of the connecting coil, as if someone had ripped it off in the midst of a frustrating conversation. Nadim groaned. Everyone used cell phones now. Surf Avenue was crowded today; he considered asking one of the passing tourists if he could borrow one, but they would surely turn him down.

Finally he found a working phone and called Malik. He got his friend's voice mail and left an excuse for his recent disappearance. "Please tell the others," he said, "I'm still in on the plan. I will definitely do my part."

As he hung up, an amplified voice boomed out behind him. "Bump it! Bump it! Bump it! Come inside! *Everybody* rides!" Nadim stepped to the inner edge of the sidewalk and peered in through a grille at a big dark hall full of careening bumper cars.

Someone tapped him on the shoulder and he spun around.

"Yo buddy, you got a light?"

It was a wiry man wearing grubby cargo shorts and no shirt; he held up a half-smoked cigarette he'd probably just found on the sidewalk.

Nadim shook his head and edged away. The people around here, the regulars, they frightened him. They looked pugnacious, jittery, undernourished yet strong enough to win a street fight. They seemed to be always pushing some scam, ever on the lookout for potential victims.

He turned into an alley, back into one of the amusement parks, eager to get back to his hiding place.

AS JACK AND THE young policewoman walked into Deno's Wonder Wheel Amusement Park, they entered a blizzard of sights and sounds. This oceanside end of the park was filled with kiddie rides: little trains and fire trucks, grinning plastic clowns and dinosaurs, brightly colored, all spinning. In fact, the entire visual field was in motion: the hordes of families cruising through, the Tilt-a-Whirl tilting and whirling, the giant Ferris wheel revolving overhead. Bells clanged; pennants snapped in the breeze; tinny music blared from crappy speakers. The two cops waded into this maelstrom, searching for one particular brown face.

Above the frenetic scene on the ground, several perennial landmarks loomed. Aside from the Wonder Wheel, Jack could see the Astroland tower, a tall white rod encircled by a rising, donut-shaped observation deck; farther east, he caught glimpses of the Cyclone, its cars full of screaming riders bucking and plunging as they whipped around its snakelike coils. Jack thought of Nadim Hasni's knapsack. He could only pray that the bag would not soon provide a different cause for terror and screaming.

His new partner wore her hair in tight cornrows. Her arms and thighs were big and muscular; some of the old-time NYPD cops had been less than thrilled with the advent of women on patrol, arguing that they wouldn't be able to subdue a fleeing or belligerent suspect, but this one looked like she could more than hold up her end. They moved north, toward the Surf Avenue end of the park. It seemed like a lost cause, but Jack knew that they had several advantages. Though the two amusement parks were densely packed, they were small; they took up only three or four blocks. And the best part was that they were bounded by high chain-link fences, so there were only a few ways in and out.

The two cops moved down a concrete ramp in the middle of the park, which led to the base of the Wonder Wheel, where attendants sorted the riders into its little cars. An alley there passed beyond the ticket booth, then veered into a lane full of game booths, where grizzled carnies surrounded by crappy plush toys separated the park's visitors from the contents of their wallets.

Halfway down that lane, another alley split off to the left. Jack's partner reached it first. She glanced down it, then waved frantically for him. He hurried over, threading his way through gaggles of little kids.

"Down there!" she said.

Straining to see over the crowds, Jack spotted a brown-skinned male forty yards ahead, carrying a knapsack, wearing a blue jacket, headed toward the west side of the park—and an exit onto West Twelfth Street.

"Radio the others!" Jack shouted to his partner, and they set off in pursuit.

They made it through the crowds and then, breathless, burst out onto West Twelfth, which featured much less foot traffic. Jack had lost sight of their suspect; he scanned right, toward Surf Avenue, then left. *There!* About halfway up the block he saw the man, still moving at a casual pace, pointed toward the boardwalk. But then, farther ahead, out of the mouth of the

Wonder Wheel lane emerged two men. One of them was the tanned stranger Jack had noticed on the boardwalk. The other he recognized immediately: it was the crew-cut fed who had approached him outside of Nadim Hasni's apartment. Charlson's man.

Jack's head spun. The tanned agent must have been tracking him earlier. But how could they have known he was here? Had Charlson's team tailed him and Richie? No—if the fed and his men had them under surveillance, they wouldn't have rushed off to Jackson Heights. A possible answer came to Jack: he had been talking to Ray Hillhouse all the way out here. Recent technology made it possible to triangulate the source of a cell phone call within about a fifty-meter radius. A phone company ping of the GPS chip in newer phones could be even more precise, but real-time tracking required a court order. Had Charlson misused his Homeland Security powers to follow an NYPD detective?

There wasn't time for further speculation: both feds stopped in their tracks as they spotted Hasni walking toward them. They drew their guns. Jack's heart rate kicked up. He remembered the bullet traces in Hasni's home driveway, and it occurred to him that these men were all too likely to shoot first and ask questions later.

He ran forward, past a swirling ride blasting incredibly loud hip-hop music. Up ahead, it seemed that Hasni had also noticed the feds. He stopped and looked to his right: a high fence edged the entire lot on the opposite side of the street. He spun around and saw Jack and his partner running toward him. He turned to his left and veered off the sidewalk.

The feds ran forward, but Jack got there first.

As he skidded to a stop, he saw that their suspect had disappeared into the entrance to the Ghost Hole, a haunted-house ride. The façade featured paintings of leering demons, above papier-mâché statues of a bloody alien monster and a devil stirring a cauldron. A little train of what looked like bumper cars was rolling inside through a couple of swinging doors.

Jack dashed in behind it.

BEYOND THE SWINGING DOORS, Nadim had found himself in near-total darkness. He ran forward, smack into some kind of heavy rubbery curtain. He found a wall to his left, so he turned right and scrambled up a long, narrow ramp. He had run about forty feet when he heard the swinging doors bang open behind him, letting in enough daylight for him to see a little train full of people rattling upward. He pressed back against another curtain; as the train shuttled past, a loud cackling came out of the ceiling and a bright light flashed on overhead. Right next to him, Nadim beheld a near-naked man strapped to a chair. The chair buzzed, electrified, and the man screamed.

Nadim almost fainted with fear. Down the ramp, the doors swung open a second time—one of his pursuers ran through. Nadim scrambled on through the hollow darkness, barely able to make out the rear of the train swerving around a corner ahead. As he followed it, demons in rags loomed out at him, reaching for him with jerky motions, and something brushed against his face. He reeled around another corner, and a bloody, naked body dropped down from overhead, suspended by its ankles.

Nadim gasped. If he didn't get out of this horrible place right away, his heart was going to explode.

JACK CURSED AS HE tentatively made his way up the dark ramp, following the little train. Up near the top, an animatronic dummy was shrieking in an electric chair. The detective looked back and saw the swinging doors burst open below. One of the feds ran in, holding up his gun. Jack ran on, smack into a heavy rubbery curtain. He felt his way around the corner, nearly tripping over the train track at his feet. He felt his way around another curtain, past a couple more animatronic ghouls, and came around another corner, where a vomiting specter rose up out of a trash barrel. He stumbled past it, almost into the back of the stalled little train, which was filled with confused, grumbling customers—evidently the operator had finally stopped the ride. Jack turned, disoriented, and under a flashing strobe light he saw Nadim Hasni disappear behind one of the rubbery curtains.

NADIM CLOMPED DOWN a little wooden staircase he discovered behind the curtain. It left him in a little hallway lit by only one dim bulb. That in turn led to a door, and he ran forward, slammed it open, and hurtled out into daylight, into a grubby concrete backyard, right toward a mangy gray pit bull, which cowered, startled, in front of a ramshackle trailer, under a big fernlike ailanthus tree. Nadim looked around, blinking in the sudden light, and realized that he was in the middle of the amusement park, in some kind of hidden employee area.

The dog quickly recovered from its surprise. It leapt forward, barking and snapping just like the dog in Nadim's dream. Nadim spun around. He felt a weight pulling him backward; the dog had fastened its jaws on the bottom of his knapsack. He twisted and turned, trying to dislodge it, but the animal held on. Nadim lurched back against a wall, stunning the beast, and it dropped onto the concrete. Taking advantage of the animal's momentary setback, Nadim bolted for the side of the trailer, leapt up onto an overturned shopping cart, grabbed for a branch of the tree, and hoisted himself out of reach. He reached out and pulled himself onto a high chain-link fence. He scrambled up and over, then dropped onto a circular tented roof, above another amusement park ride.

JACK BURST OUT INTO the little back area only to find that his suspect had vanished again, as if he had the power to turn himself invisible. Next to a dilapidated trailer, he saw a pit bull barking up at a tree. Jack squinted up but didn't see anyone.

One of the feds came running around the side of the haunted house, gun drawn.

The pit bull turned, growled, and leapt forward.

The fed didn't miss a beat; he raised his gun and fired.

Jack didn't wait around to see what happened; he ran off in the other direction.

CHAPTER THIRTY-FOUR

The race was on.

Jack rushed back into the park, where he found Richie and his patrol partner near the base of the Wonder Wheel.

"I spotted Hasni a minute ago," said Richie, breathless. "He was moving south."

"We've got company. Charlson's boys."

"How the hell did they know we were here?"

"I don't know, but we better find Hasni fast. I don't think he's armed, but these goddamned cowboys don't care—they'll take him right out."

He turned to the uniform. "Call in for backup. Here: show them this." He handed over the photo of their suspect.

The cops fanned out and combed the rest of the park.

No luck.

As they reconvened for a quick powwow on the board-walk, the sun was bright in their eyes. Jack looked up and down the wooden walkway, which was thick with roving crowds. When it came to trying to spot a suspect out in the open in New York City, only Times Square would be worse.

"Me and my partner will go this way," Richie told the uniforms. "You two go south."

"Wait a minute," Jack said. He was looking down by his feet. Between the wooden slats of the boardwalk, he could just make out some sand and trash below. Back in his youth, he had smooched it up with girls in that shadowy realm—under the boardwalk, just like The Drifters' song. At that time it had been open to the public and there had even been a few concessions down there. In the mid-nineties the city had raised the level of the beach almost to the southern edge of the walk, and blocked the other side with a fence, but there was obviously still space below.

He looked at the uniforms. "You ever get people down there?"

The patrolwoman shrugged. "Some homeless. They find ways to peel back a corner of the fence or clip a few links."

Out of the corner of his eye Jack spotted the two feds, who had almost completed their own scan of the amusement park and were moving this way. He figured that if they spotted Hasni up in the crowds, they might not dare to shoot, but under the walkway would be another story. "How can we get down there fast?"

"The easiest way is through *Shoot the Freak*."

"Let's go," Jack said to Richie. "If you find him," he warned the uniforms, "don't let him put his hands anywhere near his knapsack."

OVER AT THE CRAZY boardwalk amusement, the barker made the two detectives before they even opened their mouths. "I got a license," he growled, covering his mic with a beefy hand.

"This has nothing to do with you," Jack said. "We just need to get down below."

The barker was happy to send the cops on their way. "Climb

over the railing there—there's a ladder on the side." He asked his customers to hold their fire as the detectives clambered down.

As they entered the space beneath the boardwalk, it took a few seconds for their eyes to adjust from sun to gloom. The hubbub of the resort above quickly faded away.

The dim alley, walled with sand on the other side, was densely littered with plastic bags, swatches of towels, and other debris. Massive wooden crossbeams, raised by thick columns planted in the sand, supported the walkway above. Tiny strips of sunlight came down through the boards and striped the sand, which was densely packed underfoot. The place offended Jack's sense of hygiene, but at least it didn't smell so bad; beyond a certain briny tang, most of the trash was so old that it had long ago lost its odor.

"You wanna split up?" Richie asked. "You head west and I'll go east?"

Up above, the two uniforms had similarly divided, covering the boardwalk.

"Works for me," Jack replied. He watched his colleague plod off down the dim corridor, and then Jack turned the other way. The air down here was damp, with a ghostly chill.

The visibility was poor, as mounds of sand rose up occasionally, and the forest of columns would offer Jack's suspect lots of potential cover. He pulled his service revolver out of its holster and walked carefully on for twenty yards, listening to the thump of feet on the wood overhead and the muffled sounds of the amusement parks.

At his hip, his phone vibrated. He ignored it. Twenty yards on, it buzzed again. He picked it up and checked the source of the call. Ray Hillhouse.

Holding his gun with one hand, he flipped the phone open

and pressed it to his ear. "What's up?" he said, keeping his voice as low as possible.

"You're not gonna like this," the FBI man replied. "I asked around: there's no word here about any investigation into a dirty-bomb plot. And the JTTF has never heard of it either."

Jack stopped in his tracks. "Are you sure?" He was stunned, but he reminded himself that he needed to keep moving. Ahead, the gray sand rose up in a sloping mound. At its peak, he'd only have a few feet of clearance.

"I'm sure," Hillhouse said. "I know a top guy at Homeland Security and he also swears he's never heard of this case."

Jack felt dizzy, as if the sand had shifted beneath his feet. For days now, he had been wondering if Nadim Hasni was really part of a terrorist cell. But did the cell even exist? "Did he say anything about Charlson?"

"He says the guy creeps him out. Charlson was a security contractor back in the first Gulf War, and there were rumors that he was involved in some kind of bad scene that got hushed up. I also checked out—"

"Hold on a sec," Jack whispered. He had reached the top of the mound; on the other side, it sloped back down, revealing a cluttered little vista. About forty yards ahead in the dim alley, someone had set up a small blue camping tent on the sand. Scattered around it, he noticed other objects: a plastic lounge chair, a pile of plastic milk crates, and . . . he squinted to see better . . . a fiberglass shark, lying on its side, perhaps salvaged from some old concession stand or amusement ride. Ahead, the tent flap was closed. Jack was trying to imagine if Nadim Hasni might have gotten hold of such makeshift lodging when he saw something stir on the sand just twenty yards away, to the right. A prone human body. Young, male, with brown skin. A knapsack lay on the sand next to him.

"Jack?" Hillhouse said.

He hung up, stuffed his cell phone in his pocket, and gripped his revolver with both hands. He was just beginning to descend the slope when he spotted another figure in the shadows, stepping around the side of the tent.

A mild, grandfatherly, very reasonable-looking man.

Brent Charlson was also holding up a gun. He noticed Jack just as he caught sight of their mutual prey.

Jack accidentally stepped on an empty soda bottle and it crunched beneath his feet.

Nadim Hasni whirled to look at him.

"Put your hands up!" Jack said. "Don't move!"

Nadim complied.

Charlson spoke. "Good job, Leightner."

Nadim kept his hands up, but as he turned to see the federal agent, he visibly recoiled. He started to scramble backward, leaving his knapsack behind.

"Don't move!" Jack repeated, pointing his gun.

Nadim stopped.

"You found him," Charlson said. "I can take it from here."

"I don't think so."

Charlson's voice stayed eerily flat. *"You don't think so* what?" Strips of light glinted against his spectacles.

All of a sudden, Jack thought about the bomb underneath his car.

"You can go now," the fed told him.

Jack reached back with one hand and pulled a pair of handcuffs from his belt. He kept his voice calm and steady as he spoke to his suspect. "Nadim, I want you to stay very still, all right? You're going to be okay."

"I'll take him into custody," Charlson said to Jack. "Why don't you go get your partner?"

"No!" Hasni cried out. "I do not go with this man. Never again!"

A sudden zipping noise. A grimy head poked out of the tent. "What the hell's all this racket? I'm tryin' to get some sl—"

"Gun!" Charlson shouted. "He's got a gun!"

Jack turned back to see a flash from the fed's pistol, accompanied by a sharp report.

Still holding up his empty hands, Nadim slammed backward onto the sand.

Charlson spun around and pointed his pistol at Jack.

But Jack Leightner had his own gun up and at the ready. And he did something that he had never done in all his years with the NYPD: he fired his service weapon in an attempt to kill a man. As instructed on the departmental firing range, he aimed for central body mass. And hit it.

Charlson jerked backward and then looked down in disbelief at the red spot on his immaculate white shirt. And then he toppled back and splayed out, immobile, glasses askew across his pale white face.

Jack rushed over and felt the man's neck for a pulse. He couldn't find it but didn't have time to ponder the complete and utter strangeness of the moment—he had just killed another human being—because he had someone else to check on. He hurried across the odd little encampment to the body of his long-sought suspect, also sprawled out amid the trash.

NADIM HASNI GURGLED FOR breath. He pressed his hand to his chest and then held it up before his eyes: it was slick with his blood. His head fell back and he moaned as he felt his life draining away, down into the cool sand.

Now he would never take part in the plan. Malik and

Aarif and the others would buy the two Taxi & Limousine medallions. They would never again have to shift-lease their cars from other owners. But Nadim would never know what it felt like to be his own boss.

His eyelids slid shut.

"Abbu?"

He heard his daughter's high, sweet voice in the darkness. And then he saw some shifting pink and orange points of light. As he moved closer, he saw that they were huge transparent umbrellas, glowing jellyfish, pulsing through an endless black sea.

CHAPTER THIRTY-FIVE

The call came a week later, as Jack sat at his desk in the Homicide squad room typing up a report on his latest investigation.

After an endless series of debriefings with NYPD brass and with freaked-out bureaucrats from Homeland Security and the Department of Justice, not to mention a mandatory post-shooting session with a police therapist, he was finally back to his normal rounds, the daily influx of sad, dumb, run-of-the-mill killings: the drug dealers popping each other in battles over turf, the spouses reaching the end of the line in their marital wars, the robberies gone bad, and the teen gangstas vying to impress some curvy little homegirl.

Jack's first new case, thankfully, had been an easy grounder to the infield. (It involved no terrorists, federal agents, or Mafia kingpins.) At a house party in East Flatbush, one Ronnie Parris, twenty-two years old, had shot and killed one Brione Terrell, nineteen, in a scuffle over a Tommy Hilfiger jacket, in front of seventeen witnesses. Excess of testosterone, shortage of good judgment, overavailability of firearms: open-and-shut case.

Jack paused in his typing and considered getting up and going into the supply room for his third cup of coffee. He listened to the usual comforting clatter of detectives banging away at their keyboards, taking phone calls, ribbing each other about their personal lives.

His phone rang.

As soon as the brief conversation was over, he called Richie Powker, and then he went out and jumped into his car.

TWENTY MINUTES LATER, HE and his former partner were standing in a hallway of the Kings County Medical Center. Through a big window, he looked into a Critical Care room and saw a thicket of IV stands, tubes, and life-support machines. A couple of hovering nurses blocked his view of the bed.

The attending physician stepped out into the hallway, removed his face mask, and gave the NYPD detectives an update. "He's finally able to talk, but don't stay long. He's very weak and we're still not sure he's going to make it."

As Jack entered the room and saw the haggard, brown-skinned young patient, he remembered his own days lying—perhaps in this same bed—after he had been shot during a late-night ambush. He felt a rush of empathy but tamped it down; he was here to find out why the man had committed a homicide.

He and his partner tugged chairs closer to the bedside, pulled out notebooks, and began their interview.

Nadim Hasni was very wary, but when it became evident that they were genuinely interested in his story—and actually seemed to believe him—the words spilled out. He struggled for breath but managed to tell them all about his arrest and incarceration back in 2001.

Jack glanced out the window and saw a couple of men in business suits bustle down the corridor, probably bureaucrats from Homeland Security. He could see them arguing with the doctor, and they tried to get his own attention, but he ignored them. The connection between Hasni, Brasciak, and Charlson had finally been uncovered; of course it led back to the detention center in the days after 9/11. In the wake of Charlson's death, a couple of scared witnesses had finally stepped forward to describe the dark things they had seen inside that hulking, windowless building. The feds were spinning it as a tale of a couple of rogue guards gone astray, but reporters had begun gathering information about the broad abuses that had taken place—and about the system that had actively encouraged the bullies to run free.

Everybody wanted a piece of Nadim Hasni now, but this time the feds would have to wait their turn.

Richie interrupted the young man. "You're positive that the voices in the other cell belonged to Charlson and Brasciak?"

"I am positive," Hasni said, almost weeping with relief; finally, he could tell what had really happened. He resumed his story. The detectives had a hard time keeping up their usual stoic front as he reached the part about his daughter's death. Mercifully, then, some opiate drip kicked in; the man's eyelids closed and he was fast asleep.

Jack and Richie sat in silence for a minute, contemplating the suspect they had desperately tracked across two boroughs, their supposed terrorist.

"Poor bastard," Richie murmured.

Jack nodded. If Hasni managed to pull through, he would face homicide charges for the attack in the deli. But maybe he could plead temporary insanity. That could send him to a psych ward, but at least he might finally get some professional help to ease his anguished mind.

* * *

AFTER WORK, JACK STOPPED in to Monsalvo's for a beer. The place was quiet—just a couple of old-timers chatting companionably at the far end of the bar. Jack took a seat and stared up at the dusty deer head mounted on the wall. With its big sad eyeballs, it seemed to be staring back.

He sat there, sipping his beer, still musing about Nadim Hasni. He pictured the actual contents of the man's deadly knapsack: two pairs of socks, some underwear, a couple of dirty T-shirts, and a half-eaten box of Oreo cookies. Simple things owned by a simple man, caught up in forces way beyond his control. The guy's entire life had been ravaged. Who could possibly make that up to him?

Jack thought about the stranger who had showed up on his doorstep one recent Sunday morning, and he recalled the man's crumpled piece of paper. What had it said? Something about taking stock of one's life, and something about a Ninth Step: *making amends.*

And then he was thinking not of his recent cases at all but of his father, of the many times he'd had to practically carry the man home from bars like this one, of the rages and the shouting. But he also remembered the time his father had helped him and Petey build a raft made of scraps of wood "recovered" from a construction site; they had actually managed to float it in a little waterfront cove. And his father holding him up in the Red Hook pool, then crowing to his friends when his son managed to dog-paddle a few feet on his own. His father, lifting three semiconscious men out of the hold of a burning, explosives-packed ship. Jack shook his head. He'd spent the past few days chasing a phantom threat to his beloved city, while all his life he had been completely ignorant about his own father's role in saving the entire New York area from a very real and much greater cataclysm.

A 45 dropped into place in the jukebox: Bobby Darin, "Beyond the Sea."

Jack sat there listening to the old tune, and he thought of Michelle. Most of his life, he had carried a heavy grudge against his old man; now he was carrying one against his former love. He pondered his visit to the little Buddhist nun and what she had told him about forgiveness. Yes, Michelle had cheated on him, but maybe she had just acted out of her own fear, her own insecurities. Maybe she was just another fallible human being. Who didn't make mistakes?

He ducked his head and stared down into his glass. He knew now who he really needed to forgive: a fifteen-year-old boy who had said something stupid in an offhand moment. He hadn't said it in order to cause any trouble for his brother. He had just been a kid, and the slurs had hopped out of his mouth like little wild sparrows. Petey was dead. No one could change the past, could make it right. But almost forty years had gone by. It would never be time to forget. But it was time to set his burden down.

And perhaps it was time to make some other changes, to find out what broken things might be repaired. He knew just where to start. He got up, strode across the bar's faded linoleum floor, settled into the old phone booth, and shut the accordion door. Then he took out his cell phone and tapped in a number.

"Jack?" Michelle answered before he even said a word.

He blinked, wondering if his ex had somehow known he was about to call. And then, old-timer that he was, he remembered: there was no magic to it. Just caller ID.

"Is that really you?" she said. He could have been wrong, but he thought she sounded pleased.

For some silly reason, Jack thought about the homeless guy who'd earned three bucks off him in midtown Manhattan. "I'll tell you where you got your shoes," the man had said. "You got 'em on your own two feet."

And so he did.

AUTHOR'S NOTE

A crime writer friend insists that he never researches his novels. "They're *fiction*," he says. "The important thing is to tell a good story. Who cares if the details are accurate?"

I've never been able to share that blithe approach. In part, that's because I derive too much pleasure from the process of research, of going out and talking to real people, treading real settings, investigating real events. It's also because I learned a lot about writing from working as a freelance journalist, and I know that I can pick up details from real life that are so rich, odd, and intriguing that I could probably never make them up.

That's certainly the case with *The Ninth Step*. It's a work of fiction and I hope it's a good story, but—more than any of my other books—this one is based on a number of the most amazing true stories I've come across in two and a half decades of professional writing.

A few years ago, while working on a waterfront feature for *The New York Times*, I took a boat tour of little-known spots in New York Harbor. A four-sentence note in the accompanying leaflet mentioned the site of the near-explosion of a munitions ship called the *El Estero* back in 1943. I was captivated by this historical tidbit, which I had never heard of. My subsequent research culminated in a long and very pleasant interview with an eighty-eight-year-old man named Seymour Wittek. He had been a Coast Guardsman during that incredible event, and he was one of the volunteers who rushed to the burning ship, and he told me the tale which I have put into the mouth of my fictional character Frank Raucci.

Incredible as it may seem, except for the involvement of Raucci and of one particular Red Hook longshoreman and father, the story as told here is essentially accurate. Like the brave firemen and cops of 9/11, a small band of firemen and Coasties rushed forward when most of us would probably have been running as fast as we could in the other direction—and they saved the New York area from what could have been the greatest disaster in human history. It was one of the most astounding examples of human heroism I had ever heard of—so why, I wondered, was it not in every history book?

One reason, perhaps, is that—unlike 9/11—it was the tale of a catastrophe that *didn't* happen. Also, the incident occurred in the middle of World War II, at a time when the U.S. Navy was hardly eager to broadcast the vulnerability of New York Harbor, so the story received little press attention. I'm glad to report that Seymour Wittek finally received a Coast Guard medal for his bravery on Veteran's Day in 2008. He said that he accepted it on behalf of all the other guys who were no longer around.

Next true story. The Italian Mafia—in conjunction with a corrupt longshoremen's union—really did have a stranglehold over the Brooklyn waterfront during the early and middle years of the twentieth century. A number of the notorious mafiosi mentioned in this book (Carmine Persico, Paul Castellano, Albert Anastasia, etc.) were real historical figures. A Red Hook native told me about his own father's disappearances into the night in a car full of wiseguys—he never found out why—and that "Crazy" Joe Gallo really did have a front door presided over by a little person named Armando, and that overdue debtors in his loansharking operation were sent down to the basement to "talk to Leo."

Third, the population of Little Pakistan in the heart of Brooklyn really was decimated by overzealous "anti-terror" raids in the months after 9/11. (I live a few blocks away.) I'm especially sorry to report that there was a real detention center that was used to hold suspected terrorists in Sunset Park, and that the civil and legal rights of hundreds of Muslim residents of New York City—many of them completely innocent—were thrown to the wind when they were rounded up, often without probable cause, and imprisoned there. I didn't hear of any killings of prisoners at that facility, but a number of its guards later went on trial for subjecting prisoners to physical abuse and sexual humiliation, and it's clear that a systematic breakdown in the rule of law occurred inside. These sad abuses were detailed in 2003 in a document (easily accessible online) called the "Supplemental Report on September 11 Detainees' Allegations of Abuse at the Metropolitan Detention Center in Brooklyn, New York," issued by the U.S. Department of Justice's Office of the Inspector General, and in three hundred hours of secret videotapes which surfaced during the trials. (As someone who was living in New York just a couple of miles from Ground Zero on 9/11, I would never argue that there is not a real need for vigilance against terrorist acts or that a real threat does not exist. I *would* argue that abusing innocent civilians is not a good way to combat it.)

In late 2008, I stumbled across a few rather dubious news reports which claimed that Somali pirates who had captured an Iranian ship that summer subsequently began to die of what seemed like radiation sickness. I have no idea if there was *really* any truth to this story, but it certainly fired my imagination— and that of my fictional character Brent Charlson.

Last but not least, when I was doing my research for *Red Hook*, the first book in the Jack Leightner series, I spent some time going to meetings and otherwise exploring the fascinating world of Alcoholics Anonymous. I was hugely impressed by the courage of its members, who strive every day to face the reality of their problem, to be honest with themselves and others about their behavior, and to regain control of and to repair their lives. That's when I learned about the Ninth Step.

Gabriel Cohen
Brooklyn, 2010

ACKNOWLEDGMENTS

Invaluable assistance with this book was provided by Reed Farrel Coleman, Robert Smith, Jonathan Green and Keisha Jones, and Gerard Raccuglia. Thank you!

A huge thanks to Seymour Wittek, member of a band of true heroes, who kindly shared his memories of one of the most incredible days in the history of New York City.

For information about a real terror plot in NYC, I turned to *Two Seconds Under the World: Terror Comes to America—The Conspiracy Behind the World Trade Center Bombing* by Jim Dwyer, David Kocieniewski, Deidre Murphy, and Peg Tyre. For information about the world under the Coney Island boardwalk, I perused the photographs of Nathan Kensinger, at kensinger.blogspot.com.

Thanks to Roxanne Aubrey, as always, for help with my Web site.

And a special thanks to Vicky Bijur, for wise advice and extraordinary representation.